Sunshine's Grump

By Merri Bright

Sunshine's Grump

The Billionaire's Betasitter

Merri Bright

Bright and Dark Publishing

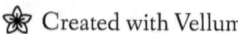

For Raewyn
Have a sausage.

Contents

Content Advisory

W elcome to The Billionaire's Betasitter series! If you love to laugh while you read, and you're not afraid of spicy stories, dive in. If you are easily offended by explicit, on-page sexytimes, profanity, or age-gap storylines, put the book down and back away.

Still here? Okay, even for you experienced spice lovers, be aware that this book is chock full of naughtiness... and *knottiness*. The characters in this human Omegaverse romcom are called betas (normal humans), omegas (typically women with soothing pheromones and ramped-up sex drives), and alphas (men and a few women who are assertive, respected, and attracted to omegas). Omegas and alphas together make up around ten percent of the population.

This "one-sausage special" has a lot of spicy ingredients, including, but not limited to: unique identifying scents, annual

Merri Bright

fertile heat cycles for the omegas, unusual peen, accidental pregnancy, "make it fit" knotting, so much dirty talk, claiming, spanking, breeding, light BDSM, power imbalance, backdoor knotting, and oh crap, I think my mom is reading this.

Have fun with the knots and yachts!

Chapter 1

Sunshine

"Okay, Sunshine, it's time for you to decide. Are you a spit or swallow girl?" An evil smile curling on her face, my best friend Rain waved a shot glass filled with warm, raw oysters back and forth under my nose. "Spit? Swallow? Throw up the eleven petit fours we ate before the meeting?"

"You're so cruel." I struggled not to inhale the stench that wafted all around us, and put a hand over my stomach. "But I'm not giving my petit fours back, no matter how bad the funk." The brunch at Chez Palette before the Omega League meeting had been exquisite, and I would not disrespect the desserts I'd consumed.

I stopped talking as Mrs. Cantervale walked past, lecturing on how to overcome aversion to odors. Specifically, how an omega could learn to get past the way most alphas smelled to us. "Now, we all know omegas' perfumes appeal to all alphas." The room tittered in agreement. "And alphas who are better matches can smell just as lovely to us. But unfortunately, not all of your suitors' aromas will be ideal." She tapped her nose.

3

"Even a casual embrace or a goodnight kiss can be disastrous in the early stages of getting to know an alpha that your biology doesn't recognize as a compatible suitor. A dinner date may pose unique problems, as some find it difficult to eat in the presence of less pleasant pheromones."

That was the truth. Most alphas smelled sort of mildew-y to me, like they'd been left in a laundry basket overnight.

Bored, Rain lifted the shot glass full of oysters closer to my nose. "Spit or swallow, my sunny Soleil. What kind of omega are you?"

I bared my teeth in the worst smile I could—which, according to her, still made me look like a kitten, just a mad one—and shoved her hand away. "You already know I'm a spit girl. You're the one who hasn't tried giving a blow job." Or anything, actually.

Rain arched one dark eyebrow. "I'm almost positive I'd be a swallow girl," she said, and picked up her own cup of oysters, slamming it back. She wiped her mouth on her linen napkin, then gave a tiny burp, smirking. "Anyway, oyster jizz is my favorite."

I covered my face with my hands and groaned. "Tell me why we're doing this again?"

"Honestly, Soleil, you tell me. You're the one who hired her for this gig."

She was right. As the Vice President of the Southern Georgetown Omega League, the oldest and most well-respected organization for omegas from eighteen to twenty-five in the city, it was my job to plan our weekly activities and monthly educational visits.

"Because Mrs. Cantervale is a widowed omega who needed money to keep from being evicted. And she's old school."

"She's a sadist," Rain murmured. "Valentine and Flora both

just vomited in their napkins, and she's already pouring them more hot oysters." We both stared at the table. We'd been given three shot glasses apiece, and they all smelled particularly ripe. "Must have been a day-old sale at the fish market."

Another omega raced from the table to be sick in the bathroom, and I sighed. I needed this day to go well, especially since last month's speaker had failed to turn up, and I'd been forced to entertain the group for two hours with an impromptu lesson on napkin-folding. It was weird how all our cloth "roses" had turned out looking like squat dicks with enormous knots.

Well, that was omegas for you.

The chestnut-haired woman on Rain's left was the newest League member, and I fought to remember her name as she muttered, "Every alpha I've met stunk like three-day-old roadkill. I'm sure as hell not gonna kiss one. I'd hurl in his mouth."

I almost snorted. The alpha my parents wanted me to marry, Tarquin Gotto-Cambert, smelled like sweaty socks and old cheese.

"I don't have time for this." Rain leaned down, grabbing something from her purse. Her long, straight hair made a dark curtain between us, so I couldn't see what she was up to.

"Rain, do you have nose plugs in there? Because you know a real best friend would share. I only need one."

Before she could reply, Mrs. Cantervale spun on her four-inch heels and returned to our table. We all straightened up, and I smiled brightly at her. "You may find that certain alphas are an acquired taste." She tapped a finger lightly against her lips, shushing us. "In fact, you may find the safety an alpha provides can make up for much more than a lack of scent compatibility." When she drifted away again, I twisted in my chair and saw the phone on Rain's lap.

The image on her screen—a rain cloud with a sun peeking

through—was the business logo for our new, secret, slightly illegal enterprise: the Blue Skies Concierge Agency.

It wasn't technically illegal for omegas to own a business, though according to the county tax office, we were required to have a parent or guardian give permission, even after we turned eighteen. Even though Rain's mom had signed off for her, I'd skipped that step. My parents held very traditional views about omegas and would never have agreed to let me try it.

We'd started in December as an online-only business, offering everything from virtual assistants to life coaches to in-home meal prep. But ever since our other bestie, Candy, had taken a job we'd thought was PA work but had ended up being childcare, our focus had changed. Mainly since we'd only been contacted to provide workers to cover one sort of temp position.

Betasitting.

We didn't have many beta friends. In our experience, the instant an omega started perfuming, most of her beta friends ghosted. We were considered less emotionally stable, less reliable with the heat cycles that kept us locked away in our nests for a week at a time, and less intelligent. Which was bullshit.

So we'd filled the betasitting spots with omegas. Omegas who took scent blockers while on the job, or if, like me, they were allergic to those, they wore enough eau de parfum to dull even an alpha's nose. For some reason, most people thought omegas didn't like other people's children, which meant no one expected the woman showing up for the job to be one of us.

Maybe it wasn't legal for omegas to represent themselves as betas while working, but it was a calculated risk. As long as no one found out their "betasitter" was an "omegasitter"? We would be fine.

"What's going on?"

She didn't answer.

"More jobs? Answer me, Rainbow."

"Four more requests, and we can't cover them, especially with Candy still on her honeymoon." She ran her fingers through her hair, like there might be extra employees hidden between the strands. "And if you call me that again, I'll leave you to do the books on your own this month."

I shuddered. I hated doing the books, even if there wasn't much to deal with. Yet.

"I apologize. Please don't make me handle the accounts payable stuff. You're so much better at it, anyway." I shot her my million-dollar smile, but she just scratched her nose with her middle finger.

Mai, the woman on my right, was obviously eavesdropping. "Wait, you got a job? Where? How?"

Rain gave an aggrieved sigh, tucked the phone away, and lifted an eyebrow at her. "A job, Mai? How could I possibly have a job? I'm an omega. I'm not even allowed to go to college, or have a bank account in my own name, for heaven's sake. My sole purpose in life is to hook up with an alpha and squirt out an infinite number of new alphas until my vagina shrivels up like a raisin."

Mai gasped and stood. "Bless. Your. Heart, Rain Torres."

It was Rain's turn to gasp. "That was rude."

Smirking, Mai excused herself to sit at another table, but not until she gave me a hug, invited me to lunch the following week, and promised to send me the name of her new manicurist.

Rain crossed her arms over her chest. "What is it about you?"

I shrugged. Six years before, after I turned eighteen and began smelling like coconuts and hibiscus, people had started to be attracted to me. Not just alphas, either. Rain teased me that it was because everyone who met me fell in love a little bit.

She might not have been wrong, which worried me slightly. Were my omega pheromones out of control?

Mom believed they were, and that's why she was pressuring me to say yes to marrying her best friend's son, Tarquin Gotto-Cambert. Once I said no—if I could muster up the courage to do that—I knew I'd need to move out.

Rain and I were close to having enough to rent a room in an omegas-only facility, and Rain's mom had already given her permission to move out if she could afford it on her own. I didn't really want to live in sketchy, government-funded omega housing, and I was quietly terrified at the idea of moving out once I told my parents I wasn't going to marry Tarquin. Or maybe anyone. All I'd ever wanted was to have my own business. Something I'd made, and could be proud of.

"Does anyone have any questions? Comments?" Mrs. Cantervale called out.

"Yes," Rain said, and I cringed, knowing what was coming. "Are you kidding? You think the way to find the right husband is to put up with wanting to throw up for our entire married lives? Why not just recommend we all get 'special nose jobs' and remove our ability to smell entirely, or—"

The speaker, her face rigid with anger, stalked toward our table.

Trembling, I stood, placing myself directly in between the two, and forced a gentle smile. Mrs. Cantervale took a breath to speak—or shout—but I held up one open hand and very, very subtly, sent the tiniest bit of my calming omega pheromones into the air around us.

It was considered incredibly rude to do this to another omega, but I hoped she wouldn't notice the hibiscus and coconut underneath the hot, raw oyster stench. She exhaled, then took another breath, her pupils dilating the tiniest bit.

Got her.

I lowered my voice almost to an omega purr, but not quite. "I am so curious, Mrs. Cantervale. The oysters were warmed for us to experience a truly strong odor. That was masterfully done. If we can socialize politely when surrounded by such a unique odor—which is obviously very difficult—then we should have no trouble getting to know all sorts of alphas, regardless of scent compatibility. We could even find... the one." While I blathered on, releasing the tiniest thread of the mood-altering scent all omegas had to some extent, Mrs. Cantervale began to calm down.

"Yes, exactly. Have you tried your oysters, Miss Soleil?"

"Um, not yet."

She reached out and handed me a shot glass, then took one of her own off the table. "Bottoms up!" She watched to make sure I drank mine as well before walking away.

I made it almost a minute, just long enough that the applause thanking Mrs. Cantervale covered up the sound of me throwing up a half-dozen oysters and eleven petit fours onto the carpet at my feet.

"Well, there's that question answered," Rain muttered. "You're definitely a spit girl."

"Shut up and drink your own oyster jizz," I groaned, and went to call the janitorial services.

Chapter 2

Sunshine

"Damage control, damage control," I muttered, as I sent a frantic SOS text to my best friends. My heart was hammering, but I could still hear Tarquin and my parents laughing and talking downstairs. Planning the wedding.

My wedding.

"Why am I such a pushover?" I ran my fingers through my hair in frustration. I'd styled it in long, loose curls, and worn the sunshine yellow Valentino dress and new heels Mom had bought me the week before.

The hideously huge diamond solitaire Tarquin had slipped over my knuckle a few moments ago suddenly caught in one of my curls. I tugged and pulled, but couldn't get the prong that had snagged my hair to come loose.

"Ouch!"

I took a few deep breaths, fighting back tears. I knew I had to go back downstairs in a minute, and whenever I cried, my pale skin turned an awful, mottled red and my eyes puffed up like I was having an allergy attack. "Sunny girls should never cry," Dad always said. "Smiles only, my buttercup."

"The heck with that," I mumbled, resting my left hand on the side of my head while I checked Rain's reply.

> Rain: What's wrong? Sock breath try to kiss you?

Thank goodness she'd texted back. I angled my phone so I could send a picture of the ring.

> Rain: Fuck. WHY???

> Candy: WTAF take it off! Stop messing around.

I set the phone down on my vanity table to type.

> Didn't mean to. Didn't know how to say no.

> Candy: Take it off. The longer it stays in, the harder it is to take out.

I stared at the screen in confusion.

> WHAT?

> Rain: Stop talking about loverboy's knot, Mrs. Paxson.

I laughed in spite of myself. Candy was on her honeymoon in the Seychelles, and half her texts over the past two weeks had been gushing about how glorious sex with her alpha was. A few had been beachy vacation pics. The ones Rain and I had discussed saving for blackmail were the drunk texts of her husband's butt, along with one impressive, blurry nighttime snap of his monster peen. I swear to god, the knot at the base of his dick had been the size of a damned grapefruit.

> Candy: OMG sorry... The longer it stays ON, the harder it is to take OFF.

> I will. But how do I tell him no?

> Rain: Try "No. You stink. I'd rather slurp hot oysters."

> Candy: Tell him you have PTSD from eating bad cheese. And from gym class in middle school.

> Rain: Just say no.

> Candy: What the tiny, mean lady said.

> Rain: Fuck all the way off, Candy.

> Candy: Love you too! GTG time for couples massage class. Soleil, SAY NO!

> Save me please...

> Rain: Calling.

The phone rang, but when I answered, all I could hear was a burst of laughter from downstairs, where Tarquin and my parents were still eating brunch and planning my doom.

"Rain, seriously. It's an emergency." I choked off a sob.

She stopped laughing. "You have time, Sunshine. He's not going to ask you to run off with him today."

"Oh, really? Mom was talking about romantic elopements. She and Dad eloped the day after they got engaged, and they're giving Tarquin ideas. They were giving him *directions* to their chapel in Vegas! Please come over." When Rain was around, I felt stronger. Her omega energy had this fierce, give-no-fucks-take-no-prisoners edge to it, and it was almost like I channeled it.

"I can't, remember? I'm covering that three-week betasitting gig over in Buckley Place. Get back in there and tell him to eat shit, girl. Tell him how you feel!"

"I can't!" I yanked my left hand down and pulled the ring loose, along with some of my hair.

Her tone darkened. "Why? Did he bark at you?"

"I'm not sure Tarquin has ever barked, Rain. It's just... you know how I get." My voice had risen to a squeak, and she shushed me.

"You'll have to tell him no eventually. You can't marry him."

"I know. But I can't do it tonight. His parents are on their way over for champagne. I can't face... all of them." Especially Tarquin. He was my good friend, and sweet as pie. But the few times we'd kissed, I'd had a visceral understanding of the phrase *it felt like kissing my brother*.

And honestly, I'd caught him wiping off his lips on his sleeve, so I had a feeling it wasn't just me.

Rain cursed into the phone, then exhaled. "Okay, two birds, one stone. Between Flora, Val, and me, we were able to cover three of the betasitting jobs that came in."

I hummed in reply. Rain had taken a longer-term job a few days before. I'd been the one to send our company's apologies to the final, last-minute request from the personal assistant of an unnamed businessman. The guy wouldn't give specifics about the job until whoever took the work signed an iron-clad NDA. No details meant that job fell to the bottom of the list.

Rain went on. "That just leaves—"

"I'll take it." I cut her off, grabbing a suitcase from my closet and stuffing random clothing and shoes into it. I dumped my whole underwear drawer in, then pulled half of them back out. I was packing like a lunatic, but I really didn't have time to pick and choose. "How long was it for again?"

"Ten days, starting tonight," Rain reminded me with a sigh, "and the PA pinged me again this afternoon, desperate. He doubled the rate."

"I said I'll do it."

"You can't. We don't have any details, except that the pay is astronomical."

When she said the number, I gasped. "That would cover an apartment for a year!"

"*Three* years and utilities in my neighborhood. Sun, I don't like it. It's too much. It could be a cartel, for fuck's sake."

"I'd betasit for Satan if it got me out of marrying Tarquin," I vowed, grabbing my bottle of Hawaiian Magique perfume from my dresser and spritzing all my pulse points. Normally, omegas didn't wear synthetic stuff; it made us feel slightly sick. But all our sitters needed to cover up their individual scents. Whether that meant using expensive scent blockers, or just cheap perfume to make people mistake us for betas who were trying too hard. "I'll fill out the NDA and sign the contract. Can you get your shady rideshare guy to pick me up two streets over?"

"Monty? Yeah," she said. "But if he asks to see your tits again—"

"I know. Punch him in the nuts," I replied wryly. For years, Rain had been trying to teach me how to be assertive and badass like she was. It was never going to happen. But I humored her. "I'll totally break his balls with my ninja-style moves. I'm a trained martial artist, you know." It was true; the League offered enrichment classes to all its members.

"Sun, you trained in meditative tai chi. If a sloth attacks, you'll win every time. I mean it; don't fuck around. Take the pepper spray I got you."

"Yes, Mother," I snarked, but stopped when someone yelled in the background on her end. Not a child. A grown man, a stranger. He was yelling her name over and over, demanding to know where she was. Practically barking at her.

An alpha? Shit. We'd both been so busy this week—me with damage control at the League, and her with Blue Skies bookings and helping her mom—that I hadn't asked about her gig. Come to think of it, she'd been mostly radio silent for a few days now, except for our morning meme check-ins.

That wasn't like her.

"Rain, are you okay?" When she didn't answer quickly, my heart raced. I fished the pepper spray out from under my dresser. For *her*, I would fight dragons. Or even alphas. "I'll fuck up whoever that is. Just shoot me the address."

"Oh no," she practically purred. She sounded the same way she did when she was about to dive into a giant bowl of pistachio ice cream. "This asshole is all mine. And he's going to pay, at last."

I had no idea what she meant, but I heard Tarquin's parents arrive and knew I had to go. I said goodbye, promising to call later. Then I left a note for Mom telling her I had to leave, but I'd be at my friend Candy's estate for the week, at the other end of our gated community.

Then I snuck down the back staircase, holding up a finger to my lips when our live-in cook looked up from the television in the kitchen. "Where are you going, Miss Soleil? Your fella's in the dining room." Her brow furrowed as she stared at the ring.

Shit! The ring.

"Belva. Keep this for me?" I pulled it off to hand it to her, but she backed away.

"Oh, honey, no," she said firmly, shaking her head. "I'll do a

15

lot for you, but I'm not breaking that poor boy's heart. You put that back on now."

"I can't marry him, Belva. And you know I will if I don't go. They'll talk me into it." I looked around for somewhere to leave it, but she glared at me.

"You'll give that back to him in person when you come back?" I nodded fervently. "And you're going somewhere safe?"

"I promise."

"Then I never saw you," she murmured, zipping her lips with a finger.

I slid the hateful ring back on and watched her slip into the powder room. Then I tiptoed to the back door, my suitcase wheeling soundlessly behind me, and ran away from my nightmare life.

Two hours later, I was standing at the end of one of the private piers on King George Bay, staring at an even worse nightmare. The pier was well-lit, but the yacht sitting at a short distance from it was even more so.

A brilliant, enormous white behemoth of a luxury vessel, it had to be four hundred feet long, and looked like a futuristic starship had landed in the bay. There were four levels above the main deck with an observation deck on top, a helicopter pad up front, and what looked like a dance club with colored lights flashing near the back. The shining brass fixtures all along the sides were almost blinding, even at a distance.

The smaller boat waiting at the pier matched the yacht, down to the strange nautilus shapes on the windows. Someone had decorated it with white silk bunting and gold ribbons, mixed with fresh white peonies, calla lilies, and white roses with what I was almost certain was real gold foil pressed onto the petals.

My parents were millionaires, thanks to a few software patents my dad had filed a long time ago, and I was used to a level of luxury. But this was light years beyond anything we could afford, not that Dad would ever buy a boat. Or gold-leaf roses.

"Miss, are you here for the wedding?" A man stepped out of the small boat, dressed in a crisp white maritime uniform.

The wedding. The NDA had said this was a wedding gig. But this couldn't be the place.

Not by the water. The *ocean*. The most dangerous place in the world for a person like me.

I'd rather be in the dentist's chair.

I'd rather be slurping warm oysters by the bucketful.

I'd rather be marrying a man who smelled like the runniest blue cheese in the world, stuffed inside the dirtiest old socks.

"No, not me! No boats for me, thanks!" I chirped, walking backward while I fished in my purse for my phone. I'd sent off my contracts, but hadn't received any details other than the address, length, and event type. I'd assumed the job was in a mansion near the waterfront. If I'd known it was a boat, I would never have taken it, no matter how much it paid.

The sailor called out again, "Miss? Can I at least help you with your case?"

I waved him off again, pulling my suitcase backward like a demented crab. "All a terrible misunderstanding!" I replied, starting to turn. But my heel caught on something, and I slipped. My knee buckled as I began to fall.

My suitcase tipped over with a thump, but I never hit the ground.

Something warm, hard, and smelling like warm chocolate and coffee, pressed against my back. I peered down at my waist. Massive, firm hands wrapped around me, the skin slightly darker than tan. No rings, but a sprinkling of dark hairs and—holy hell, I'd never seen fingers that looked like they worked out. But if I squinted I could actually see... *definition.*

"Finger muscles?" I murmured, touching one of them. "Who has finger muscles?"

"Finger *what?* Who the hell are you?" The deep, alpha voice had every single one of the hairs on my entire body standing on end. I sucked in a breath to answer, got a lungful of that rich, decadent scent, and the words I meant to say came out as a moan.

The man actually *growled.* "Are you on drugs?"

Holy crud, I was acting like I was in heat! I shook my head and pulled away from the addictive warmth of the arms that held me, and turned to face my rescuer. "I'm so sorry, Mr...." I began, before I saw him.

I tried to speak, but my lips were no longer listening to my brain. No, the only parts of my body that were answering any sort of call to action were my ovaries. I pressed one hand against my abdomen as a thrumming pulse below my waist began to beat out the ancient, doubled drumbeat that chanted: *Al-pha. Al-pha. Al-pha.*

He was tall, well over six feet, dark-haired, with an olive complexion and near-black eyes that flashed in the lights from the yacht. His cheekbones were high, his jawline chiseled. A hint of silver flashed at his temples. The wind blew a lock of hair over his forehead like a scene from a Hollywood blockbuster, the shine on it as iridescent as a raven's wing. His muscley hands flexed as he crossed his arms impatiently.

I'd never used hard drugs, but now I wondered if the ride-share driver had slipped me something. I had to be hallucinating. This man was the most beautiful, perfect, gloriously honed specimen of alpha-ness I'd ever seen. And he smelled like my favorite mocha latte. My mouth watered.

He wore a white dress shirt, open at the collar, over an obviously muscled chest that stretched the fabric slightly. A loosened gray silk tie hung around his neck like a promise. Or a threat. Or both. A pair of dark gray, pinstriped trousers that clung to his thighs ended in shining black dress shoes.

"Answer me now," he demanded, a hint of his alpha bark in the words.

I whimpered slightly, but still couldn't speak. The drumbeat in my abdomen had moved lower, to my clit, and now it was a jazz drum solo, the pulsing so irregular and fast I wondered if I was having some sort of attack. A *clit* attack. This had to be a medical condition. I'd never felt anything so intense before. Like I could have an orgasm by mere proximity to this man.

My eyes trailed back up his body, but caught on the front of his trousers. And the ridiculously huge lump that was suddenly growing there, destroying the perfect line of his suit. As I stared, I could almost make out the widened knot at the base of a wine-bottle-thick erection.

There was no way that was real. But what if it was?

Everybody had a party trick, and mine had always been to fit my entire fist in my mouth. But that was probably wider than my fist. I chewed at my lip, considering hypotheticals. Maybe, if I used enough lip gloss, and came at it from an angle... I blinked furiously, reminding myself that I was not here for an alpha.

Think of the children, Soleil. Think of the money.

I shivered as he inhaled sharply, and my eyes returned to his face. "Who are you?" he repeated, a phone out and in his hand already. "This is a private pier and a private event, girl."

I frowned. I'd liked him better when he kept his mouth shut. "I'm not a girl. I'm twenty-four. I'm from the Blue Skies

Concierge agency." I pulled my own phone out and turned it to face him. He stopped typing on his own and snatched it away, reading aloud.

"Soleil Annette Fairweather, twenty-four years old... betasitter?" That sharp jawline clenched as he sniffed. For some reason, he began to growl slightly, as if there were some threat I couldn't see. I glanced around, my pulse jumping, then inched away. He growled louder. "I hope you're a more accomplished *betasitter* than you are a liar, Miss Fairweather."

I forced my features to smoothness. Did he suspect I was an omega? "How rude. I don't know who you are, but I have a job to get to. So if you'll hand back my phone, Mr..."

"Grantham." He stepped closer, so that I had to crane my neck to meet his stern gaze. "Giovanni Grantham."

"Oh crap," I breathed, now that my brain had started working again.

This was Giovanni Grantham? The notoriously private, billionaire co-owner of at least a quarter of the cruise ships in the world. Chosen as Bachelor of the Year five times by *Alpha Roll* magazine until he bought out the entire parent media company and dismantled it, just to stop the annual articles about him. Supposedly, he'd hated the nickname the magazine had given him, when they reported that the gorgeous man before me had never once been seen to smile.

Unfortunately, that's what slipped out of my mouth as I greeted my new boss. "Grumpy Grantham?"

Chapter 3

Grumpy

I knew I was a miserable asshole. I had to be. At forty-two, I'd spent two full decades at the helm of Duchess Cruises, the company my father had dumped in my lap with a casual "Don't fuck it all up," on his way to retire to a small island near Bali. He was living his dream, but there was no place for that sort of frivolousness in my life. Dreaming only led to mistakes. In my work, a single fuckup could cost thousands their jobs or even their lives.

In my personal life? Well, I'd learned the hard way not to allow the slightest deviation when it came to navigating my way through the dangerous waters of being one of the wealthiest unmarried alphas alive. It was unbelievable what women and even some men would do to try to lure me to them. As if being at my side at a gala, or in my bed, meant they owned some part of me.

So I embraced my asshole nature. And except for one notable exception, I'd managed to stay on course for decades, keeping my family afloat financially, my friends few enough that I knew who I could trust, and everyone else as far away as possible.

But now, not two full minutes after meeting a young woman in a modest, bright yellow lace dress that promised innocence—though the curves underneath hinted at wild nights of debauchery—I was lost.

First, in her scent, coconut and some lush tropical flower, that lay under a heavier layer of awful, cloying perfume. Her own underlying notes emerged when I touched her, though, and sank like a stone straight to my cock. That part of me had been half-hard after one brush of her silken skin, and now was threatening to tear its way through my favorite suit to get to her.

Her thorough inspection hadn't helped one bit. My knot had even begun to swell at the base, like it wanted to make sure she noticed it, too.

Then, I'd made the mistake of looking into her eyes, the green and blue swirls of her irises like some sort of tidepool that trapped unwary men. The long lashes that framed them. The innocence that shone, along with curiosity and a blooming sensuality.

She was every fantasy I'd never allowed myself, come to life.

My fucking teeth ached like I'd bitten into something cold, and the only thing that could soothe the pain was her hot skin under them. Her soft flesh, breaking slightly as I bit down, claiming her as mine. Marking her forev...

I stopped breathing, a frisson of dread running down my spine. It wasn't possible.

I didn't believe in true mates. Only one alpha I knew claimed to have met his, and she'd been standing at the altar with another man at the time. But he'd told me what it felt like once, when we were drunk. "Like getting kicked in the dick so hard you forget how to breathe, forget your name," Victor had mumbled. "And all you want is for her to keep kicking until you die from the pain."

Of course, ridiculously sappy movies and books portrayed it far more romantically. Supposedly, if you met yours, you just *knew*.

But this woman... One breath of her, and my cock ached.

I clenched my fists as she stared at the front of my trousers. A small bead of sweat rolled down her temple, dampening her golden curls, and her lips moved. She whispered something about children, and then, when I leaned in closer, breathing in that ridiculous tropical scent that made me want a drink with a fucking umbrella in it more than I ever had in my life... I heard her words clearly.

"Think of the money."

Think of the money? For some inexplicable reason, I couldn't breathe. Like she'd punched me in the gut.

She couldn't be my true mate. She was a fortune hunter.

I'd already dialed security when she thrust her phone at me, and I saw a familiar document. My PA made every employee sign one. I scanned it quickly. Her name, Soleil Fairweather, suited her. The golden hair, the sun-kissed skin. The smile that kept peeking out, even now when she was so obviously nervous. I stepped closer to her, liking the way she shivered and dropped her gaze when I did so.

Think of the money. The little gold digger.

If I had time, I'd teach her to try and play those sorts of games with me. She would look gorgeous on her knees, wearing nothing but a diamond collar, tears on her pink cheeks, my cum dripping from one corner of those soft, pretty lips... *Fuck.* I tore my gaze away and adjusted myself discreetly.

Even if she hadn't revealed herself inadvertently, she was still a temporary employee of Duchess Cruises, so I wasn't allowed to touch. And I couldn't fire her now. Damnit, I *needed* someone to keep an eye on my niece.

But this fresh, young omega, who looked like a literal ray of sunshine...a *betasitter?* I almost choked. This woman was no more a beta than I was, though the strong perfume she wore may have been her attempt to disguise her status.

I knew omegas. My sister Lorelei—who was getting married on my private island in a week unless I could stop her—was one. When she went out, she also wore a heavy scent.

Omegas were supposedly soft-tempered and emotionally fragile, but the ones I'd known had been territorial and protective. Would Lore even allow this stunningly beautiful woman to be in such close quarters with her alpha fiancé? I doubted it.

My teeth ground together as I thought about Alphonse Dubois, my sister's latest poor choice, but possibly her most dangerous one. He set off every alarm bell I had, though I'd called Storm Halder, who owned almost every private investigative firm in the Western Hemisphere, and he hadn't been able to dig up any real dirt on the alpha. Yet.

I'd confided my misgivings to my sister, but she'd brushed them aside. Lore was an adult, a mother, and ten years older than me. If she wanted to ignore her younger brother, that was fine. But I'd insisted on hiring a sitter for the cruise, thinking it might give me a chance to speak to Lore again, before the damned ceremony. Get her to listen.

Time was running out for me to discover what set my instincts blazing around Alphonse. Something about the brutish alpha made me think he might take pleasure in hurting others.

For a moment, my vision blacked out as the image of Alphonse manhandling Soleil, injuring her, flashed before my mind's eye. I bit back a growl, and noticed Soleil edging away carefully.

I wouldn't let that happen. He would never so much as touch her, or I would flay every inch of skin that...

Fuck. I was growling louder now.

I cleared my throat. "I hope you're a more accomplished *betasitter* than you are a liar, Miss Fairweather."

When I accused her of trespassing on my private pier, she acted innocent, then claimed not to know who I was. She seemed to be telling the truth—though she couldn't be, not with that whispered remark about money—but then she froze when I told her who I was.

"Grumpy Grantham?"

That fucking nickname again? Suddenly, I wanted to turn her over my knee and spank the brat out of her. But what else had she...?

"So, you're a liar *and* a fortune hunter. What else are you, little omega?" I crossed my arms over my chest, alarmed at the growing urge I had to hold her. Or shake the truth out of her. "How the hell did you end up here?"

Those blue-green eyes flew wide. "I was hired. And I'm not any of those things—except an omega. I know it's unusual for one to take a position as a betasitter. But your PA was extremely persistent—" The yacht's horn sounded, and over the omega's shoulder, the Little Duchess's co-captain tilted his head toward the waiting tender in a silent question. "...and I was the only one left at the agency who could cover this job. I can go now, if you think I'm not suitable."

For some reason, the thought of sending this young, deceptive thing back out into the late afternoon where I couldn't see her, know what she was doing and with whom, caused something in my gut to twist. I leaned down, grabbing her suitcase, which was surprisingly light. "Do you at least have experience with children?"

"Before I became... this"—she waved a hand at her body as

if it were not a sumptuously delectable package—"I was a summer camp counselor every year. I love children. Well, loved. After I turned eighteen, I wasn't given the opportunity to be around them much." My heart ached slightly at the way her lip wobbled. But then she forced that cheerful smile back on her lips. A smile I was starting to hate, since it wasn't real.

Her eyes met mine, and I longed to force a genuine reaction. A frown. A shout. Something. I sneered at her obviously designer shoes, yellow lace dress, and the soft leather purse in her manicured right hand. "Poor omega. What a difficult life you've had. Such a lack of opportunities. You have my deepest sympathy."

Her smile dimmed slightly, then brightened. "No. But I find that how you see life has a lot to do with how you decide to look at it. Like my dad always says: chin up, heart open, smile on. That's all anyone needs to make it through a storm."

"What the fu— What a *ridiculous* aphorism. Like a failed fortune cookie. Daddy's girl, you've got a lot to learn." Shaking my head, I walked toward the wide, carpeted gangplank. Someone had tied ridiculous silk banners all over the railings. "Get on the boat, Sunshine."

"Sir, yes, sir," she replied, with a mock salute.

A salute that drew my attention to the diamond ring that twinkled on the fourth finger of her left hand.

Fuck.

Chapter 4

Sunshine

M om liked to tell the story of how I smiled in the hospital the day I was born, and never stopped. "All the nurses loved you," she would say. "Even if it was probably gas."

Sometimes it seemed I'd spent all twenty-four years of my life smiling, and after only an hour on board the superyacht, I knew I was going to need all those years of practice to hold onto my temper.

Or my sanity.

That insufferable man had interrogated me, growled at me, and stared at me all the way to the yacht. Then he'd practically dragged me onto the boat before vanishing, dumping me on a steward at the very first opportunity. Grumpy Grantham indeed.

"So, why is this boat called the Little Duchess XI?" I asked the dark-haired twelve-year-old inside my room, who stood with her arms crossed and a suspicious glare on her face. She was dressed in all black from head to toe, including her long-sleeved top, floor-length skirt, Doc Marten boots, and what looked like a hand-drawn neck tattoo. I hoped it was Sharpie markered on, but who knew what billionaires' children were allowed to do. Apparently, they had free rein to enter the staff bedrooms unannounced. "Do you know? I hope the first ten Little Duchesses didn't sink or something."

No response.

I glanced up from the pile of clothing and shoes on my bed. So far, besides the ones I had on, I only had one other pair of shoes that matched—five-inch red heels that Rain had bought me as a joke. I'd managed to bring enough socks and underwear for three weeks, except I'd only grabbed lacy thongs and two pairs of my day-of-the-week granny panties—Thursday and Sunday.

My clothing options were even worse. Instead of bringing my go-to casual outfits, I'd managed to pack the things I'd pulled to the front of my closet to give away. Everything was either too tight, not my style, or something my friends had given me to try and get me to stop dressing in what they said were "Quaker-approved" outfits. They'd bought a bunch of dresses at an online boutique that specialized in discreet bondage wear, but I'd never been drunk enough to wear them.

"Not enough tequila in the world," I mumbled, hastily stuffing a top that sported tiny padlocks all the way down the front behind the one dark blue formal gown I'd packed. I shoved my wallet and engagement ring in the safe, then turned back to the messy bed.

I had ten minutes before I was expected back in the main dining room to meet Lorelei Grantham, the bride on this wedding voyage. According to the crew member who'd escorted me to my room, she would give me my detailed instructions for the duration of the cruise.

Well, at least I had one outfit that wasn't ridiculous. I smoothed the front of my bright yellow dress and peered down at my feet. The new shoes I'd worn all day had rubbed blisters in my heels, and I'd almost cried with relief when I realized I'd actually packed sandals.

Maybe no one would notice one was gold and one silver.

I slid the empty case under my bed and stood, addressing my cabin guest again. "Is your name... Serena?" I'd been given a list with all the children's names and ages onboard. I hoped I wasn't in charge of all nine of them, though it would explain the ridiculous compensation. I wouldn't remember any of the names until I could put faces to them. But I could learn this one. "Eleanor?" I widened my smile as the girl's scowl grew deeper. "Blaire? Devon?"

"No, I'm Sylvia." She left the words *you idiot* unspoken.

"That's a lovely name," I said, holding out my hand to shake.

She backed up slightly, but didn't move out of the doorway. "I'm going to change it as soon as I can."

"To what?" At this range, I could see the neck tattoo was definitely done in permanent marker, and more than that—it was words.

"Ennui," she drawled, with a lovely French accent. "I want everything about my person to reflect my inner miasma."

I bit the inside of my cheek to keep from smiling. "So you're an intellectual. And..."—I hazarded a guess—"a poet, I would think." She tilted her head at me, her lip curling on one side like she'd smelled something rank.

"What would a betasitter know about poetry?" She arched her neck up, and I read the first words of the tattoo aloud.

"'I shut my eyes...'"

A wicked smile curled up as she yanked her collar tightly around her throat and buttoned it so I couldn't read the rest. "And all the world drops dead," she intoned, overdramatically. She paused, as if waiting for a reaction.

I just smiled and gestured for her to go ahead of me. "It was one of my favorite poems when I was younger. I'm surprised you like it so much."

She scoffed, trotting nimbly up the narrow stairs to the next deck. "You don't need to pretend, Betasitter. I'm not going to 'bond with you,' or whatever you have in mind. My mom just asked me to make sure you came straight to the family lounge."

"Your mother?"

"The *bride*." She practically spat the word.

Oof. "That was kind of her. Is she worried I'll fall overboard?"

She arched a black brow. "More likely that you'll pinch some wedding guest's jewels."

I fought to hold onto my smile. "Well, I'm more worried about the former. Slightly terrified, in fact." I kept walking, wondering if she would take the bait.

She did. "Why does that terrify you, Betasitter?"

I lifted an eyebrow as we reached the third level, where the map in my room had indicated the bar was located. "Because I don't swim."

She stopped, gaping at me, her tongue pink against the near-black lipstick. "You don't know how to swim? Why would you come out on a boat? There are two pools. And the entire ocean. We'll be swimming every day. Snorkeling."

"I won't," I said, shuddering at the thought. "And I know *how* to swim. I just can't." I lowered my voice so she had to get closer. "I'm a sinker."

"A what?"

"A sinker," I repeated. "I have negative buoyancy. High bone mass. It means when I go into the water, unlike you, I don't float. I sink." I stopped and tapped my chin with one finger. "Not as fast as my great-grandfather did, thank goodness. Perks of being a woman and having slightly more body fat." She looked like she didn't believe me, so I went on. "Go ahead, look it up. It's a genetic condition. My great-grandfather would vouch for me." I paused dramatically. "But he drowned, of course."

"I will look it up," she said, grasping the brass handles of the door to our right. "If you're lying, my mother will fire you. She can't abide liars."

I opened the door just as she turned to go, and met her dark eyes. "I lift my lids," I murmured, "and all is born again. I think I—"

"—made you up inside my head," she finished, following me now into the bar. "You really know it?"

"Yes. I memorized it in my senior year of high school. Did your mother name you for Sylvia Plath?"

For a moment, I thought she might laugh, but her face went flat and eyes wide, as she peered over my shoulder.

"What an inappropriate personal question, Miss Fairweather." I whirled to see Giovanni Grantham standing against the back wall of the wood-paneled room, next to a seated woman that had to be his sister. They both watched me like I was a venomous spider, and they weren't sure if I was the jumping kind or not.

Lorelei half-stood and asked, "You're Soleil Fairweather? The betasitter?" She sniffed, then peeked down at her phone, as if to check.

"Oh, it's her," Giovanni growled. He had changed into another suit, a darker one, for some reason. Lorelei wore a shimmering sapphire cocktail dress that I was almost certain I'd seen on a television awards show recently.

I glanced down at my mismatched sandals and shrugged internally. I was never going to measure up to these people, at least not in their eyes. And all I was here for was a job. "Excuse me, Mr. Grump—Mr. Grantham," I said with a nod. Next to me, Sylvia snorted. "I didn't mean to be rude. I was getting to know Sylvia. She is incredibly intelligent—"

Another voice, with an odd, quasi-British accent, interrupted me. "Did someone die?" A man I hadn't noticed moved out from behind the bar. He was a huge alpha, dressed in a suit with diamond cufflinks winking at his wrists, but his face looked like he'd made his fortune in a boxing ring. He laid a hand on Lorelei's waist and kissed the side of her hair as he moved past. "I asked you a question, Sylvia. Did someone die?" His voice was warm, but I noticed a slight tremor run through Sylvia's thin frame, and I stepped slightly in front of her instinctively.

He narrowed his eyes at me. I didn't move, though. I had no idea who this man was, but the instant the other adults in the room couldn't see his expression, it changed. His smile grew sharp edges, his eyes lost their sparkle, and even his scent grew slightly thicker, a boiled cabbage odor that forced me to breathe through my mouth.

"No, Alphonse," Sylvia finally replied. "No one died."

"Then why are you dressed for a funeral, my little crumpet? We've spoken about this already."

Giovanni started coughing then, almost covering Sylvia's muttered, "Call me a crumpet again, and there *will* be a funeral."

"Sylvia!" Lorelei hissed.

Alphonse laughed. "Now, now, is that any way to talk to your new dad?"

There was a moment of silence, before Sylvia's enraged shout filled the room. "My dad is dead. You'll never be anything like he was. You're nothing."

The spark of fury in the man's eyes had me moving even more squarely in front of the little girl. I pasted on my million-dollar smile and held out a hand, even if touching this man was the last thing I wanted to do. "Hello, I'm Soleil Fairweather. I'm betasitting on board this week. We haven't met?"

He grabbed my hand, but instead of shaking it, leaned down and pressed his lips to the tops of my fingers.

A strange rumbling noise came from the corner of the room.

"I'm Alphonse Dubois," the alpha said, squeezing my fingers so tightly it hurt. "And the luckiest man in the world." He dropped my hand, leaving a smear of his alpha stench behind. I tucked it behind me, rubbing it roughly on the back of my dress.

Suddenly, Lorelei was there at his side. "What was that, Fons?" Her eyes flashed at her fiancé, then at me.

"Trying for sophisticated," Alphonse said, pulling her into his side. "You're always saying I'm too uncivilized. How am I ever going to fit in with your family if I don't learn to behave?"

Lorelei laughed, a high trill of sound that was as beautiful as it was brittle. "Maybe I like you uncivilized. But don't crowd the... *beta*sitter."

The perfume may have covered my omega scent, but Lorelei obviously recognized my nature. Any omega with an intended mate would be territorial. I wanted to assure her I had no designs on her alpha, that I was probably going to decontaminate my hand the first chance I got.

But then I caught sight of Sylvia slipping out the door and racing back down the stairs. "Uh-oh." I glanced up at Lorelei. "Should I go after her? Wait... are there more children for me to watch over? A playroom onboard? It wasn't clear how many I would be taking care of."

She wasn't paying any attention to me, though. She'd pulled Alphonse close to whisper into his ear, her face wretched with concern and anger.

"Your only charge is my niece," Giovanni said, walking past

me. "The other children came with their own au pairs and beta-sitters."

I was being paid this much to watch one child?

"Get your instructions from Lorelei. I'll go take care of Sylvia." He stopped next to me and whispered so quietly that only I could hear, "Flirting with my sister's fiancé, Sunshine? What would dear Daddy say about that?"

My jaw dropped, but before I could formulate a reply, he was gone. I took a deep breath, drawing the remnants of dark chocolate and espresso into my lungs, then faced the angry omega in the room. "Do you have instructions on Sylvia's care?"

Oh, *did* she. Thirty minutes later, I had an impending migraine, a downloaded document listing what had to be twenty minor medical conditions and food sensitivities, strict parameters for what she was allowed to wear while on board, and the knowledge that no matter how hard I tried, nothing I did this week would pass muster with Lorelei Grantham.

I almost wanted to text Rain to let her know I'd finally met someone who hated me on sight. Well, two someones, if you counted Lorelei's painfully attractive brother.

"I'm not sure where Giovanni's PA dug you up, Miss Fair-weather, and if we weren't already three hours out to sea, I would have you disembark and find another betasitter." Her exquisitely made-up face wasn't nearly as attractive with that expression.

I smiled wider, hoping she'd take the hint.

She looked at me like I'd lost my mind. Maybe I had. "My daughter is the most precious thing in the world to me," she said, enunciating each word. "And she has been through more than any child should. If anything happens to her..." Her voice trailed off, and Alphonse embraced her.

While staring at me.

Her face was buried in his shoulder, but his eyes roamed all over my body in a way that felt like a violation. I practically ran for the door.

I fixed a smile on my face when I passed a couple sunbathing on deck, and waved at two young children playing in a wading pool with a small fountain. Sure enough, even though their respective parents were present, each child had a designated au pair watching from the pool's edge.

I stopped on my way to my cabin at a bathroom near the pool, and scrubbed at my hands. They still stunk like cabbage even after the first two times, so I used more soap, scrubbing all the way up to my elbows. While I washed, my mind wandered back to Giovanni Grantham.

Why had I felt so attracted to him? After all these years of thinking alphas had some sort of amazing PR team telling everyone they smelled great, when I knew they smelled like moldy towels at best, I'd finally met one who made me want to roll around in his sheets. Made me want to take those sheets, and his shirts, and wrap them around me until I couldn't smell anything but... "Oh *shit*," I whispered, inhaling. My own scent filled the tiny room, and I realized to my complete mortification that my panties were damp.

No, soaked.

I ran to the toilet and used as much toilet paper as I could to wipe the slick away from both the thin silk and myself. It was far more liquid than I usually produced, which had me counting in my head back to my last heat cycle. *Hmph.* I had plenty of time. Months. It couldn't be that.

I sighed in relief and went back to work on the panties, but gave up after a minute. They were a dead loss. I threw them in the trash, then washed my hands again. I'd finally managed to get rid of the cabbage smell, but my camou-flaging eau de parfum was now also a distant memory. I'd need to go to my room, spray myself down, and put on one of the scent-blocking pantyliners I'd packed. Did I have enough for a whole week on board a yacht with Giovanni Grantham?

Definitely not. I'd need to learn the layout of the boat, and take pains to avoid him. Maybe Sylvia and I could hunker down in her room, or a side galley, and memorize Plath and Poe. "He's a butthole, Sun," I whispered to myself as I opened the door. "A rich, rude"—I swallowed, and used one of Rain's favorite phrases—"fucking alphahole!" I said with a bit more confidence as I stepped back out onto deck.

"Are you cursing, Miss Fairweather?" The alphahole in question was right outside, leaning up against the side of the boat, looking like the next cover of *Yacht Guild* magazine.

I put my hands to my cheeks, covering what I knew was a blush. "No," I told him. "I'm... practicing a line from a play." My cheeks grew hot, and I knew they were bright red.

"That's cute," Giovanni said with a sexy sneer. Ugh. How could a sneer even be sexy? "Do your cheeks go pink every time you tell a lie, little betasitter?"

"No," I gritted out through clenched teeth, fully aware that my blush was deepening.

"Oh, they do." He straightened and crossed the deck so that he was right next to me. I backed up against the wall, and he set one hand on the outside of my shoulder, boxing me in. Then he leaned in until his dark hair brushed the side of my face, and sniffed. "Naughty, naughty. You deserve pink cheeks everywhere for telling lies. Need to be punished, don't you?"

What. The. Hell.

Was Grumpy Grantham checking on my kinks? Because I'd never been spanked in my life, but all of a sudden, it was imperative that I find out what his hand on my ass would feel like. Just for research, of course.

I stifled a whimper, clenching my thighs together, but still felt a tiny trickle of wetness.

"Smell that? Luring me with that scent." Giovanni leaned closer, grasping my left hand and glaring at it for some reason. "Is that what you like to do? Use that sweet face, that perfume, to get you what you want? Get alphas to fall for you, give you pretty things? Give you what that curvy little body is begging for?" He went still, waiting for something.

Waiting for an answer. My mind spun as I tried to make sense of what he'd been asking in that sinful, dark chocolate voice.

"That's what you are, isn't it? A fortune-hunting honey trap? You chase wealthy alphas often?" He ran a finger along my neckline. "Or are you going to pretend this is your first time?"

My blood turned to ice. He was calling me an opportunist, at best. Maybe even a whore.

"No," I replied evenly, my lust evaporating. "I do not chase alphas."

He blinked, obviously surprised at my answer. His hand moved to my cheek, as gentle as his words had been cutting, and he murmured something that sounded like, "No blush now."

I ducked under his arm. "Please leave me alone, Mr. Grantham. I have a job to do." I looked around. "Where is Sylvia?"

His eyes were practically drilling holes through me, but he eventually answered. "Safe. I left her in her cabin. You should go there. Her name's on the door."

I blinked. "Which direction?" This wasn't a cruise liner, but there were dozens of cabins and staterooms on the yacht, and I didn't want to wander for an hour knocking on every door.

"Port side, aft." He nodded curtly, then turned to go before I could reveal I had no idea what aft and port meant. "Miss Fairweather? Please dress *appropriately* for dinner. And make sure my niece does as well."

A small, molten ball of anger began to churn in my gut. "Appropriately. And what *precisely* does that mean?"

His gaze slid over my dress. "Whatever the nicest thing you have to wear is. Just... cover yourself." With one last frown, he was gone, greeting the couple by the pool with a wave before he vanished through a door.

Cover myself? Like I was dressed in a thong bikini? I glanced around. Half the people on deck were wearing just that, and no one blinked.

I wanted to chase him down and punch him in his perfect face. Tell him to stick his chauvinistic, alphahole attitude right up his portside aft. Instead, I went straight to my room and screamed into a pillow so loud that a crewmember passing by knocked to make sure I wasn't being murdered.

Once she left, I washed my face, texted Rain and Candy, and replaced my underwear before going in search of my charge. For a boat that supposedly had eighty wedding guests, ten "guest employees" like me, and forty crewmembers on it, there was a decided lack of people to ask which direction aft was. I returned to the pool.

The smile I shot the other au pairs as I approached them must have been more bared teeth and less good humor, since they both recoiled slightly. "I'm Soleil Fairweather," I said, holding out a hand to the taller one, though both women had at least five inches on me. They were elegant, dark-haired twenty-somethings who could easily have pursued professional modeling.

Of course, before I knew what I was saying, I'd told them both that. "You may be the most beautiful women I've ever seen," I blurted out, my mouth still going. "Please tell me you're not also med students, or PhD candidates in aerospace engineering or something?"

I fidgeted as they glanced around. Possibly looking for my keeper.

"May we help you?" one of them asked after a long moment, her accent every bit as gorgeous as her face.

Naturally, I told her that, too. They both laughed out loud then, drawing the attention of everyone on deck, because of course their laughter was also beautiful. "I promise I'm not crazy, I'm just lost. It's my first betasitting gig on a boat. First *anything* on a boat. Can you help me?"

The taller one, whose name was Clotilde, and who was in fact a graduate student in biochemistry when she wasn't nannying, gave me directions to the "aft" of the ship, which just meant the back, and told me the port side meant the left. The other one, Veronika, who came from Hungary and wanted to be a pastry chef, warned me away from one of the hallways, where the highly strung wedding coordinator had her rooms, and was known to be a "bitch of iron."

In five minutes, I was standing outside a door with *Sylvia Grantham-Standish* engraved on a brass plaque. The last name made me pause. An actor named Simon Standish had passed away two years before, while working on a superhero movie. Had he been her father?

My heart aching for her, I knocked on Sylvia's door. A few seconds later, the lock slid, and I pushed the unusually heavy door open. When it closed behind me, the sounds from the ship were muffled, almost like there was soundproofing.

Of course there was. *Billionaire, Soleil. He can afford anything.*

"You do know you say a lot of stuff out loud," Sylvia remarked from the bed, where she sat cross-legged next to an old-fashioned sewing basket, in a pile of colorful fabric scraps. She had a pair of silver scissors in one hand, snipping pieces from a swath of pink silk into thick streamers.

"I do not," I argued, even though I knew it was true.

A tiny smile peeked out. "You do. And you can't lie to save yourself." She held up a scrap of fabric. "Same color as your face right now."

I sat on the edge of the bed. "Okay, you got me. I can't lie. But I figure, why bother? Lies always come back to bite you in the butt, don't they?"

She just raised one dark eyebrow and handed me another pair of scissors from the basket. "Can you help me?"

"What are you making?" I asked as she handed me a length of butter-yellow fabric. I started cutting it into long strips like she was. It was surprisingly therapeutic.

"Yes, it was my therapist who suggested sewing as a way to channel my aggression and depression into something positive." Her mouth twitched again, almost into a smile when I groaned. "You said that out loud, too." We cut for a while, then she said, "So, tell me about yourself. How did a woman like you get hired as a betasitter?"

"A woman like me?"

She pointed at my hands with her scissors. "You may be wearing mismatched shoes, but those nails have never done a hard day's work, *Miss Fairweather*. I know a two-hundred-dollar manicure when I see one."

A hard day's work? I tried not to smile at how much she sounded like a disapproving great-aunt. "Okay, so yes. Manicures are my weakness." I held my nails up to the light, admiring the shimmery glitter in the polish. "It costs that much if you don't want to have to get them done every week."

"Quality is expensive." She held up the pink bolt of fabric, and I noticed something. It was attached to what looked like a scrap of a waistband, and at the other end, a collar. I pulled the yellow fabric off the bed and realized that mine was also not just fabric.

It was clothing, a girl's dress, and when I found the discreet label sewn into the collar and recognized the designer's name, I felt dizzy all of a sudden. "Sevartina? These are couture." I'd never even dreamed of buying a dress by Sevartina, but my mom had always wanted one. They started at thirty thousand dollars. "We're destroying Sevartina dresses?"

The room filled with gleeful laughter, and I blinked at the tiny demon who was snipping again. Cutting her clothing into tiny scraps.

And having fun doing it. My heart was still racing, but for the first time, Sylvia was truly smiling. And she sounded like a real twelve-year-old when she said, "It's actually the best therapy I've ever tried. And I've done a lot."

"Sylvia. Are these your clothes? Not old clothes, but... the ones you're meant to wear this week?" A high-pitched giggle escaped when she nodded. Her eyes slid up to my face, more than slightly nervous. I set down my scissors and groaned. "What are you going to wear now?"

"I'm not going to dinner," she stated. "I've decided to go on a hunger strike." She inhaled, but there was a little hiccup in it. "Maybe then Mom will wake up and listen to me." Her lip quivered as she attacked the fabric more ferociously.

"What is it you're trying to get her to see?" I asked quietly.

"That the jerk she's marrying isn't a nice man."

Something in her voice had the hairs on my body standing on end. "Sylvia. Has he done something to you? Has he touched you, or hurt you..." I had the scissors gripped in my fist like a knife before I was done asking the question.

She slumped down, her shoulders rounding. "No. But he told me after he marries Mom, he's going to make sure I get the 'best education possible.' Which, according to him, is some boarding school in Austria. He's good at making it sound like he cares. But he just wants me gone."

"If you tell your mom—" I began, but she cut me off. Her eyes were shimmering with tears.

"My mom hasn't listened to me for two years." Her breathing hitched again. "When I try to tell her how bad things are... when I tried to talk to her about Alphonse, she said to act happy, and I'll be happier. But that's not how it works."

"No, it's not," I agreed, thinking of all the times my own dad had said things very much the same.

We both went quiet. I set down the dress I'd been ruining and walked over to her closet, opening it and pushing through her racks of clothing. Every remaining dress was similar to the ones we'd cut up: pastel-colored, made of fabric that felt amazing but would ruin if even a drop of sauce splashed on it, and... none of them were fun.

"Who picked these out for you?"

"My personal shopper," she said, her voice grim. "She hates me." I couldn't disagree. I peeked through the rest and noted there weren't even any play clothes, or tennis shoes.

"Where did the black clothes come from?"

"I traded my phone to a girl on my swim team for them."

"What about the Doc Martens?"

"Uncle G. For my birthday."

"Hmmm." I tapped my chin, thinking. "So, if I don't get you dressed for dinner, I'll be fired. And I need the money from this job."

She rolled her eyes dramatically. "No you don't, Miss Manicure."

"Shows what you know. I really, really do need the money." I started combing through the racks, looking for anything that she might want to wear. Nothing. "Right, stand up." She hesitated, but after a minute did as I asked. "You're only an inch shorter than me," I said aloud. "It's not fair."

"You have boobs," she replied with a shrug. "Life's not fair, is it?"

"You're not wrong." I handed her a pair of silver flats I found in the bottom of the closet. "Take these and come with me, Miss Ennui. We don't have much time."

"For what?" I loved that the flat, dull look in her dark eyes was gone.

I winked at her as I grabbed the sewing basket off the bed. "To become the kind of 'Mad Girls' the original Sylvia would approve of."

Chapter 5

Grumpy

S he was late, not that I should care. Or notice.

The main dining room was packed, every seat filled with a glittering member of the elite, with enough alphas and omegas that the air purification units were having trouble filtering out all the different scents.

Every chair and bench was filled except the one next to me, where I had asked my niece to be seated, though the scrawny, overdressed wedding coordinator had tried to argue. Stupid woman. I was spending over a week away from my offices for this charade, and the only good part about it so far was getting to see Sylvia.

And *her*. Soleil, that ridiculously sweet-smelling, innocent young omega who had fallen into my lap. Or weaseled her way into it, like so many other women had tried. Though if she was attempting to be some sort of seductress, she was doing a piss-poor job of it. Where the hell was she?

I had more questions for the little liar now than I'd had on the pier. After I'd gotten her safely aboard—she'd seemed inordinately afraid of falling in when the tender pulled up alongside the yacht, and I'd had to pry her fingers off my arm—I'd gone straight to the conference room and called Storm Security to get answers.

"What is it, Grantham?" Storm panted through the phone. He sounded seriously out of breath, which worried me. He'd looked like shit the last time I saw him, and had confided that he'd developed some sort of heart condition.

Then he let out a groan. "There she goes again. Wearing that damned bikini."

"Oh, I'm sorry," I drawled. "Did I interrupt? You watching porn?"

"Practically," he growled. "What do you want now?"

"I need to know more about Soleil Fairweather." He'd sent over all her relevant information a few hours before. Her school records, her past history with the Omega League, her medical history. Even her parents' tax returns, which had shocked me the most. By most people's standards, they were wealthy. Why the hell would she take this job? "I need to know everything about her."

"About your betasitter who isn't a beta? I sent her files right after you texted."

"I want to know her first kiss, her first heat, her text messages, her social media passwords, every fucking detail there is." It was illegal as hell, but I didn't pay Storm Security a retainer of ten million a year for nothing.

He laughed, wheezing slightly. "I've never heard you curious about a woman. I thought you'd given up on omegas after that Zoe woman."

I cursed. Zoe Henning was an up-and-coming starlet I'd dated a few years before. The last omega I'd touched. I'd thought she was a good actress, but I'd had no idea. Every day had been

45

filled with laughter, every evening with parties, and the nights with her crying out around my knot, though she seemed to enjoy the sex more than I did. She'd smelled of lavender and vanilla, not my favorite scents. But all omegas smelled pleasant to unbonded alphas.

She'd almost convinced me to marry her, that she loved me. Then I'd caught her ordering filtering nose plugs and having them delivered to her massage therapist's office. According to the masseuse—who was happy to share every detail for a few hundred thousand dollars—I smelled like rotting onions to Zoe. But she was willing to live with it, for the money. The prestige.

It's why I never trusted a smile.

"What is it about this one, Gio?"

"I don't know," I finally admitted. "I'm... concerned, is all."

"Concerned?"

"Intrigued, maybe."

"If you're asking for every detail of her entire life, you're crossing into obsessed, friend."

I swallowed the insults that wanted to pour out, then muttered, "She had on what looked like an engagement ring."

He cursed. "I've got you. You'll have everything within two days. All known family, friends, dating history, name of the fiancé." I cut off the growl that emerged at that, but he heard it. "If there is one, okay? My people didn't find any record of a fiancé." He mumbled something that sounded like, "Her best friend will know," then said more clearly, "Some advice, Grantham? If she's who I think she might be to you, what it sounds like? Don't let her get away."

I had no intention of letting her get anywhere. Not that she could, a hundred miles from shore, but the longer she was absent from the dining room, the more agitated I became. Where the fuck was she?

The head waiter glanced at me again, waiting for my signal to bring out the first course. I shook my head and stood. I'd go find the little brat, and show her exactly what happened to—

At that moment, the door opened. But it wasn't Soleil.

Sylvia stepped in, alone. I blinked, beyond surprised at her appearance. I'd rarely seen her in anything besides black clothing for two years—though god only knew where she was getting them from, since Lorelei sure as hell wasn't buying them for her. The few times Sylvia had worn a dress, they'd been expensive but also young, like something a ten-year-old would wear. Sylvia had looked miserable in pink, baby blue, and yellow at the three family events Lore had dragged her to.

"I'm firing that betasitter," Lorelei muttered next to me. "She swore Syl would be dressed appropriately."

"She is," I replied softly, placing one hand on her arm to keep her from storming across the dining room. Sylvia was walking toward us, her chin jutting out in defiance, but her eyes dancing with mischief and something else.

Happiness.

"What do you think?" she asked her mom when she got close enough, but before Lore could answer, I stepped up to her and bowed.

"I think that may be the most beautiful dress you've ever worn, Silly." Our eyes met, and she wrinkled her nose at the pet name I'd given her when she was a baby. But she didn't complain.

"Look, Uncle G," she said softly, then turned so I could watch the skirt flare out. She'd always done that as a little girl, too.

Upon closer inspection, the dress wasn't black, but a dark, midnight blue, that flowed from a collar of rhinestones at the neck down her arms to matching rhinestone cuffs, and all the way to her feet. Silver flats peeked out at the hemline when she finished her turn, but the ship pitched slightly. I caught her before she fell, and murmured, "Please tell me you didn't sneak any champagne?"

"Uncle G, I'm *twelve*." She giggled, and a second later, I heard Lorelei smother a sob. It was the first time I'd heard Sylvia laugh in two years. It might've been the same for Lorelei.

"Where did the dress come from, Sylvia?" I asked.

"The betasitter made it for me," she said with a strange smile, directed at her feet. "She's the weirdest person I've ever met."

Where was she? My eyes flew to the door.

"What do you mean, weird?" Lore asked. "And how did she make you a dress?" Her tone was slightly sharp, and I squeezed her arm gently.

Sylvia's chin jutted out mulishly. "She's weird in a nice way. And she used Nana's sewing stuff. She cut up one of her own dresses." A tiny giggle escaped again. "She didn't even have to hem it. Soleil is short, for a... beta. Betasitter, I mean." She winked at me, and I frowned back.

"Where is she now?"

"Oh, um." One silver-clad toe rubbed at the teak floor. "This was her only fancy dress—she said she had no idea she was going to be on a boat, right? So she stayed in her cabin. I'm going to bring her some food later."

My heart stuttered in my chest. "No, Silly. I'll take her some dinner."

She grabbed my hand as I began to do just that. "I like her. Don't be grumpy at her."

"Me? I'm not grumpy." I scowled ferociously at her, making her smile once more, then strode to the door as fast as I could.

The yacht was rocking slightly more than I liked, given that the weather reports had been mostly clear. I ordered dinner to be served to the waiting diners, and two additional meals to be plated up and delivered to Miss Soleil's cabin. Then I texted the captain to keep an eye on the weather and left, ignoring my sister's calls and the fluttering complaints of the photographer who seemed to think I'd care that their head table shots would be ruined.

The night was warm and when I reached the cabin—which was unacceptably far from mine—I was already sweating at the thought of the woman inside, and half-hard from the floral, tropical scent seeping out into the hall.

The door swung inward after my second knock, and Soleil's voice greeted me. "Sylvia, didn't you— Oh! Mr. Grantham?"

I blinked, then rubbed my eyes. "What... what is this?" I stepped into the room, letting the door swing shut behind me. I couldn't process what I was seeing. The woman I'd been obsessing over, the dazzling creature I'd been imagining, was dressed in... "Ducky pajamas?"

The most ridiculous printed tank top I'd ever seen—yellow rubber ducks sitting in duck-shaped inner tubes—floated across her generous breasts and coasted down to a pair of bright orange shorts that hugged her ample thighs. My teeth began to ache again, and my mouth began to water at the thought of biting those luscious thighs, leaving my marks on her. She would be *mine*.

Shit. Not mine. This woman, this innocent-looking, possibly duplicitous woman was a stranger. Maybe an alpha-chaser, for all I knew. Maybe taken. Definitely too young for me.

Fuck it, a dark voice growled inside. None of that mattered. I would let myself have this, have her in my grasp, just once.

49

Touch her, taste her. I didn't care if she had a thousand fiancés back home.

"Mr. Grantham?" she repeated, confused. "What are you doing here? Didn't Sylvia get to the dining hall? I walked her halfway; I saw her go through the door—" I set one finger over her mouth.

"Shh." I took in every inch of her, memorizing each detail. Glittering pink polish decorated each nail on her bare feet. Her legs and arms were gleaming and smooth, her hair tied up in a ridiculously high ponytail, her face scrubbed clean, and her skin... "Damnit, you're so young, Sunshine. So bright, and soft, and forbidden."

As I stepped further into her cabin, that last word seemed to shimmer in the air between us. I had held on with an iron grip to my own instincts, my desires, for so long. Had kept myself separate from women, especially omegas, with one notable exception. And I'd never approached a woman this young.

But her breath was already coming fast, her perfume blooming, merging with my own scent. Telling me she was receptive.

I'd spent my life hiding what I desired. Emotions, desires, hopes... They were all weapons that could be used against you in business, and in bed. I'd crafted the stony face I showed the world, keeping my true feelings hidden to everyone. Maybe too well hidden. It felt like a part of me had petrified. My heart, maybe.

And perhaps that was for the best. But it was almost impossible not to feel when I was around Soleil. Painful, to hide the desire that mounted inside.

I wanted to be with this deceitful omega more than I'd wanted anything in so long. To feel what it might be like not to be alone, just once. I was so damn tired of holding on, holding back. She was a perfect temptation. I wanted to strip her bare and do every filthy, depraved, forbidden act I could imagine... and that she had probably never even dreamed existed.

I wanted to break her down, leave her sobbing on the floor, begging my forgiveness for trying to entice me into her bed. For making me feel desire again. I wanted to own her, then leave her gasping for more.

But I knew if I went too far, I might be the one who was left aching and alone.

Though maybe I could have just a taste. A touch.

My control slipping, I threaded one hand behind her neck, tangling my fingers in the hair at her nape. A shiver ran through her, and her nipples beaded, like they were trying to reach through her shirt for me. Those pink, bow-shaped lips puckered into a small moue of displeasure, and she inhaled as if to complain, but I circled her waist with my other arm and hauled her face up to mine.

"No, brat. I told you to be on time, dressed appropriately for dinner. And this is where I find you? Dressed like this?" The pupils of her innocent, blue-green eyes were blown wide with desire now, and her breathing came in short rasps. "Well, what do you have to say for yourself?"

She fought to maintain her small frown, but the heady rush of her scent betrayed her arousal. Her throat worked as she swallowed hard before answering, "I'm... I'm sorry?"

"Not certain? Do you understand that you did something wrong, Sunshine, and now you need to make up for it? Didn't you ever learn how to take responsibility for your actions?"

I tightened my hand at her nape slightly, and she leaned her head back, her eyelids dropping closed. I brought my lips to her neck, rubbing my own scent over her skin, scraping her soft neck with my teeth. Our scents mingled together on her skin, and I felt a deep sense of satisfaction. Any alpha would know I had marked her.

"Or do you need me to teach you? Show you how you make it right?" I nipped lightly at the base of her throat, where her pulse hammered furiously.

The room exploded in a bloom of tropical scent. "I don't know," she managed to say. "What do you want me to do?"

I trailed my fingers over her tank, the small buttons at the front pulled tight. "I think you should start by taking off the inappropriate clothing, don't you?"

Her eyes met mine, and the flash of mischief there shot straight to my groin. "Yes, sir. I definitely think I should."

Without dropping her gaze, she lifted her hands to her top and slowly undid the buttons, one at a time. The cloth of her sleep shirt fell open, revealing the most perfect breasts I'd ever seen. Heavy and full, with dark, tight nipples that jutted toward my lips.

I pulled her waist closer but let her head fall back so she was exposed to me, bent backward like an offering. "Fuck, Sunshine, those are for me, aren't they?"

She mumbled something that sounded like assent. I lowered my lips to the outer swell of one breast, then moved my tongue in wide circles around the outside edges of her areolas, coming close to the tight nipples, but never quite touching them. She gave a strangled moan, arching her back even farther.

"Tell me what you need. Tell me exactly what you want from me."

"You know what," she whispered, and I delighted as a flush of pink covered her chest.

"Oh, my little Sunshine is embarrassed? Have you never had to ask for what you wanted before?" My balls ached, my knot pulsing, as I realized just how innocent she might be. But she was engaged... supposedly. "Do you have a lover, Omega?"

"No."

"Have you had lovers?"

She tried to nod her head, but I held her nape, a shockingly fierce growl emerging from my lips. "Who?"

"Just one," she murmured. "In high school. A beta."

The compulsion to find whoever had dared to touch what was mine was almost overwhelming. Instead, I lowered her onto the bed, taking in the vision she presented. "Did he make you come, Sunshine? Did he touch you, bring you pleasure?" The need to kill the unknown man increased at the thought of it.

Her short bark of laughter cleared my mind slightly. "No. I had to learn that on my own."

A wave of heat ran through me at the vision of her in bed, teaching herself how to find her pleasure, spending her nights, her heats, alone. "Then that's how you'll apologize to me, brat."

She blinked, her green-blue eyes hazy with lust and curiosity. "W-what do you mean?"

"You're going to touch yourself. You're going to do *exactly* what I tell you, and then all will be forgiven."

A hint of uncertainty in her gaze, she swallowed hard. "You want me to touch myself. Now? While you..."

"Yes, while I watch," I told her, standing back and crossing my arms over my chest. "Take off those shorts, brat. Show me that naughty pussy."

I wasn't certain she would, but after a moment, she closed her eyes and reached down, pushing her sleep shorts to her ankles, then to the floor.

"Good girl," I murmured, as a blush rose on her cheeks. She liked that, being praised. "Now, spread your legs. Let me see that pretty pink cunt." Her face went bright red at that, and she started to shake her head. I stepped closer. "Maybe you're not a good omega. Maybe you're a bad girl who doesn't deserve an orgasm. Not even with your own hands."

Her lips tightened at that, and with her eyes still shut, she spread her thighs, her knees dropping to the sheets on either side.

"Ah, there it is," I groaned, leaning over and inhaling as her scent pervaded the room. Her folds were pink and swollen, and a trickle of her wet slick had already begun to drip from her opening. "Look at that mess. Dripping for me, naughty girl? Touch yourself. Open yourself up so I can see every inch." She hesitated. "Do it, Sunshine. Now. Touch yourself for me. Rub that aching little clit, show me what you do when you're all alone, being so fucking bad."

She reached down with both hands, parted her lips, and dipped a finger into that honeyed slick. She brought it to her clit and began making small, light circles, moving closer, then slightly faster after a moment.

"God, look at that," I breathed, unbuckling my belt. Her eyes flew open at the sound of the metal buckle, tracking the belt as I removed it. I felt a wicked rush of heat at the uncertainty and desire in her shocked gaze. "No, sweet one, not that. Not today. I'm just going to give you a little something extra." Her eyes were cloudy and confused, and she let out a small whine as she went back to circling her clit. "Look at you all swollen. So close," I murmured, pulling my cock out and pumping it. I stepped right to the side of the bed, pushing her legs even wider, and jacked my cock over her.

Her eyes flared wider as she took in my erection. "That's... That's..." A flicker of panic appeared in her gaze, and I felt my lips curl up ever so faintly in a dark smile.

"That's for you, Sunshine. But not tonight. I'd have to train your little pussy to take me." I ran a hand through the slick that trailed from her channel, then rubbed it on my cock, using the thick liquid as lube. "I'd have to stretch this tight cunt wide so you could fit me inside." I purred, and she went back to touching herself, getting closer. "It would still hurt, princess, when I stuffed my cock into you. When I pushed my knot in that tiny, perfect pussy. You'd probably even cry the first time." I purred louder when her shocked eyes met mine.

"I'd lick your tears up, like I'd lick your swollen cunt. But you'd get used to the stretch, the burn. I promise. You'd *beg* me for it." Her chest was flushed now, her breathing erratic, as she slipped close to the peak. "That's it, baby, you're almost there. Show me what my bad girl does when she's all alone, hungry for her alpha. Empty inside."

Her small noises of pleasure were soft. So soft, the kind a woman makes when she's afraid of being heard. If I was going to touch her again, I'd have to train that out of her. Teach her to yell, to call my name. Not that I could let that happen, let this moment happen again.

My balls drew up, my knot thickening, as I grew closer to my own orgasm. "Come, Sunshine," I demanded as I felt the first spurts of my release begin to spill. I set one hand on the bed so my cock was directly over her cunt. "Come now!" I demanded.

She cried out as she obeyed, her body shuddering under me as I painted her stomach with pearly ropes of my own release.

"Good girl," I crooned, while she lay there, panting, trembling. "Shush now, hold still," I said when it seemed like she might try to move, or speak. Kneeling between her thighs, I reached one hand behind her plump ass, lifting her toward me. Then I rubbed the cum I'd draped across her into her skin, massaging it into her soft stomach.

"Lower," she murmured. "Touch me there." She put a hand over mine and led it to the swollen lips of her cunt.

Merri Bright

"You want me to stuff you full of my cum, princess?" She nodded, her eyes still shut tight, and pushed my hand down, pressing my fingers almost inside her. "As you wish," I growled, and with our fingers overlapped, began to gather up my seed and slip it into her swollen channel, one handful at a time.

Fuck yes. That was where it belonged. Inside her.

My vision grew hazy, my thoughts muddled. Our mingled scents were so strong, it felt like breathing syrup. I wanted nothing more than to breed this omega. My omega.

I grabbed my still enlarged knot and squeezed it roughly over her bare mound, watching the white cum run from the top down to her ass. "You want more, princess?" She moaned and opened her thighs wider. "Good girl," I praised, purring while I scooped up more of the liquid and fed it into her incredibly tight pussy, twisting my fingers inside her as I shoved them in, squeezing her ass in an almost painful grip when she tried to shift away. "Hold still and take it, Omega. Take every drop."

I knew this feeling. I was on the verge of a rut, a mating frenzy.

And I didn't fucking care.

"Wait," she said, her voice rising. "What am I... What are we *doing?*" She sat up, her eyes wide with apprehension. "I'm not on birth control."

"Good." For a moment, my alpha nature roared out inside me. *Mine to fuck. Mine to claim.* Suddenly, I could see her, pregnant with my child, milk flowing from those perfect breasts, her eyes shining with love for me...

"Mr. Grantham?" Her hand had slipped to my wrist, and I stopped moving with my hand pressed against her opening, cum leaking out around my fingers.

Mr. Grantham. Not Gio. Not Alpha.

"Y-you can't want that. I'm just the betasitter."

56

The haze of my impending rut cleared like smoke in a strong wind. *I'm just the betasitter.*

What. The fuck. Was I doing?

I was her boss. She was eighteen years younger than me. And she was most likely engaged, but hiding it for some reason.

I knew better than this. I had been fooled by an omega before. I knew better than to get caught in the trap of their beauty, their scents that turned normal, sane alphas into knotheads with alimony payments and broken hearts. I was *better* than this.

I'd lost my mind. "What the fuck was I thinking?" I finally managed to say, and tore myself away from the bed, staring down at my cum and slick-soaked fingers. Frantic, I fastened my trousers, turning to go.

"It... it was me, too. I knew better." A soft sob from the bed had me freezing. She'd curled into a ball and was huddled on the mattress, as if she were ashamed. Ashamed of herself, and her response to me.

A matching shame rocketed through me. Her scent had gone bitter, and it was all I could do not to go to her, hold her until she relaxed. But that was falling back into the trap that omegas were for me. I had to be strong. Or at least cold. Distance myself, no matter how hard it was.

"Apology accepted, Miss Fairweather. Next time, be at dinner, dressed and ready. I won't be lured down to your room again."

She lifted her face, her cheeks streaked with tears, her eyes flashing with what looked like betrayal. "Lured? What do you mea—"

Knock knock! Before she could finish her question, a voice called out, "Dinner, Mr. Grantham?"

"Leave it outside," I replied, pressing her back onto the mattress as I stood. The vision before me—the naked, supple limbs, ripe with my scent and hers—was everything I had ever wanted.

But I couldn't have her. She was too young for me. Too innocent.

And too fucking tempting by half.

"You look unwell, Miss Fairweather," I gritted out. "Rest and eat." I knew my tone was harsh; she flinched as I all but barked the command.

When she shifted on the bed, and a final rush of our combined scents flooded my senses, it took all I had to muster the internal strength to make it outside the door before I knotted, bit, and claimed her.

Sniffling, she kept her eyes lowered, but reached for a tissue to rub at the drying streaks on her skin. "Don't rub it off. Leave it there," I demanded, shocking her to stillness. Shocking myself. My feet were made of lead, my teeth aching almost as much as my knot, my pulse a wild drumbeat clamoring for me to stay. "Let it be a reminder of what happens when you don't follow your employer's instructions." I slipped out the door while she sputtered, pushed her tray inside, and left her alone.

It was the most cowardly and most selfless thing I'd ever done.

Chapter 6

Sunshine

Rain's voice was glitchy, and it sounded like she was talking from the bottom of a well as she lectured me the next morning. She'd called a few minutes before, her "best friend radar pinging hard," or so she'd said.

I'd already confessed everything that had happened the night before to Candy and Rain via texts, and we'd covered the most important topics, like how enormous Giovanni's cock had been and how we'd almost had filthy hot sex.

I didn't tell them all the things he'd said, though. For one thing, they'd never believe I wasn't straight up quoting a porno. Training my naughty pussy? Even remembering it had my panties soaked.

For another, if I'd told them all the mean stuff he'd said afterward, they'd probably both swim across the ocean to avenge me.

Why, oh why, had my lady parts fallen in everlasting lust with Grumpy Grantham? Obviously, my pussy had no common sense or taste in men. Those cruel things he'd said to me at the end... Lured? I'd somehow lured him, like a wicked temptress? I wanted to lure his face right into my fist, if I didn't think I'd probably break a finger punching him.

What an asshole. A sexy, sexy asshole. With really muscular, talented, thick fingers. That I could almost still feel inside me.

"Are you listening to me, Soleil?"

"Of course," I lied. Rain had been losing her shit for a solid three minutes, because I'd accidentally mentioned the cum-stuffing thing.

"Then tell me what in the hell you were *thinking?* Why would you even let him in your room? And his sloppy, contaminated, baby-making fingers in your business?" Her voice was shrill. I could almost see her, pacing up and down as she fumed, her nearly perpetual frown transforming her face into a picture of diminutive rage. She always reminded me of a tiny, dark-haired pixie warrior when she was railing against the world.

I didn't know what to say. I wanted to tell her that I thought he might be my true mate. His scent was just so perfect, and the way I'd felt when he'd commanded me to touch myself, and when he'd watched me, was unlike anything I'd ever experienced.

But I knew too much about her past to do something so thoughtless. Because while meeting your true mate was so rare that it almost seemed like a fairy tale, meeting him and being rejected by him? It was a horror story she'd lived.

And if it was happening to me, I might die of humiliation. I'd had enough of that the night before, anyway.

"I'm sure I'll be fine. It wasn't that big of a deal." Giovanni had made certain I understood that. To him, it was a lesson taught to a stupid omega.

"You listen to me now, Soleil Fairweather. You and I both know you can't take birth control pills because of your allergies or sensitivities, or whatever. You don't have a damn IUD. And apparently, they don't make condoms big enough to fit that alpha's torpedo. You know *better* than this," she ranted just as my phone buzzed.

It was Mom texting, again. I ignored her, again. Somehow, she'd figured out I wasn't in Georgetown. She was enraged, insisting I come home immediately.

Rain was still talking. "...and you know as well as I do how fertile omegas are. Remember, Misty Mumstack got pregnant from a hot tub—"

I sighed. "She got pregnant *in* a hot tub, Rain. It wasn't just jizz floating around in there with her."

"It could have been. Alpha jizz is *dangerous*. Remember what we promised each other?"

"That we'd never partake in high-fructose porn syrup without protection, I know."

"That's right. Now you will promise not to let his baby batter near your muffin maker again. If you come home pregnant, and you haven't even gotten to feel what a wine bottle dick could do to your poor little ladybits—"

"Rain, stop. I can't think about it." I'd just put on new swimsuit bottoms, ones Rain had left at my house the year before. I stood and pulled them out of my butt crack. I had no business wearing my teeny-tiny bestie's bikini.

She snorted. "Was it really that big? Are we talking a sauvignon blanc? Or, like, a limoncello bottle... Please tell me not an Italian chianti."

We both laughed hysterically for a long moment.

"Okay, Rainy, real talk. You know that bottle of Campari you got me for my birthday?"

"Of course."

"Mmhm. Every bit as wide, and almost as long, so not actually wine-bottle-sized. But so thick. I don't know." I shivered. "I guess with a peen, there's some give..."

"Holy shit, girl. There's not enough give in the world. There may not be enough *lube* in the world. If you could swim, I'd tell you to jump overboard. Your poor vagina needs to get to safety."

"It's not going in my vagina, apparently, since he's my boss," I muttered, yanking a brush through my hair with so much force, it pulled a few hairs out.

Pulling my hair. *Oh, fuck.*

I remembered those thick fingers tangled in my hair, tugging my neck back, his teeth on me... "God bless America!" I shouted. "I'm going to have to change my dang swimsuit again!" I pulled the red bikini bottoms off and flung them onto my messy bed, purposefully not looking at the mounded-up sheets that were starting to form a very obvious nest shape. Against Giovanni's final command, I'd wiped myself down last night with washcloths... but I hadn't put them into the laundry. No, I'd slept with one of them shoved right against my face all night, and another one in between my legs, like some kind of desperate omega.

Okay, that was precisely what I was. I shoved a wad of toilet paper into my crotch while I scrambled naked around on the closet floor to find my gold and silver sandals. Rain was laughing so hard she sounded like a hyena, and I told her so.

"Stop thinking about your Abominable Cock Monster, you thirsty ray of sunshine, and tell me about the job."

"The job kicks butt." I told her all about Sylvia as I pulled on my second outfit of the day, an even-smaller gold bikini bottom with a mismatched daisy-printed top, and a white sundress that had fit me back in eighth grade. It worked as a cover-up, though.

"Oh my gosh, she sounds like a mini-me," Rain said when I was done. "What are your plans for today?"

"Well, I'm staying away from wine bottles of all kinds," I

declared, checking my lip gloss in the mirror and hiking my sundress over my boobs. I asked Rain about her gig, but she just mumbled something about chickens coming home to roost, rushed out a goodbye, and hung up. *Hmm.* There was something going on with her.

A soft knock at my door kept me from calling her back and forcing her to tell me. I'd locked the door after Gio had left, and hung the discreet Do Not Disturb sign on the handle, so I knew who it must be. "Hey, Sylvia."

She had on the black outfit from the day before, along with a shy half-smile. "Good morning, Miss—"

I stopped her with one hand. "No. I can't be anything but Soleil today. At least not until after coffee. Are you Sylvia or Ennui?"

Her eyes sparkled even as she flattened her smile. "Definitely Ennui."

"How did the dress go?"

"They loved it." Her nose wrinkled. "Can I keep it?"

"What use would it do me?" I asked as we entered the hall. "It's been custom altered for you." Her smile grew, and she practically skipped ahead to open the next door. "What lies ahead of us today, Ennui?"

A real frown creased her small brow. "Breakfast, swimming, group activities, and then dinner. Same boring thing every day, until we get to Uncle G's island, and then the wedding." She said the last two words with a tone most people saved for talking about serial killers or tax audits.

I replied using the same tone. "Breakfast?"

She peeked back at me. I sighed heavily and rolled my eyes, dragging my feet on the shiny teak so hard my sandals squeaked. "It's so tedious, isn't it? Having to go to a mundane breakfast, as if muffins can feed the existential hunger in our souls."

"Precisely," she agreed, making a terrible expression between amusement and disgust. "How can toast address the spiritual starvation these people inflict on me every day?"

My stomach growled audibly, and we both smiled. "You know, cheesy scrambled eggs can sometimes fill both physical and metaphysical voids," I suggested. "Or so I've read."

"I suppose we'll find out," she replied, taking a breath as she held open one last door, like she was steeling herself. But what for?

I glanced around curiously as we entered a medium-sized dining room, filled mainly with children and people I assumed were au pairs, though a few bleary-eyed parents sat here and there as well, mostly checking their phones. I called out to Veronika and Clotilde, and they waved back, but no one else greeted us. A few of the other children glanced at Sylvia, then turned their backs.

Huh. Weird.

I waited until we'd filled our plates at the extensive buffet that had everything: kimchi, omelets, Greek yogurt with honey and fresh berries, vegan bacon, thick ham steaks, even rice congee. Not that anyone was eating much of it. Not even the children had more than a few bites of food in front of them, though a few of them were glancing at the buffet as if they wanted more.

When we sat at a table, alone, my plate was piled high, while Sylvia only had two strips of vegan bacon. "Not hungry?" I asked.

Her eyes flitted to the au pairs who were drinking black coffee and eating a similar, carb-free meal. I knew without asking what that look meant, and I silently cursed the media, the patriarchy, and the clueless adults who were responsible for ruining one of the best parts of being wealthy.

Really good food, with no dishes to do afterward.

I dug my fork into my food, taking out my aggression on the pillowy-soft scrambled eggs. And stopped. "Oh... my... god." I swallowed and flagged down the crew member who was waiting on the tables. "Could I speak to the chef please? About what's in these eggs." He raced away.

"Are you allergic to something, Soleil?" Sylvia whispered. "Do you have an EpiPen?" She looked panicked. Way more panicked than she should be.

"No," I soothed her. Before I could explain, the chef was on her way through the double doors to the galley, and she looked pissed. Before she could say a word, I rose and held out my hand. "Are you the one who made these amazing eggs? I took a course with Master Chef Stella Del Raspici in Florence a few years ago, and she made eggs that tasted exactly like this!"

The chef's broad face widened into a huge grin. "What a compliment! Stella is a friend of mine. We studied in Lyon together." We switched to French and then Italian, speaking about the eggs and then about the different ways to prepare them.

Something tugged at my sleeve. "Why are eggs such a big deal?" Sylvia asked. "They're just... eggs."

"Oh, no," I said, shocked. "If you want to know if a cook has truly mastered their craft, you can tell that by tasting their eggs." The chef smiled and introduced herself to Sylvia.

Sylvia's eyes narrowed, but she took her fork and tasted a bite of my eggs. Her eyes widened. "Those are really good." She swallowed, and snuck some more while I spoke to Chef Juliette.

"Chef, I believe that every young person should know the basics of cooking. Is there any way I could bring my young charge into your kitchen so she could watch a Master Chef prepare eggs correctly?"

Juliette was already shaking her head when we looked

down, and saw that Sylvia had eaten all of my eggs. "Please?" she asked in a whisper. "I've never tasted anything so good in my life."

I didn't turn my head, but could sense that all the other children, and the adults as well, had gone silent. Listening.

"I cannot bring children into my galley. But!" She winked at Sylvia. "I can bring my galley to you, Mademoiselle." She gestured to the wait staff who sprang into motion, while I cleared our table for the impromptu cooking lesson. In minutes, there was a small propane burner, a copper-bottomed sauté pan, and all the ingredients for scrambled eggs sitting in the middle of our table.

A soft, cleared throat at my elbow got my attention. "Miss, can we... can we watch, too?" It was another girl, probably about ten. Two women hovered a few feet behind her, and the girl, Devon, introduced them as her mom and her aunt. The aunt was a female alpha, who smelled... I blushed. Her scent wasn't as good as Giovanni's, but she smelled of sour cherries and heavy cloves, and the glint in her eye told me she'd noticed my reaction.

I peeked back down at Devon, who was smiling shyly at Sylvia. "Sure, sweetie. Sit by us."

In seconds, a whole group of children had clustered around our tables and the other au pairs were pulling up chairs all around. When Chef Juliette came back out, she laughed at the crowd. "I will need a sous chef with this many." She pointed at Sylvia. "Miss Grantham-Standish?"

"M-me?" Sylvia stammered, but stood at Chef's beckoning hand.

"Yes, you. Put this on." She draped an apron over Sylvia's neck, wrapping the ties around her small waist twice before tying it in the front, and plopped a white hat, smaller than her own chef's toque, on Sylvia's head. "When I ask you to do

something, you must obey immediately, and say 'Yes, Chef!'"
The chef's eyebrows danced up and down, then she leaned
over and whispered something in Sylvia's ear. "Do you
understand?"

"Yes, Chef," Sylvia replied, her narrow shoulders shaking
slightly. I was worried until she turned, and I could tell she was
suppressing laughter.

Chef Juliette took over, instructing the assembled group as
if she had taught wedding guests how to scramble eggs a thousand times. Maybe she had. What made me grin so hard my
cheeks hurt was how Sylvia responded to the attention. She
was intense, as always, but when her turn came to demonstrate
the lesson, she did every step perfectly.

Her dark eyes shone with pride as she placed the finished
eggs in front of me. "Well, Soleil? How did I do?"

I took a bite, and the flavor exploded in my mouth. "Oh.
My. Goodness. Sylvia, you could be a chef yourself. What did
you put in these?" She rolled her eyes, but the light shining
from her face was brighter than any smile.

"Make me some, Sylvia?" a red-haired boy, who looked
about twelve or thirteen, asked. "I'm starved."

The adults all moved away, and I joined the au pairs I'd
met and chatted with them for a while. Some of the other kids
were looking bored, but the pools outside hadn't been uncov-
ered yet, so I asked the waiters for clean napkins, and spent the
rest of that hour teaching them all how to make swans and
teddy bears. I was probably prouder than I should be when I
realized that not one of my examples ended up looking like a
dick.

Then the pools opened, and everyone rushed out of the
room. Sylvia asked permission to go out with the boy, Alexan-
dre, and I sent her on. From the bench seat at one end of the
room, I could watch them through a window, so I relaxed. I was

finally getting my first cup of coffee—with a healthy splash of cream and a tablespoon of dark chocolate—when a low voice interrupted me.

"The pretty little betasitter is all alone? We can't have that. I'll join you." I blinked up at Alphonse Dubois, who was wearing a too-tight pair of Hawaiian-print swimming trunks, a stack of gold chains over a hairy barrel chest, and... nothing else. I peeked at the ground. Well, he had on leather flip-flops. As I scrambled for something to say, he lowered himself onto the cushioned bench next to me.

"Oh, you don't have to do that. I was just heading out."

"No, I know you must be lonely. You and me, we're not like these others. Billionaires, so spoiled they don't know how to wipe their asses without a butler and a maid holding the roll." He laughed, like he'd told a great joke. I tried to laugh as well, then took a breath to excuse myself, but Alphonse slid closer.

I wasn't stuck in the corner—there was another way out—but I felt trapped. Suddenly, my coffee tasted bitter and rancid. He waved at the waiter to bring him some, and I took the opportunity to scoot away slightly. The alpha's presence felt like a threat, but his smell... between the rocking of the boat and the cloud of funk that was now roiling around me, I worried I might get to see what perfectly scrambled eggs looked like the second time.

I held my breath, a closed-mouthed smile pasted on, while Alphonse drank his coffee and stared at me. It made my skin itch.

"So, what's your angle, sweet thing?" His mid-Atlantic accent had faded somewhat. Now it had a hint of Jersey Shore.

My eyes met his bloodshot ones, and I swallowed hard. "What do you mean?"

He rubbed a hand over his stubbled chin. "What are you on this boat for?"

"For a job," I said quietly. "For money."

"Yeah. Yeah, I get that. But sniffin' around Giovanni? That won't do you any good. He's been through the wringer. He knows about women like you."

"Like me?"

"Omegas, looking for a sugar daddy." My cheeks flamed, and he snickered at my obvious shock. "You could bathe in that perfume you've got on, but it still can't cover up your delicious little scent. What's your game, little girl?"

"I'm sure I don't know what you're talking about. If you'll excuse me..."

"I'm not judging you. I get it." His meaty hand gripped my arm as he leaned close, speaking low. "Listen, sweets, I don't know why you would get on a yacht this close to your heat, but if Grantham won't help you out, I'll make sure you don't have to suffer alone, eh? Just keep it our secret."

"You... I'm not—" I spluttered, trying to pull away, but he tightened his grip. My stomach lurched. "Let me go."

But he didn't. Rain was right; my tai chi wasn't going to help me now. And I had left my pepper spray in my room.

I only had one way to defend myself. One weapon. So I inhaled as much of his musky, hot cabbage smell as I could, and used it.

Chapter 7

Grumpy

"**W**hat the hell is she *doing* here?" I said aloud, not for the first time, as I read the report Storm had sent that morning. The words on the built-in screen on the mahogany tabletop mocked me.

...engaged to be married to Tarquin Gotto-Cambert, heir of Cambert Comestibles, reported to the Georgetown police as missing this morning... tracked her phone signal to your location... parents are demanding her return...

The words blurred. I'd already ordered Storm to inform both her parents and the police that she had been brought on board as a temporary employee, and sent copies of the contract she'd signed to allay the authorities' suspicions, as well as the video of her embarking the boat.

Video. I had promised myself I would stay away from her, but I needed to see her. Make sure she was well.

Apologize for being such an unbelievable asshole the night before.

No, that wasn't happening. I had to stay pissed at her, or keep her angry at me, or I'd be in her room again in minutes, trying to see what the vivid dreams that had kept me up in more ways than one last night would feel like in the real world. How she would feel, wrapped around me.

Slamming the door on the way out of my private office, I stalked to the security room down the hall. "Sir?" My head of security greeted me as I walked in. "You said to keep an eye on Dubois. See if he made inappropriate advances to any of the au pairs on board?"

"Yes?" I snapped out, glad of the distraction. This was what I needed to focus on, not the alpha chaser. Alphonse Dubois, who I knew in my gut was a con artist. Possibly worse. It seemed too much to hope for, but I prayed he would slip up in the traditional way of unworthy grooms. "Is he in one of their rooms? I'll make sure Lore sees—"

"No," the man said, pointing to a screen. "He's in the smaller dining room with one, but he hasn't made his move. Although... Yes, here we go. He's touching her." I leaned over the monitor and saw him.

And Soleil.

I couldn't see her face, but his was a study in lust. His eyes dropped to her chest, his tongue moving over his lips as if he planned to kiss her.

He was already touching her.

The world blacked out. I couldn't remember leaving the room, only vaguely heard the shouts of people as I leaped over railings and deck chairs. The ship was a haze of red, white, and gold, blurring as I ran faster.

He had touched my Sunshine. *Mine!* The word echoed inside my skull. As I reached for the handle of the dining room door, intent on murdering the alpha who dared approach my omega, it opened abruptly.

I stumbled back just as Alphonse came storming out. "Fucking bitch," he spat, wiping at something on his front. I had a handful of his tacky gold chains wadded in my fists, before he could say another word.

"What did you do to her?" Something squelched under my fingers, and I smelled a revolting odor. Like scrambled eggs, coffee, and vomit? "Fuck's sake, man, what the hell is this?"

"That bitch threw up on me." He jerked away, his cheap chains coming loose in my hand. I flung them back at his reddened face.

Suddenly, Lorelei was there at his side. "Gio, let go of him! Who did this, Fons?"

"The betasitter," he said with a huff. "I was just trying to get some coffee. The bi—" His eyes flew to my face, and he broke off. "I need a shower, honey." My sister fussed over him, taking him back toward their cabin.

"Is Soleil sick?" Sylvia stood beside me, dressed like a tiny mourner at a funeral, as usual. Her gaze was on Alphonse, her small white teeth bared. "Is she okay?"

"I'll go check. Stay out here." She nodded and slunk back to a deck chair beneath an umbrella. There was a stack of what looked like napkins on the poolside table, and for some reason, she and two boys around her age were folding them into odd shapes.

I pushed the door open, taking in the scene. The room was empty, except for a waiter who was cleaning up something on a bench by the window. He noticed me when I grabbed a stray napkin to clean my hands, but before he could greet me, I held a finger to my lips. Soleil's voice filtered through the door to the galley, and I walked quietly back, listening just outside.

"... if they teach one thing in the Omega League, Juliette, it's how to deal with alphas."

The chef who had worked for me for eight years, and had never once allowed me into her kitchen, or spoken to me with anything but a sneer, laughed. "*Ma petite ange*, you cannot tell me they teach you to vomit on alphas who come too close!"

Soleil's laughter joined hers. "No. In fact, we recently had a lesson in how *not* to throw up around alphas who smell bad. But that guy, Alphonse? He stinks like—"

"Rotten cabbages in the sun," Juliette finished for her.

"You can smell him? But you're a beta."

"I may not be an omega like you, *ma belle*, but we chefs have noses almost as keen." Their voices dropped to near whispers. "Have you ever smelled an alpha whose scent you liked?"

"Liked? No," Soleil replied.

I sucked in a breath. Why would that word feel like a knife stabbing into my gut, creating a wound that would never heal? She didn't like my scent. But the night before, she had responded as if... Had she been pretending, like Zoe had all those years ago? I turned to go, but Soleil's soft voice stopped me.

"But *loved*? Yeah."

"Loved? Oh, sweet one. I know that look. Like you are lost and found all at once. Your world shaken, and your feet off the ground. You are in love?"

"No." Soleil gave a sigh loud enough to carry all the way to me. "Not love."

Juliette cursed in French. "Ah, I have seen this before, one time, long ago. You have found your true mate, *oui*?"

"Well, I don't know about that. But yesterday... You know how you have a favorite scent in the world? Like one thing, and if that was the only smell you were ever allowed, it would be just fine? That's what that alphahole Grumpy Grantham smells like to me. A mocha latte, with just the right amount of dark chocolate." My heart almost stopped beating as she moaned, "Yummmmm. But it's not fair. He's such a giant douchebag; he's probably ruined my favorite drink forever."

Wait. I wasn't a douchebag. I only acted that way to keep people from taking advantage. And where did she get off, calling me that? Disrespectful wench.

Juliette laughed. "*Ma petite*, that alpha—you say alphahole, yes?—that alphahole is far too old for you. *And* too grumpy. Though you could loosen him up with some olive oil, maybe, and this lemon reamer?"

"Oh, that's mean, Juliette! He could get a splinter in his chocolate starfish. Though the idea has merit..."

I bristled at the laughter that spilled out the door as I pulled it open. "Chef Jul—" My voice broke off as I took in the scene before me.

Soleil stood in a mismatched bathing suit, a flowered top and a bottom that was no more than strands of shimmering gold dental floss attached to a piece of fabric the size of a condom wrapper. And nothing else.

Thank god she and Juliette were the only two in the room. If a man had been in there, I would have scooped his eyeballs out of his head with a grapefruit spoon.

"What in the hell are you *wearing?*" The words flew out of my mouth before I could think of anything else to say. "Is this what you consider appropriate?" My cock apparently thought it was just fine, as it was already trying to salute her sartorial choices. I crossed my hands over my front, ignoring Juliette's sudden fit of coughing.

"Good morning, Mr. Grantham," Soleil replied coolly, spots of color rising high on her cheeks. "I'm afraid you caught me changing clothes." She waved to a pile of white fabric in a bucket on the floor. "I was... ill." She wobbled a little and swallowed hard.

I walked toward her, my hand rising to feel her brow for fever before I knew what I was doing. I checked the motion at the last minute, and she smirked as I ran my fingers through my hair instead. I'm sure I looked like an idiot. I didn't care.

Up close, I could see her face was flushed, with sweat at her temples. "Are you running a fever? I have a ship's doctor; he's been with my family for decades. I can have a helicopter on board in two hours if necessary—"

"I'm not sick," she interrupted. "I mean, I was sick to my stomach. But I'm fine now." The air around us filled with the combined scents of coconut and tropical flowers. That wretched perfume, and her own addictive aroma.

I moved toward her. "No. You're flushed. You're feverish. I'm taking you to the ship's doctor now." I lifted her in my arms and had her halfway through the dining room when I noted the waiter staring at her chest. "Fuck," I growled, pulling a table-cloth off the nearest table and throwing it over her head, obscuring her entire body from view. She sputtered and complained the entire way to the medical office, and when I set her down in front of the elderly doctor, she managed to claw the starched fabric away from her face.

"Dr. Rimbolt, this is Soleil Fairweather. She's ill. Please examine her," I said with a nod to the shocked man. He stood and smiled at Soleil.

Who rolled her eyes. "I'm not ill. I'm fine. My *boss* has lost his mind. I don't need an exam. I just threw up once."

My fingers itched to pick her back up and shake some sense into her. "Remember that I *am* your boss, Sunshine. And your safety on board is my responsibility. You could have some communicable disease." I frowned, knowing I was a hypocrite. I wouldn't have rushed anyone else to the infirmary; I would have confined them to their cabin. What was it about this woman?

"Could be something simple," the elderly doctor said in a soothing voice. "Seasickness?"

"Sure," she agreed, that telltale blush spreading over her chest. I reached over and tugged the tablecloth back up over her shoulders, covering her chest. I glared at the doctor. He might be a beta, and old enough to be her grandfather, but he wasn't dead. Fuck, hers was the kind of beauty that raised the dead. An entire army of zombies. I knew my own cock hadn't gone down for more than a few minutes since I'd met her.

"Keep it professional, Doc," I whispered.

Dr. Rimbolt coughed in his hand. "Let me just take a few vital signs, put all our fears to rest. Would you like privacy for the exam, Miss... Fairweather, was it?" His icy blue eyes met mine. "I may need to ask questions that are personal."

"Well, I don't have to answer them, do I?" she asked. "And call me Soleil."

"Thank you, dear, and no, you don't have to answer." He patted her hand. "But if you'd like the alpha to go, I know he'll respect your decision."

I swallowed a growl, but when she shook her head and muttered, "He can stay," I felt a wave of satisfaction.

He puttered around her, checking her heart rate, taking her blood pressure, frowning slightly when he read her temperature. "I need to ask one of those personal questions now, Soleil. Are you sure—" She covered her face with her hands, and I walked to the far side of the room, reading the medical degrees on the wall and listening as hard as I could. The doctor scowled at me, and spoke very quietly. "Your elevated temperature makes me wonder. When was your last heat cycle, dear?"

"Three months ago. I'm not due for another eight months, at least."

"Ah, your cycles are regular? I see. And you're single?"

"Yes," she said, then gasped. "Well, I mean... I guess technically, I'm engaged." Her hand went to her bare ring finger.

Technically? What the hell did that mean?

"Congratulations, dear. Well, you may need to get back to shore sooner rather than later, if you want to spend this heat cycle with your fiancé."

"Heat cycle? How can I... Oh." Her voice sounded so small, and I felt her gaze on me, burning holes into my back. "You mean a mini-heat?"

"Yes, dear. You haven't experienced one before?" His eyebrows rose as he waited for an answer. She shook her head.

I fought to remember what I'd learned about omegas' heat cycles, but it had been decades since the mandatory sex ed classes all alphas took in our teens, before our first rut. Everyone knew omegas had an annual heat, where they were most fertile. But I remembered something about shorter mating heats, which were extremely rare. They occurred when an omega was in the presence of an alpha their body perceived as a very close scent match.

The doctor's voice drew me back to the present. "...and as you know, until the omega is bonded with her alpha, the mini-heats can recur. Flare up, if you will. But usually not when the alpha is no longer physically present. When did you become engaged?"

"The, um, the day I boarded the ship."

"Ah, that must be it. Your fiancé triggered this heat. It happens, as I'm sure you know, with some very lucky omegas and their alphas. But the timing is unfortunate, with you here and him at home. It could fade with time and distance. Or, perhaps, if you ask Mr. Grantham, he'd take you to the nearest port so you can fly home and spend the next few days with your intended?"

I wasn't sure when I'd stopped breathing, but the room had gone so quiet, I had a feeling everyone else had as well. "I don't... I don't want to go back to shore," Soleil burst out.

"I see," Dr. Rimbolt said gently. "I have some heat suppressants."

"I'm allergic," she half-whimpered. "They give me terrible hives. And I need to stay here; I need to earn this money. I can't... I can't go home."

I wheeled around. "Why not? What do you need money for?" Her eyes met mine, and she tried to paste a smile on that gorgeous face, but it trembled. I stepped up to her, and her shoulders were in my hands before I could stop myself. "Tell me what you need. Now. I insist."

"What I need?" She breathed deeply, not answering, her eyelids fluttering shut.

"Anything. Anything at all." I gripped her chin in one hand and moved the other to the back of her neck, tilting her face up to mine. Her skin was still too hot. I blew a stream of cool air over her forehead, and the air between us filled with my own alpha scent, and even more of hers.

Her mouth fell open, inhaling. Tasting the air.

Dr. Rimbolt murmured, "Ah, I see," and backed toward the door, leaving.

Leaving? "Doc, where are you going?"

His eyes sparkled. "There's nothing I can give Miss Soleil, other than some ginger ale and saltine crackers for her stomach. In fact, I'm fairly certain she has everything she needs right here." And with that, he was gone.

Neither one of us moved, though my breathing was harsh, as if I'd run a race. And hers was short, quick pants that made me worry that she truly was ill.

"Are you... are you going to just keep holding me?" Soleil gripped the white plastic bench beneath her, as if she wasn't certain what to do with her hands.

"Why?" I said at last, the word exploding out of me. "Why are you here? Why would a privileged omega like you take a nannying job, leave her *fiancé*"—I spat the word out like a curse —"to work on a boat? Are you playing games with him?" The security video I'd spied came to mind. "Or were you playing a game with my sister's groom? Taunting him. Flirting?"

My gut churned. Was she even more duplicitous than Zoe, than the countless other omegas who'd put up with my sour disposition in hopes of snaring my billions?

She couldn't be, though. The longer I was with her, the more I knew she was mine.

Or feared it.

She seemed to go rigid in my grasp, her eyes bright now, but with anger. "A game, huh? What is it with you alphas? You're the ones playing games." She closed her eyes and murmured, "If you can't find the sunshine, be the sunshine."

I backed away, uncertain. "What the hell are you talking about?"

"Just more of my fortune cookie sayings," she said, her tone brittle. "I won't bore you with them. Am I free to leave, sir?" She wore that hard mask of a smile now, and I wanted nothing more than to wipe it off her face.

"Why were you sick?" I demanded. "Why throw up?" She didn't answer, just smiled at me like a lunatic. *Fuck.* I slammed out of the room, my cock stiff, my knot aching, and my mind buzzing with questions that I had no answers for.

I called Storm again the moment I was alone in my office. He answered with his usual good humor. "What the fuck do you need now, Grantham? We're not friends. I'm not your personal hotline." There was the sound of banging pots and pans in the background, and I waited for him to finish cursing me out.

"She's not wearing the ring," I said furiously. "You said she had a fiancé. Fuck, even she said it. She got engaged the day she boarded my yacht. Why did she run? Do you think the guy"—I couldn't make myself say her alpha—"did he try something? Was she coerced?"

"Did she say something like that happened?"

"She hardly says a word about anything to me! Nothing but fucking fortune cookie platitudes and sunny motivational poster quotes! I demanded she tell me what happened, about him, why she's here, and she just... smiled at me!" I paced the room in quick circles. "She told my chef she liked my scent—no, she loved it."

"She told you that?"

"No, I eavesdropped. She also said she'd never met an alpha she was attracted to before me. So why *the fuck* is my Sunshine engaged?"

Silence met my shouted question. "Are you done?"

"Yes," I bit out.

"You need to calm the fuck down. Her best friend says she's engaged. But she won't tell me anything else, and if I press her... Well, I'm not going to risk another attack from that woman again."

I waited for an explanation, but none came. "Her best friend assaulted you?"

"Assault by bikini," he groaned. Before I could ask if he'd been drinking, he went on, "Listen, I can try to find out more. But I know where you can get all the information you need. A source close to you. Very close."

"Who?" I asked, but I knew.

"Your Sunshine, as you say. Who is most likely your damned true mate, so you need to not fuck this up, Grantham. If you meet her, and she leaves... you know there will never be another woman for you again. You will literally die alone, and a lot sooner than you would otherwise."

"It can't be," I said, my voice breaking. "I'm too old for her." For some reason, he started choking, or laughing. "She's... she's chosen someone else already." I'd seen pictures of her fiancé and read the file Storm had sent. Tarquin was twenty-seven, six feet tall, a bit scrawny. The kind of muscles you got from golf and a once-a-week personal trainer. But in every picture he'd taken—and I'd found one with the two of them together, though I'd thrown my laptop across the room when it had popped up—he was smiling like he'd won the biggest lottery in the world.

And she'd been smiling, too. But had her smile been real?

Storm stopped coughing and cleared his throat. "She's not too young, if she's already engaged. You said she wasn't wearing the ring. Find out why. She's the only one who knows. Try asking her instead of demanding, asshole. Don't yell at her. I know it's expecting a lot, but if you could even muster a smile for the woman, my guess is she'll tell you everything you need to know."

I hung up and went to find answers.

And my omega.

Chapter 8

Sunshine

"Why did your parents name you Soleil? Are they French?" Sylvia peeked up from her sewing when I didn't answer at first. I put a few more basting stitches in the hem of a full-length skirt Clotilde had loaned me. We were sitting in Sylvia's room, since my bed was still nest-like, though I'd stuffed the dirty washcloths and linens in the back of my closet. I'd found Giovanni's belt under the bed, and had stashed it as well. I didn't want to think about why I was hoarding his scent.

So Sylvia's room it was. Her bed looked like an explosion of fabric and craft supplies, and she'd asked me to play some of my favorite music. We'd been listening to the new Babymetal album on my phone, and she looked happier than she had since I met her.

Dinner was only an hour away. I was supposed to go with Sylvia—her mother had sent a note to her cabin to make certain I knew to show up—but I'd altered my only formal dinner dress for her the night before. Luckily, I had a spangly golden sequined top with no back, a gift from Rain for my twenty-first birthday. But the only bottoms I'd packed were shorts, one pair of ripped-up jeans with a patch on the ass that said *Knot Thot*, and a purple Versace miniskirt that had been too short four years before. Thank goodness Clotilde had been such a sweetheart when I told her my problem.

"Are you from France?" Sylvia asked again. "I heard you speaking French with Chef Juliette."

"No. My parents, Peter and Marietta Fairweather, are both from Idaho," I replied, glancing at the tiny, counted cross-stitch pattern she was making. It read *Embrace the Void* and had tiny skulls and belladonna flowers around the edges. Rain would love it. "My dad wanted to name me Sunshine, but my mom went to the baby name books to save me from that fate."

She giggled, then said slyly, "My Uncle G calls you Sunshine. I heard him."

"He's making fun of me," I replied, my gut churning. "Playing a game."

"Oh no, Soleil. He wouldn't. He likes you, I can tell." She fluttered her eyelashes at me. "We all could, when he carried you like a princess all the way through the ship. Uncle G is strong. Do you like him?"

"He's very grumpy," I told her, hurrying my stitches. "He mostly growls and shouts at me."

"He's like that to most people, except me and Mom and Grandma M. He used to smile a long time ago, Mom said."

"Why did he stop?" I wondered aloud.

"Why does anyone?" she said after a long moment. "When there's nothing to smile about, why bother?"

I sighed and started packing the sewing kit away. "My dad always said not to let the shadows of yesterday spoil the sunshine of tomorrow." She made a choking sound, and faked her death very credibly on the bed. I poked her in the side. "He also said the sun never had to go to college because it already had a million degrees."

She didn't move.

"And he told me why the sun was mad at the clouds."

The corners of her mouth twitched.

"Because they throw so much shade."

She snorted quietly.

"And of course, he made sure I knew what the sun drinks out of." I waited until one dark eye opened. "Sunglasses," I yelled, tickling her side.

"Oh my gosh, your dad sounds like the hugest dork," she said, jumping off the bed.

"Totally."

I slipped into the bathroom to change, but heard her say softly, "My dad was a nerd. He told stupid jokes, too."

"Tell me one," I called back.

"What did the ocean say to the beach?" I waited, until she added, "Nothing. It just waved." I pretended to groan, but my heart was aching for her.

When I walked back into the room, she was dressed as well, in the navy gown I'd cut down for her the night before, but with a pale blue satin capelet made of couture dress streamers we'd tacked to a collar. I prayed her mother wouldn't recognize the fabric.

Sylvia was staring out the balcony window. "Dad was a computer nerd. He was teaching me how to code in Python before he died. He said I could be anything I wanted. An astronaut, or an engineer."

"He sounds like a wonderful man."

"He was," she said. "He had an allergy attack. He was stung by a bee, but no one knew he was allergic. Not even us. He didn't have an EpiPen."

Suddenly, her earlier panic in the dining room made sense. "I'm so sorry."

"Nobody talks about him now. Mom locked herself in her room for a year, and slept all the time. But Uncle G was there every day. He drove me to school and picked me up most days, and when it was the school Father-Daughter dance, he flew me to Hawaii and took me snorkeling with manta rays instead. He went to my parent-teacher conference one time when Mom was too tranked out to wake up for it." Her eyes glittered when they met mine. "He may not smile much, and he may even yell a little, but Uncle G is the best man... Well, the best one still alive. Don't judge him by how much he frowns."

I took her small hand in mine. "I'll try not to."

The dining room was almost entirely filled when we arrived. Sylvia seemed slightly overwhelmed, so I whispered that I'd escort her to her seat at the head table. She squeezed my hand in thanks. As we wound through the tables, the other au pairs called out greetings, and more than one of the younger guests nodded or said hello to Sylvia. She seemed somewhat shocked, but pleased.

"Here you go, Miss Ennui," I murmured as we reached the main table. Giovanni had stood the moment we walked in, and had already pulled out Sylvia's chair. I ignored him, nodding to Lorelei as I stepped back.

"Miss Fairweather," Giovanni called out. "Are you well?"

"Yes, thank you," I answered without looking back. Veronika had made a place for me beside her and some other au pairs, and we chatted about our favorite pastries and the most unusual flavor combinations we'd tried. I was delighted when Chef Juliette came out of her kitchen. After applause, and a short conversation with those at the head table, she made a beeline for my chair.

"Veronika, you must meet Chef Juliette," I said, standing.

"Chef Juliette, Veronika is from Hungary and she's passionate about pastries. Would you have any advice for her on how to start her own business? A shop perhaps, or some place to do more training?"

"Oh, I could never—I would never presume," the au pair sputtered, her accent growing thicker. "Chef Juliette is world renowned. She opened Le Petit Voleur in Paris; I've followed her career for..." Her sharp cheekbones were darkened with embarrassment, or something like it. "Well, I'm just... It's a dream. I could never—"

Juliette cut her off with a tsk. "Have you done any formal study?"

"Only a few classes. But I watch videos online all the time."

"Can you make croissants?"

"Of course," Veronika replied.

"Come to the galley tonight. I will judge for myself." She raked Veronika with a glance that held something more than mere professional interest.

As soon as she was gone, Veronika stared at me with disbelief. "How did that happen?"

I shrugged. "Juliette's incredibly nice. And her kitchen is amazing. She showed me the setup for the morning pastries, and I just thought—"

"She allowed you in her *kitchen?* Not even her employers are welcome there—not Mr. Grantham himself, not even the captain of this vessel." Veronika took a huge gulp of wine. "Chef Juliette is famous."

"Infamous," Clotilde broke in from across the table. Every au pair near us was listening intently. "She became the Grantham personal chef eight years ago, when she stabbed her previous employer in the hand for sticking his finger in the soup pot for a taste."

I took a bite of sorbet. It was scrumptious, lemon curd and

wild blueberry, and I wished there was more than a tablespoon-ful. "I might stab someone for Chef Juliette's cooking."

Clotilde giggled. Veronika was still staring at the door to the kitchen with wonder. And lust, though I wasn't certain if it was for the room beyond the door, or the chef inside it.

"She seems to like you, Veronika. I hope your croissants are as beautiful as you."

Over the next hour, I got to know all the other au pairs and nannies. A few of them were a little cold at first, but by the end of the meal—and after the copious application of a gloriously complex tempranillo wine—even the most starched of them all were smiling and sharing their contact information.

Then the table went quiet. "Miss Fairweather, a word?"

I twisted in my chair. Lorelei Grantham was behind me, a peculiar expression on her face. I glanced past her to see Sylvia still seated at the high table, chewing at her lower lip, her arms wrapped around her tiny waist. Alphonse was next to her, but he was smirking in my direction. Giovanni had risen and was speaking to the captain.

I forced a smile and replied to Lorelei. "Yes, ma'am. On deck or...?" But she was already halfway out of the room. I pushed back my chair and followed her, unsteady as the boat began to pitch slightly.

Once outside, Lorelei whirled. "I gave you a schedule. I expect you to keep it. I need to know where Sylvia is at all times. And where you are."

"Where I am?" There was something I didn't understand in her expression. Suspicion, and fear. I sensed my omega pheromones beginning to spill out, and tried to control them.

"Where were you today, Miss Fairweather?"

I frowned slightly, trying to think. "I had breakfast with Sylvia this morning. I was ill shortly afterward, and your brother kindly escorted me to the medical office. Dr. Rimbolt said it was probably just a touch of seasickness," I rushed to explain. I didn't want her to think I'd been taking care of her daughter while I was truly ill. "Then Sylvia and I spent the rest of the day together in her cabin, doing needlework. She has a hundred colors of thread. A very interesting collection for a young girl."

Lorelei's eyes softened, and turned her gaze to the ocean. "She used to do that with my husband's mother. Cross stitching."

"Yes," I said. "She's working on a pattern she found online. She's very talented with a needle; the back of her design is almost as clean as the front." I didn't mention her talent with scissors, or how evenly she'd sliced up all of her gowns.

"And she was with you all day," she said, her eyes boring into me. "You were together."

"I already told you that, Mother." Sylvia's voice emerged from behind me. "Not that you pay attention to anything I say."

Obviously flustered, Lorelei stammered, "I-I only needed to be sure, Sylvia."

"I've never lied to you. Not that I expect you to listen to me, or believe me, or care. But leave Soleil alone. She's not a liar either." Sylvia brushed past us, and I tried not to stare as Lorelei's face transformed into a mask of pain.

The ocean around us began to pound against the yacht, and we both grabbed onto the sturdy railing. After a long moment, Lorelei spoke, though I wasn't sure she was addressing me. A swirl of burned cinnamon and marshmallows swept past my face. "She doesn't understand. I'm so lonely."

I took a breath, knowing it wasn't my place. "Sylvia is, too. Perhaps you could join her tomorrow morning for breakfast. Swim with her."

I shouldn't have said a word. "Isn't that what you're here

for, *beta*sitter?" She spat out the word *beta*. "That perfume you wear will fool most betas, but not an omega. Not an alpha. I'm still not certain what is it that you think you're doing."

"A job, and that is all. I understand. I'll keep Sylvia out of your hair and make sure she follows the schedule to the moment. I'll go check on her now, to see that she arrived at her cabin safely." Before she could say anything more—and before she noticed the calming omega pheromones that were swirling around us in the ocean breeze—I gave a half-bow and left.

Sylvia was safe in her room, and I went straight back to mine, fuming. I scanned the most recent dozen of my mom's angry texts. Apparently, Mr. Grantham had informed her of my employment, so she was no longer filing missing persons reports. But the all-caps demands to *RETURN HOME IMME-DIATELY* and her reminders that I had not had permission to sign the contract—therefore making it void—had my heart racing at what exactly waited for me back there.

Normally, I would have rushed to answer them, to assure Mom I was okay. To do what she wanted. Like I always did.

But I was just tipsy enough to go against all my years of training.

So I deleted them all and texted Rain instead. She'd be so proud of me.

> Feeling cute. May never come home.

I attached a picture of me in the backless gold top.

Of course, there was no signal. I threw the phone on the bed, pondering my options and folding the edges of the blankets in even pleats. The room was rolling back and forth, though that may have been the ocean or the wine.

I was hot, so I stripped off my clothes. That was better.

The mini-heat Dr. Rimbolt mentioned had been on my

mind all day. I'd been in enough Omega League educational sessions to know precisely what he'd been referring to. And it terrified me. For this grumpy jerk to be my perfect scent match... I refused to follow that thought down to the two words at the end of it. But they bubbled up in spite of my denial.

True mate.

Normally, omegas only had one heat each year, a week-long fertile cycle where they would be frantic for sex with an alpha. I'd had enough heats to know how awful going without an alpha felt. It was five to ten days of absolute torture: feeling like my insides were being blowtorched, biting down on pillows so my parents wouldn't hear me screaming, though they sometimes checked me into a secure penthouse apartment for those weeks.

A naughty part of my mind wondered what would happen if I called Giovanni to the room. Asked him for help, just for the night or two.

Ha! He'd probably throw me off the boat to cool me off, I'd sink to the bottom of the ocean, and he'd be glad.

Lots of omegas would ask an alpha they knew, or a well-endowed beta, to help them through their annual cycles. But there were so many stories of omegas either being bitten in the moment by an alpha they would never have chosen for a life-long partner, or getting knocked up even with triple birth control in place, I'd never wanted to chance it. So I'd always made do with knotted dildos, vibrators, and an assortment of other sex toys.

Unfortunately, I didn't have any of the extras I needed for a really great self-care session in my cabin. But I had some quality reverse harem smut downloaded on my phone, and two hands.

I'd just tucked myself under the covers and found my

favorite e-bookmarked spot in Grace McGinty's latest sausage-fest when someone knocked on the door. "Who is it?"

"Your employer. Open up." The angry growl in his voice made my heart rate speed up. I set my phone down, but kept my other hand beneath the covers, circling my clit. I giggled as I remembered a list Rain and I had made to talk about masturbation.

"Sorry, Mr. Jack Off, this *Jill* is off the clock." I circled a little faster as he rattled the door handle. "Jilling off," I said louder, in case he hadn't heard. "Leave me alone. I'm my own boss tonight, Mr. Grump."

"Let me in," he demanded.

"Not by the hair... on my chinny chin chin," I replied, laughing. "Come back later. I'm doing finger exercises." *Huh.* Maybe that's how *his* fingers got so muscley. I almost asked out loud, but I wasn't that drunk.

He went quiet, and I bent my knees for a better angle. The ship was rolling smoothly now, and for some reason, the movement felt sensual. I slowed my pace, as the hallway went quiet. My uterus was contracting in a way that felt slightly painful.

Giovanni's words from the night before echoed in my memory as I thrust two fingers inside myself. *It might hurt the first time, Sunshine.* With a cock that size, and a knot... I shuddered, my fingers making wet noises as my body began to prepare for that terrifyingly large cock, my slick perfuming the air.

Then he was back. "You have ten seconds to open this door, Sunshine, or you will face the consequences."

"Can't. I'm... touching up my lip gloss," I replied breathlessly.

"Open the door."

"Not now," I said, rubbing harder, faster. "I'm... sick."

"Sick?"

"Yes, hot... fever... sick." It wasn't entirely a lie. The way I'd felt ever since I saw Giovanni was a sort of sickness. Like a drug moving in my veins, changing me. And I was hot, the mini-heat driving my temperature up.

It usually took me a lot longer than this to climax, but something about his presence, even through a door, brought me close. God, I could smell him, almost taste him in the back of my throat, like a hot chocolate sliding down, and it was bringing me to the peak, almost...

And then the door opened.

"What the fuck?" I sat up straight, the covers falling to my waist. "How did you get in?"

Giovanni stood in the open doorway, panting. In his hand was a card that must have been the master key. He stepped inside, growling low, and shut the door behind him. "You're not sick at all, little lying Sunshine," he growled. He yanked the covers off the bed, leaving me totally exposed. "You were fucking yourself with those dripping fingers, weren't you? Teasing me through the door. Worrying me." His eyes practically glowed with dark fire.

My own veins hummed with liquid courage. "Yes. Like I said," I sassed, letting my fingers drop back to my mound. It was slick with my arousal, and he licked his lips as his eyes tracked my hand.

It almost felt like I could come from only his eyes on me. I took a shaky breath and closed my thighs, starting to sit up, but the movement triggered a searing cramp in my abdomen.

"Ah!" I cried out, doubling over.

"What is it?" Suddenly, he was on the bed, pulling me onto his lap. For a second, I thought he might carry me naked across the ship again to the doctor, but then he buried his nose in my hair and exhaled. "Oh, Sunshine. That glorious fucking scent.

You tempt me. Do you need me to take you back to shore? To your fiancé?"

"No," I gasped. "Please don't."

The air was charged. "Does he hurt you? Are you afraid of him? I swear I will—"

"Tarquin? No, he's a sweetheart. I've known him since kindergarten. He wouldn't hurt a fly."

"Then why, Sunshine? Why are you here?"

Chapter 9

Sunshine

Something in Giovanni's tone pulled me out of the impending heat haze. I wrapped the ends of the sheet around my chest and did some of the shallow, counted breathing exercises I knew that helped with heat cramping. He waited, and when I had myself under control—well, except for the insistent throbbing from my overexcited clit—I answered. "It's a long story."

"I need to know. Start from the beginning."

"My friends and I, we're all omegas. Most of us found out when we were seventeen or eighteen. That's when we were pulled out of our schools and lost the lives we had planned." I held up a hand when he took a breath to speak. "I know what the public perception of omegas is. We're emotional and hormonal. Not the kind you'd want in a leadership position, right? Not the kind you'd trust your children with. Or your husband around. We're oversexed and lacking morals."

"I don't think that—" he said, but I shook my head, cutting him off.

"It's literally the first thing you said to me. And every time you see me, you say something rude about my clothing, like I'm some skank, trying to lure men to me. Entice alphas into my bed." I laughed bitterly. "Hey, look! I guess I did."

"I'm sorry. That was wrong of me. Inexcusably rude." Carefully, he turned me so he could see my face. There were lines of strain on his, like it hurt him not to hold me closer. It did hurt me; a cramp of need blazed through my insides the instant he'd pulled away. I grabbed his hand and placed it on my abdomen for relief.

"Too late now, Grumpy. You're already lured." I faked an evil laugh as the cramp subsided.

"That I am," he replied, his tone still brusque. "Go on. Tell me about your life. The good and the bad, Sunshine. The truth behind all those smiles."

My breath caught in my throat for a moment. No one except for my very best friends had ever cared to know any more than the surface Soleil I presented to the world. Smiling, happy, optimistic. And yet Giovanni had noticed that my smiles were masks.

So I told him. Everything from growing up spoiled and pampered, to the very day I came home crying in the middle of my senior year of high school. "I perfumed during my final class of the day and was sent home early, with all my things."

"Were you able to finish your high school education?"

"At home, yes. Of course, an unbonded omega in a high school, even a private one, is clearly dangerous, or so they told me." I ducked my head, the memories almost as painful as my cramps. "I had a job working for a local animal rescue, but the owner was an unbonded alpha, so that was over, too. I joined the Omega League that week. I hated it at first, but then I met Rain and my other omega friends. Some of them had it so much worse than I did. I couldn't complain."

"I would have."

"Well, sure, but you're Grumpy Grantham, the man who never smiles. All you do is complain, right?" I craned my neck to look at his face.

"Stop calling me names, brat," he growled, and the ache in my core started up again. I moaned softly, and he stood, leaving me alone on the bed. His gaze drew lines of fire all over my naked body. "Clothes, now." He crossed to the chest of drawers, and opened the top drawer, pulling out underwear. "Fuck's sake, Sunshine. What is this?" He held up a pair of red crotchless panties that had a cupcake printed on the very small scrap of fabric. I didn't have time to answer, since he was already digging through the rest. "Thursday, Sunday... Today's Tuesday. None of these are organized in any way. You're a slob, aren't you?" He pulled out a few more pairs of crotchless panties and muttered, "And possibly a closet stripper."

I clapped a hand over my mouth as he started folding the underwear neatly. He pulled one of the most risqué pairs out—a gold thong that had thin gold chains on the sides and up the butt. They were ridiculous, and the most uncomfortable ones I owned. He tossed them onto the bed, then opened the next drawer down.

"What are you doing?"

"I need to talk to you, and I can't when you're naked." He flung the first t-shirt on the pile. I wriggled into it, and the underwear. Once I was more or less dressed, he sat on the edge of the bed, crossing his arms over his chest. "Now tell me. Please. What did you want to do with your life before you knew you were an omega?"

"Exactly what I'm doing now, but without all the hiding." His expression was shuttered, guarded. I went on, hoping he wouldn't shout, or tell me I was dumb. "I wanted to start a small business, all woman-owned and operated. But the laws about omega guardianship make it almost impossible. We broke some rules, and did it anyway.

"Rain is fabulous with money and websites, and I write great marketing copy. We decided to offer virtual assistant services. But it wasn't until our friend Candy accepted a week-long job that she thought was a PA spot, but ended up being a betasitter job, that we started getting requests."

"Let me guess, all for betasitting?"

"Bingo. An anonymous donor gave us enough grant money in December to afford a few necessary things—scent blockers, heat suppressants for the omegas who can take them. Of course, we had to show a proper business plan, and invest in tax software and other things, so Rain and I haven't been able to pull out any money for ourselves. Not that I would be allowed to keep it if we did."

"Your parents won't support you in starting your own business?" he asked, a hint of righteous indignation in his voice. "Do you not have your own money?"

My laughter was bitter. "You have to be kidding. Your own sister is an omega, and you don't know that we have to have a co-signer on our accounts?"

"My sister doesn't. She's fully financially independent."

"There are exceptions. She had a husband." I wrapped the blankets tighter. "My mom is a beta, and my dad is an old-fashioned alpha. He's the softest-natured one you'll ever meet, but he believes I'll only be happy with an alpha husband. I asked him to let me have my own bank account. When he refused, I came back with a list of the reasons it would benefit me to have my own money to invest. He told me to stop being hysterical."

"Your dad sounds like an ass."

I shrugged, yanking my t-shirt down. "He's an alpha. Protective, thinks he knows everything, likes to boss other people around." I fluttered my eyelashes. "Not that all alphas

97

are like that, I'm sure." I tried to smile, but couldn't quite manage it. "Some are decent."

"What about your... fiancé? Tarquin Gotto-Cambert? Is he a decent alpha?"

I froze. Had I mentioned Tarquin's name to Giovanni? "Tarquin's okay. I've known him since I was four. He probably wouldn't want me running a business, but he would never hurt me."

"You don't want to marry him?"

A scream was welling up inside me, a shouted "No!" but I breathed deeply, keeping it inside. "I have to marry someone. He's kind. He'll treat me well, and we... we know the same people. We get along."

"What if you had a bank account of your own? Enough money in it for a year of expenses, say. No, two years."

"Expenses? You mean, for the business?"

"I mean for anything. Enough that you didn't have to marry unless you wanted to. You could live in a place like... the Omega Lofts. Run your business from there." I almost choked at his casual mention of New York City's most exclusive all-omega apartment building. It had phenomenal security, an attached twenty-acre park with a lake dedicated solely for its use, and was occupied by super-wealthy single omegas from all over the world. The Lofts weren't rented out; they were purchased outright, though the residential fees were more than my own parent's mortgage payments.

"Wow, shoot for the stars. We were saving up for a shared room at the Georgetown government omega facility but yeah, I guess. If I could get a few rooms at the Omega Lofts for me and my friends—oh! Plus an extra one for a physical office space. Maybe a slush fund of a few hundred thousand for incidentals? And legal documents of course, so no one could come in and take it all away... Yeah, I'd stay single for sure." I rolled my eyes, but his own expression didn't change.

"But that would make you happy?"

"I don't know," I said honestly. "I'd miss my parents. My favorite restaurants. I love living in Georgetown." I thought for a long moment. "No. I wouldn't be happy with that. I want to earn it, right? I want to work for it, and have the company be something I'm proud of, because I built it. Not just another thing somebody else gave me."

"Of course." He rubbed a hand over his wrinkled brow, like he was trying to solve some difficult equation.

"Do you ever smile, Grumpy?" I teased.

"No," he said. "The last time I tried, I had to have emergency surgery. I almost lost a lip." His delivery was so deadpan, at first it didn't register.

"Oh lordy, Grumpy McGrumperson. Did you just tell a joke?" I clapped my hands. "You're a real boy, Pinocchio!"

"Brat, I told you to stop calling me names."

I glared at him. The blankets and sheets were completely rumpled, and I folded them back into place as I retorted, "Why should I, Grumperman? Hit a little too close to home? Don't like it? Just smile. Maybe people will start calling you Smiley. Thanks for the talk, Smiley. Now, if you could head on out, I'll get back to my downstairs DJ job." I wiggled my fingers at his face. "Bye, Smiley."

For a moment, he hesitated, his nostrils flaring as he breathed. The only movement I could perceive was his chest as he sucked in my scent. His pupils were dark, his hands clenched, like it was all he could do not to throw me down on the bed and lay down a few sick beats of his own... but then he turned on his heel and walked out.

Chapter 10

Grumpy

I deserved a fucking award—a Nobel Prize, maybe even Humanitarian of the Year—for not throwing Soleil Fairweather down on her narrow bed and fucking her until her voice gave out from crying my name, until she begged me to stop making her come, until she forgot the name of her damned fiancé and knew that she was mine.

But she wasn't mine. She wasn't even hers.

Instead of doing what I wanted, I stalked back to my cabin, took a quick shower, jerked myself off so hard my dick was probably sprained, and went to bed.

The next day, I stayed in my room and my office, getting food delivered that I had no appetite for, and watching my obsession move around my ship on the camera feeds I'd rerouted to my phone.

Then I jacked off again. And again.

I spent the morning reading through my brat's high school yearbooks and trying to find the beta boyfriend, the afternoon putting things in place to make certain she would never need to marry Tarquin or any other alpha unless she wanted to, and the evening catching up with contracts that needed reviewing for a possible merger with a competing cruise line. Then I went to find my sister and get some more answers.

She was sitting alone in the dining room bar, her asshole fiancé nowhere in sight. I checked her drink. Hot tea. Good.

"Where's the douche?" I asked, signaling the bartender for my usual Balvenie Caribbean Cask scotch, no ice.

I expected her to snap back at me, but she just took a sip of tea and shrugged. "Did you hunt me down to trash talk Alphonse some more?"

I flinched. She sounded like she had six months before, when she'd been self-medicating. She'd almost died, and I'd checked her into a rehab facility near Miami. I wished I'd chosen any other one, since that was where she'd met Alphonse. He'd followed her out of rehab and into her life, and she'd only introduced us a month before, after they were engaged. I could not get her to see the red flags that were so apparent. When I'd asked her why she'd settled on him, she'd said, "He smells green and comforting, like Simon did."

I didn't think a general smell was enough reason to get married. Of course, I didn't think marriage was all that great, in any case. Our own parents had divorced when I was seventeen, and both of them seemed happier for it. But Lore was fifty-two, plenty old enough to make her own mistakes.

"No, I don't want to talk about him," I replied after I'd had another drink. "I want to ask about being an omega. About what your life was like, after you changed." She turned on the barstool and stared at me in shock. Her eyes were red-rimmed. "Have you been crying, Lore?"

"You know what they say about omegas. We cry all the time," she said, waving a hand in the air like she was brushing away a mosquito. "Why are you interested in my life all of a sudden, little brother?"

I frowned at my drink. I was disappointed in myself, that I'd never asked her about... practically anything. We'd grown up in the same house, but she was just enough older than me that I'd been... uninterested? No. Self-centered, like most boys. I told her so.

"Don't feel bad, G. You got better over time. Well, mostly."

I mock-glared at her. "When you first discovered you were an omega, you didn't drop out of school. I would remember that." I was eight at the time, and our parents had still been together. Dad had been excited, telling all his friends about the first omega born in our family in four generations. Since fewer than one in ten women became omegas, it was rare. But I'd mostly been annoyed at her getting more of the already-inconsistent attention of our parents.

She snorted. "I was lucky. I went to St. Catherine's, remember? All girls, and no female alphas, thank goodness. Dad made sure the one male alpha teacher was reassigned so I could finish my last two years." She smiled wistfully. "And then he forced Harvard to allow me to do remote learning."

"And you used your degree. You graduated, then helped Dad with marketing campaigns for our business."

"From home," she qualified. "I wasn't allowed to go to any meetings, remember? Omegas in a meeting room, influencing all those poor, weak alphas and betas with my magical pheromones?" When I frowned, she rolled her eyes. "It's literally illegal for an omega to appear on the witness stand, G. Apparently, we can sway juries with our scent."

I ground my teeth, wondering why I hadn't cared about this before now. Before Soleil. "But even before that, before you met Simon, you helped Mom's friend with her flower shop."

"That was a stroke of luck," she said. "Working in a florist— if you can get permission from a parent or guardian to do so—is one of the few jobs omegas can do without endangering themselves." She tapped her chin. "Though I would imagine one could be a perfume seller or something like that. In a place where there are constant, competing scents—"

I interrupted, "But when we were young, you always said you dreamed of running the company with Dad. Fuck, you made better grades in college than I did. If you weren't an omega, you'd be running it all, wouldn't you?"

Her tone was half humor, half condescension when she finally answered, "Probably not. Just being a woman makes it twice as hard to get recognition and the paycheck to go along with it. Dad is not the worst, but he's still a chauvinist at heart. Being an omega? Only made that dream impossible. Plenty of state laws declare us permanent minors until we marry. Even after that, the general stereotypes make it so we... Well, I didn't end up running Duchess Cruises for a lot of reasons. I don't regret it, though. If I hadn't been working in that flower shop, I wouldn't have met Simon. Or had Sylvia." We drank in silence.

"She really likes that betasitter you hired," Lore said eventually, as we watched the bartender polishing the glasses and hanging them. The ship was rocking enough to make them swing like a strange chandelier.

"Yes," I replied, as she slid off her bar stool. "Soleil is special."

"Just... keep her away from Alphonse," she murmured as she left. But for some reason, her tone wasn't threatening.

It was concerned.

The next morning, it was pouring rain, the ship pitching enough that I had to hold a handrail on my way out of my room. My steward greeted me outside my private conference room, but instead of my usual routine of drinking coffee while I caught up on the overnight trading markets, I headed for the dining room.

It was mayhem. Steel drum music was playing from the speakers at a ridiculous volume, but even louder were the sounds of laughter and shouting.

The smaller tables along the walls had been left empty, but all the seats at the larger tables were filled, and the surfaces piled high with various breakfast foods.

One table featured an enormous stack of steaming Belgian waffles and three separate pitchers of maple syrup, surrounded by bowls of every topping imaginable, from chocolate chips to fresh berries to whipped cream. The occupants of that table were hooting and cheering as a young boy used toothpicks to create some sort of leaning tower of waffles on a platter.

The other tables were every bit as wild. One had omelets being made into abstract art as the diners used real paint-brushes to cover the egg canvases with what looked like liqui-fied vegetable purees. For some reason, the people sitting there were speaking in terrible French accents, pretending to be omelet art critics, it sounded like.

Another table had towers of pancakes, all the individual plates decorated with various sizes and shapes of snowpeople. Sylvia stood on a chair, holding a sifter of powdered sugar that she was shaking over the entire table, while shouting, "It's snowing!" Her black clothing was completely covered with bright sugar, and her face held the widest smile I'd seen since before her father died. "Uncle G!" she called out. "Come sit with me!"

The waiters in the room all froze like frightened deer. Every eye turned to me, and the noise dropped off, except the music.

At that exact moment, the omega who I knew was

responsible for this debacle backed out of the kitchen, shaking her ass. An ass that was almost completely visible, since the rainbow-patterned shorts she wore had obviously been created for a toddler, not a grown woman with curves. When she turned around, singing off-tune, "Every little bitty thing... is gonna be okeydoke now," I got a glimpse of the front of her. Which was worse than the back. Tighter, if at all possible.

"Grumpy!" she shouted, a smile covering her face. Like a sound effect from a movie, the music went silent. "Sorry, I meant Mr. Grantham," she said, her face already turning red. She held a platter of sausages that had been stuck together with toothpicks to look like people. "What are you doing here?"

"I was under the impression this was my yacht," I drawled, reading the slogan on her midriff-baring white t-shirt, which read *Knot Interested* in bold black letters with a winking happy face in place of the letter O. "But it can't be mine. This scene resembles one of our competitors' tacky cruise lines."

"You really are grumpy in the mornings, aren't you?" she commented with a fake pout. Her pink lower lip jutting out made me want to bite it. "Coffee for Mr. Grantham?" she called out toward the kitchen, then held up the tray. "Have a sausage, sir."

"Do I look like I need a sausage?" I demanded. She stifled a giggle, her eyes dropping below my waist. "I meant..." What the hell had I meant? "No, thank you." I shifted, crossing my hands over the front of my trousers.

She danced right up to my side and whispered in my ear, her breath making every hair on my arms stand tall, "How silly of me. It looks like you already have a good-sized sausage there, Grumpy. How about taking a seat?"

"Brat," I snarled, and slid into the closest seat, since her coconut scent was making the situation harder and there were children all around. She winked and carried the sausage tray over to the other tables, chatting with everyone as she went.

I took it all in silently. I knew most of the eighty guests on board. I'd socialized with them at events all over the world, but I'd never seen any of them like this. Normally, the adults ordered coffee in their cabins. But this wild feast was a collection of children, au pairs, parents, and... I almost choked. Some of the guests who didn't even have children were here.

"Croissants!" a tall, model-thin au pair called out from the kitchen as she carried out a tray.

"Croissants!" all the children echoed for some reason, in exaggerated French accents.

Soleil ran over to the woman, pulled one croissant off the platter with a pair of tongs, and raced back to my table so fast I couldn't believe she didn't trip. Especially wearing two different shoes. Why the hell did she have on one gold sandal and one silver one? Was this a trend with young people? To look like they got dressed in the dark?

Damnit, this woman made me feel old, and off balance. And perverted. All I wanted to do was throw her over my lap and spank her until she came. Inside my pants, my dick tried to nod its agreement with this plan. I shifted around on my seat. At this rate, I was never going to be able to stand up again.

"Grumpy, you have got to try this!" my tormenter panted, holding the croissant up to my mouth with her hand. "It's Veronika's audition to work with Chef Juliette after this trip, and they are the flakiest, butteriest, most delectable croissants I've ever—"

I grabbed her wrist and bit into the croissant, my teeth scraping her thumb as I tore off a chunk. Her eyes went as wide as the pancakes.

It may have been delicious, but all I could taste was her. All

I could see was her. It took every bit of my failing self-control, but I let her wrist go and mumbled, "Good," around the pastry.

She hummed something in response, looking as flustered as I felt inside, and moved away unsteadily. I drank the coffee a humming waiter delivered, and pondered the change in the entire atmosphere.

More of the guests began filtering into the room, drawn by the music, or the shouts from the children, perhaps. Crew brought in more chairs until half the adult wedding guests must have been there, seated practically on top of one another.

They should have been offended by the mess, the informality. Instead, I watched my omega weave some sort of spell of happiness over the crowd, making sure every new arrival was greeted and brought into the celebration. There were socialites and heads of industry who I'd never seen smiling, using toothpicks and cupcake sprinkles to build atrocious food sculptures on their plates, and then eating them.

The CEO of one of the largest petrochemical companies in the world was intently building pancake snowmen, his graying hair flecked with white sugar as he muttered something about needing more coconut flakes.

The co-owner of the Atlanta Alphas basketball team was giggling as she walked a sausage person around on top of an omelet painted like a golf course, complete with a little flag and golf ball made from an edible gold dragée.

The man next to her, who had just gone public with a new aerospace firm that I'd invested in heavily, was asking the four-year-old boy next to him, who'd made a smiling face with veggie paint directly on the tablecloth, "But is it *art, mon petit?* Above all, ze art is king!" The child giggled so hard, he fell out of his chair and onto the carpet.

I shook my head. Somehow, I'd fallen down a rabbit hole I'd

never even seen. Following a curvy, smiling Alice who didn't seem to notice the mayhem she caused everywhere she went.

"She's magnificent, isn't she?" I turned to see Dr. Rimbolt seated beside me. I hadn't even noticed him enter the room. "Like a Pied Piper of joy."

I glanced down at his plate, which was a pile of sausages and pancakes surrounded by a lake of maple syrup. "That doesn't seem healthy, doctor."

"What's the point of living if you don't have fun on the journey, hm?" He ate for a few minutes as I watched Sunshine start a conga line with the children, while the adults laughed, clapped, and took pictures. After another moment, the doctor spoke again. "Young Soleil came to my office early this morning."

Coffee spilled over the white linen in front of me. "Tell me why. Was she sick again? What did she need?"

"I'm afraid I can't share that information." I fisted my hand to keep from grabbing his lapels. "I can, however, make some general comments about omega biology and their needs."

"I would... be very grateful if you would... educate me."

His eyes twinkled, as they had the day before. "An omega experiencing a sudden, unexpected heat cycle will almost always take suppressants. If those were not available for any reason, well... the pain is significant, and normal painkillers only work for an hour or so, even at prescription doses. Many omegas turn to alpha friends to help them through a break-through heat."

"Alpha friends?" My voice was almost a bark, and a few people nearby turned to me. I nodded and sipped my coffee, pondering how to get the information I needed. "But if an omega has a... fiancé, for example. Then it would be reprehensible to touch her."

The doctor was grinning like a fool. "Not necessarily. An

omega's heat can be a dangerous thing. If she doesn't have access to a nest, a place she feels safe, and to enough sexual aids to help ease her need for an alpha's knot, a heat breakthrough—which usually lasts only for a few hours—can continue for days. It can weaken her, lead to febrile seizures, even brain damage if the fever cannot be contained." He sighed. "Once an omega starts building a nest, the danger increases."

The coffee cup had somehow broken in my hand, and the waiter bustled over to clean it up. When he retreated, I asked, "Is Soleil in danger?"

"I can't tell you anything about her. She seems to trust you, though. Maybe you could ask her about a nest. Check and see if there are any sexual accessories on board to help someone experiencing this need. She is so conciliatory, so unassuming, yet effervescent. She'd never ask for what she needs, not if she thought it would upset those around her. She would never rock the boat, as they say." The yacht pitched as he spoke, and everyone in the room shouted, then cheered, like they were on a roller coaster.

"Fuck that. I don't care about the wedding; I will turn this boat around right now if she is—" The doctor's hand landed on my arm.

"Calm down. A mini-heat can be resolved in a matter of hours, Giovanni. After it breaks, as long as she stays away from alphas who... appeal to her, there shouldn't be a recurrence until her next cycle. But if an omega were experiencing a breakthrough, I would counsel her to find an alpha nearby who would help her. Male, female, it wouldn't matter. Just someone she could trust."

"Female alphas are rare as hen's teeth," I replied stiffly.

As if his words had conjured an alpha from thin air, I watched Anne-Marie Jacks, the curvy red-headed sister of my CFO, approach Soleil with a wicked smile on her face.

Which Soleil answered with a blush.

My blush. The one she had when I embarrassed her.

And then Anne-Marie held up a hand, reaching toward her face. And Soleil's eyes fluttered shut, leaning in.

"I don't fucking think so, Sunshine," I muttered, flinging myself out of the chair and marching over to my omega. I grabbed her arm, growled an "Excuse you," to Anne-Marie, and dragged the troublesome minx away from the cacophonous room. Soleil called out for Sylvia to stay with someone named Clotilde, and then we were down the stairs, walking toward the servants' cabins.

"Wh-what are you doing?" Her voice was lower, sultry, and her arm in my hand was blazingly hot.

I didn't dare to stop and look at her, or answer her. I could sense the haze of a rut beginning to fog my thoughts, and if I didn't move fast, I'd be knotting her in the damned hallway. We reached her room, and I turned to face her at last. "Have you built a nest in your room?"

For the first time since I'd met her, she wasn't smiling or faking a smile, or even trying to look anything other than what she was.

Pissed off.

"Tell me. If I opened that door, would there be a nest in there?"

"I don't have to answer that."

"I know. But I want you to." I ran my nose along her neck. "Do you trust me?" She tightened her lips, refusing to answer. There was a tiny speck of whipped cream on her cheek, and I leaned down and licked it off slowly, deliberately. "Sunshine, answer me."

She lowered her head so I was staring at the top of her hair, and muttered, "If you can't say anything nice, don't say anything at all." I knew she was talking to herself.

"Your call, brat." I pulled the key card out of my pocket and ran it over the lock pad, then lifted her up and carried her inside.

The room had been destroyed. The mattress was off the bed and on its side, creating a wall in one corner of the room. Clothing was draped over all the light fixtures, and a blanket taped over the long window on the far wall, blocking out the daylight even more thoroughly than the blinds. I had no idea where the rest of the pillows and blankets had gone, but they were either in the tiny closet or...

"You *have* built a nest, haven't you?" I breathed, the heady scent of flowers and coconut making my mouth water. Underneath her scent, there were hints of my own.

"I'm sorry I ruined your things," she replied, her voice soft. "I know you wanted a betasitter for Sylvia, not an omega. And I didn't know my cycle would get so weird; I swear I've been regular for years now—"

I put a finger over her lips and lifted her up to stand on the bed's bare platform, holding onto her shoulders. "Did you go to Dr. Rimbolt this morning for pain medication?" She nodded, still not looking at me. "Is it wearing off?" When she didn't answer, I shook her gently. "Answer me, Sunshine. Are you in pain now?"

"Yes," she muttered, her voice rising in a slight whine as she fidgeted.

"And is that your nest, Omega?"

"It's a terrible nest," she muttered. "There's not enough..." Her eyes darted to mine, then down again. "There's not enough good smells in it."

I let go of her shoulder with one hand and reached behind my back with the other, pulling the shirt I'd worn off in one movement. I balled it up in one fist, then rubbed it on her neck and down her chest until she took it from me.

111

Merri Bright

"Smells like this, cupcake? Alpha scents. My scent, and yours."

She nodded, stuffing the shirt behind her back, like a child concealing something naughty. I let go of her and she scurried back to the corner, pushing her way behind the mattress, hiding.

So fucking cute. There was nowhere she could hide from me.

I followed, peeking over the divider and discovering what had to be most of the spare blankets on board covering that part of the floor. Weirdly, there were washcloths and towels in there as well, what looked like a slim, beta-sized dildo, and... "My belt?"

"Mine now," she snarled, busy rubbing my shirt over the tops of all the blankets. I watched her, my heart aching for some reason.

She deserved a real nest. A room devoted to her comfort and pleasure. With silk pillows and soft blankets, dim lighting, and an alpha she loved. I wanted to ask her if she loved him, the alpha she'd chosen, but I couldn't make the words come out.

Instead, I asked, "Will you let me help, Omega?"

Chapter 11

Sunshine

"Will you let me help, Omega?"

My thinking was fuzzy like it tended to get when my heat cycle was imminent, but something in Giovanni's voice made me stop the frenetic folding and fluffing of the pillows, blankets, and towels I'd been hoarding in secret for the past two nights.

Two excruciating nights.

I hadn't seen the alpha that my ridiculous body seemed to be fixated on for over a day, and with every passing hour, the pain of not having him in my sight—in my *nest*—had grown more agonizing.

But the painkillers the doctor had given me, as well as the dildo Clotilde had somehow managed to scrounge up from one of the crew—new and still in the packaging, thank god—had given me enough sanity to be able to do my job.

"Why?" I croaked out, seeing that bright pink dildo now, at the edge of my nest. I hoped Giovanni hadn't noticed it, right next to his belt. "Why do you want to help?"

"You're my responsibility—" he began.

113

I cut him off. "No thank you, then. Go away." My core pulsed with a painful, searing heat. "I... I appreciate the offer, though."

"Do you want Anne-Marie?" His growl made me shudder.

"Who?"

"The alpha. Anne-Marie, she's the sister of my CFO. She was touching you." His voice had dropped to a rumble so low, I almost couldn't make out his words.

"Oh. Her. Yes... I..." I lifted a hand to my face and looked up. Giovanni was trembling as he stared down at me, something in his gaze that looked like rage or angst or... fear?

What could he be afraid of?

I murmured, "I had whipped cream on my face. She was just wiping it."

Relief washed over his features, and the rioting emotions sank beneath the surface of his dark eyes again. "Omega, please, let me into your nest. Please let me help you." The words were raw and truthful, and the stuff of every omega's dreams. A strong, virile alpha begging to come into my nest? My hand slipped down from my face to my neck, and another thought came through.

He wanted to help me. But he wasn't planning to stick around. He wouldn't want to be tied to me, and there were real dangers to accepting a temporary alpha for a heat. "No biting," I said firmly. "This isn't permanent."

"I would never do that." His eyes snapped with fire. "You don't need to worry."

For some reason, I whimpered. He would never bite me? Never claim me? I knew I should be relieved, but it felt like I'd been kicked in the stomach. I couldn't speak.

"May I enter your nest, Omega?" he asked, more quietly. "I only want to help you."

Not to mate me, claim me, or love me. I dropped my eyes

and slapped a hand over my mouth, trying to breathe through the sudden urge to scream at him. To demand to know why I wasn't good enough. Why he was so closed off, so untouchable.

But then another wave of cramping hit, and I cried out. "Yes, Alpha. Help me."

For a large man, he moved gracefully. Pressing his hands against the wall, he leaped over the mattress without knocking it down. There was almost not enough room for both of us to sit in the nest together, but he sat cross-legged and pulled me onto his lap, my back to his chest, and held me quietly for a moment while the cramp passed. "Better, Sunshine?"

"Mmhm," I replied. I had my nose pressed as deeply into his arm as I could, sucking in his mocha scent. The pain and tension that had been mounting in my body began to transform into warm eddies of lust. I had on a scent-blocking pad that the doctor had found in the ship's supplies, since I'd used all mine, but it was growing uncomfortably damp from the amount of slick my body was producing. I squirmed a little, and felt teeth on my shoulder, holding me in place.

"No biting!" I squeaked, my stomach jumping like I was at the top of a roller coaster.

"I promised, Sunshine. This will just be pleasure. Hand me that toy, would you?"

Oh shit. He'd seen the dildo.

I obeyed, and he held it up in front of my face. "Did you bring this from home, naughty girl?"

"No," I admitted, squirming on his lap. His giganta-dick was pressing into my spine from my ass halfway up my back, it felt like. "This was from a crew member who had an extra."

His face froze as he dropped the pink silicone toy, like it was on fire. "You borrowed a dildo?"

"Oh my god, no! It was new! In the packaging, I swear."

He grunted, but still glared at it like it was a sleeping snake.

"Do you have one like it?" His hands moved to the waistband of my shorts, and he tucked his thumbs underneath and slid them, along with my underwear, down my legs.

"Mine are bigger," I managed to say, though he was staring down at my exposed pussy, blowing a stream of cool air over my shoulder. It was making me hotter, filling the nest with his scent.

"Bigger?" He grabbed my shirt and pulled it over my head, then deftly undid the front clasp on my bra. He snorted, almost a laugh. "I like your lingerie, Sunshine. Not what I expected." He held up the bra, reading the printed words out loud. "'Spank me, Daddy?'"

"It was a gift from my best friend," I tried to explain, but then his hand was around my throat, and he shushed me.

"You don't need to be embarrassed about anything that brings you pleasure, little Sunshine. Is that something you've tried? Being spanked?" His eyes blazed a trail over my naked breasts. "Would you like me to spank those gorgeous, soft tits, and your curvy ass as well?"

Sweet fuck, was this man going down an invisible list of every top fantasy I never even knew I had and ticking them off? "Um... no. I mean, I haven't tried it. But..."

"Yes, you want to?" he grumbled, his chest rumbling against my back, his hand tightening ever so slightly around my throat.

I nodded. "I do," I rasped, pressing my neck even harder into his restraining grip.

"I have to admit, I've had more than a few fantasies about punishing you for all the naughty things you've done over the past few days." He shifted under me. "Facedown, Sunshine, over my lap."

I wanted to do just that, but he didn't wait for me to obey. His hand stayed on my neck, gentle but immovable, as he positioned me like a doll so that I was facedown, staring at the pillow-covered floor. His hand was on the back of my neck now, and his other drawing smooth circles over my bare ass. "If you need me to stop, just say that: stop. One word, Sunshine. But I think you need this now, don't you?"

I wasn't at all certain, but I managed to squeak out, "Yes."

He purred the tiniest bit, and I relaxed. "You signed a contract you had no legal right to sign, Sunshine," he said, and raised his hand, bringing it down with a loud clap. I jolted, feeling the sting. But it hadn't hurt exactly. It just felt warm. A trickle of wetness seeped out of my opening, falling on his trousers before I could squeeze my legs together to stop it.

He lifted his hand again. "You came under my control, onto my boat, on false pretenses." Another light slap on the other cheek. As he peppered a few more gentle blows, the heat intensified, the vibrations traveling lower to where my pleasure was already beginning to build. My nipples hardened, rubbing against the cloth beneath me.

"More," I mumbled, grabbing handfuls of the sheet.

"Oh yes, naughty girl. You're going to get a lot more." As he spoke, he rained down slaps on my ass and thighs, none of them so painful that I wanted to cry, but hard enough that the stings took a moment to dissolve into a welcome heat. The ones on my thighs stung more, the burn dissipating more slowly. But I loved how the sensation sent shock waves of pleasure to my clit, and beyond. My whole body felt oversensitized, almost raw.

Hungry, for this alpha. For his hands on me, rough or gentle. When he hesitated, a soft whine escaped my lips. He answered with a sound halfway between a purr and a snarl, and squeezed one of my cheeks. "God, my marks look good on you, brat. Glowing pink." He whispered the next words, "I could bite you and leave a mark that would stay longer."

Before I could draw in a breath to protest—though the words on the tip of my tongue weren't a complaint, but a "Yes, please, Alpha"—he went on. "For some reason, you decide to wear the tightest clothing I've ever seen on a woman every day." He knocked my legs apart with his hand. When I tried to close them, a slap fell on the tender inside of my thigh.

"Ow!"

He rubbed the spot for a second, then went on, as if waiting for something. Waiting to make sure I was all right.

I chewed my lip. "Keep going."

He ran his fingers through my dripping pussy and snarled, "Oh, I will. You're gushing for me. You needed this, didn't you?" He didn't wait for an answer. "You did need it. Hold still, bad girl, and take your punishment." I widened my thighs again, feeling the stinging slaps as they grew faster. "Wider," he demanded, "and arch your back."

"Why?"

"No, you meant to say 'yes, sir,' didn't you?" he rasped, spanking even harder now. A strange, painful ecstasy spiraled up in my core as the vibrations from the blows seemed to burrow into my center.

"Yes, sir." I arched my back up, my ass high in the air, and he slapped my ass, hard enough to burn, then stopped to move his finger around my clit, circling the spot where some of the sensation had been building, gathering, though the burn was deep within now as well. I tried to press into his hand, seeking more.

"Hold still," he scolded with another sharp slap on my thigh.

He kept circling, growling. A tidal wave of ecstasy threatened to fall over me, consume me. But every time it drew close, he backed off, denying me. If only he would use a little more pressure...

A long, needy whine slipped out. "Harder. Please, Alpha!"

"Bad. Fucking. Girl," he barked. "You don't get to decide.

All you do is feel." He went back to spanking my inner thighs, and, to my shock, the wave grew even higher. I held my breath, wishing it could keep building forever.

Wondering if I would survive it when it came crashing down.

"Now come," he ordered. "Fucking come all over me, my disobedient little omega. Soak me. Do it, come from me spanking this naughty, dripping cunt." And then he moved his hand so that the blows rained down on my pussy itself.

Holy shit! It hurt, but it felt so fucking good. The climax that had been building exploded, drowning me in a pleasure that had sharp edges, and no end in sight. Stars swam in my vision as I cried out, arching my back even more, and his clever fingers returned to my clit, circling with just enough pressure now to keep the wave moving through me. I felt wetness escaping me, heard it spilling on his lap.

Before the orgasm was over, he had me on my elbows and knees, and had maneuvered behind me, his face buried in my pussy. It was oversensitive, the way it always felt right after I came, but he pinned me in place with one thick arm.

"This slick is mine. Let me have it," he demanded. His tongue was all over me, plunging into me, while I was still contracting. The wet, slurping noises he made were obscene. "Gonna drink this pussy dry, tastes so fucking good." The pleasure was so intense that I was crying, but I felt another orgasm start to build as he licked me, biting softly at my sore thighs. "No, I want to see your face when you come this time, princess," he murmured, flipping me over. He hovered over me, one hand behind my back, holding me so my back was arched off the blankets. His other hand was on me, his nimble fingers circling my clit, then plunging into me. I came again as soon as he entered me, riding out that orgasm as he watched.

"One," he murmured, his eyes almost cruel as he watched.

"That was two," I panted.

"No, princess. That was one finger." He pulled his hand out, working my oversensitive clit while I sobbed and protested that I was done. Just when I was at the verge of another orgasm, he plunged two fingers into me, stretching me slightly. "Two," he growled.

A shiver of desire and fear went through me. Those eyes bored down into me, his grip on my burning ass now almost too tight as he drove me to another quick orgasm, his thumb working my swollen clit at the same time.

"Three," he snarled, and thrust hard and deep into my pussy, crooking his fingers each time he hit that pulsing, aching spot in me.

"What are you—" I gasped as he worked those three, thick fingers in and out, building the next orgasm from inside.

"I may not be allowed to fuck this tight, pretty pussy. I may not be able to bite you, knot you, claim you. But I can teach you what it means to have a real alpha, who knows how to take care of this body, this messy, dripping slit. You'll feel me inside you for days, Sunshine. And every time you fuck yourself with one of these little toys, or your tiny fingers, your needy cunt will miss me." The orgasm had my inner walls tightening around his fingers, and I felt the intrusion grow thicker.

"Four, princess." I felt the unmistakable burn and stretch of four fingers moving inside me, roughly. His fingers alone were every bit as big as any toy I'd used, even the knotted ones. It felt so good, I thought I might pass out. But the dark promise in his eyes was terrifying.

"You can't," I whimpered. "You're not going to..."

He leaned over me, licking my neck, nibbling my ears, still fucking me with those fingers. "You worried I'm going to count to five, Sunshine? You worried I'll fuck my whole fist into you? Stretch you wide as my knot, leave you hurting for more? No, princess. I'm not going to do that today." The panic receded, and I ignored the wash of disappointment that inexplicably followed.

He moved back down and swirled his tongue around my clit, somehow knowing exactly the rhythm and pressure I needed to have another climax. I exploded around his hand, hot liquid squirting around his fingers, and he crooned as he lapped it up, cleaning me with his tongue, gentling me back down. When the last spasms were wracking me, he pulled his hand out of my aching pussy and moved me back up onto his lap, purring.

I lay there, shaking from experiencing more orgasms in the space of an hour than I usually had in a week, as he petted my hair and purred into my neck. I'd never felt so well used. So cherished. So owned.

"I like that," I managed to say. "Your purr."

"I haven't purred in a while," he said after a moment. "The last time was for my fiancée—"

"You're engaged?" The aroma of charred coconut began to fill the nest. I stifled a sob. Of course a man like this had someone. He could have kept it a secret from the world. He had power, money, influence.

Oh, god, was she on the boat? I hadn't seen him with anyone, but there were so many gorgeous women here. People he'd known for years. Stars swam in my vision as I began to hyperventilate.

He purred harder, forcing me to calm. "No, Sunshine, no. It was years ago. I'm not engaged; I would never be unfaithful." He hesitated when I gasped at the implication. "I know this is different. This is medically necessary."

I turned on his lap and stared into his face. "Are you trying to rationalize what we're doing? You think I am being unfaithful?"

His purring stopped now, and I missed it. "No, Sunshine. I just need you to know I'm not the kind of man who would act unethically."

"Whatever you say, boss," I snapped back, wrapping my arms around me, suddenly cold.

"I'm not, you know," he replied brusquely, as he pulled a blanket up and over my shoulders. "As your parents and the Georgetown authorities have stressed in our communications, the contract you signed was not valid."

"Right," I said, suddenly terrified. "Are they going to... shut down the business? Is Rain okay?"

"She's fine. I looked over the paperwork for Blue Skies, and the anonymous donor who made you file everything made sure you were protected legally. Or at least your partner is."

"Right. Rain's mother gave her written permission."

"That's correct. So it's only your connection with Blue Skies that's in jeopardy, not the entire business."

"Oh." I was still cold, the mini-heat thoroughly broken. My ass was the only part of me that was hot now. Well, that and my face, after Giovanni said the next words.

"I'm sure your fiancé will support you in your business." He stood, vaulting back over the mattress. I stood as well, my legs shaky, watching as he straightened his clothing. He was still fully dressed, the wet patch on his dark gray trousers the only sign he'd even been near me. "I'll make sure the doctor comes to check on you daily, and get your meals delivered until we're back in port."

"What do you mean? I'm not staying in my room. I'm Sylvia's betasit—"

"You are not a beta, and you are not a sitter. I told you, the contract you signed was void. You're not my employee. You never were."

"But Sylvia needs me," I said, my heart breaking at his cold expression. "I've only known her for a few days, but she's coming out of her shell, talking to the others her age. We're working on a *dress* together."

"Thank you for your help so far." He crossed to my bathroom and took a towel out, holding it folded over one arm in front of him, to hide the stain on his thigh. "But she has me, her mother, and quite a few au pairs who will all be happy to keep her company."

"I don't want to stay in here," I protested, pushing the mattress down and climbing over it. "I'm fine now."

"You must." His jaw flexed as he turned to the door. "There are alphas onboard. We don't know what might trigger another... heat event. It would be inconvenient."

Tears sprang to my eyes. "You mean it would be inconvenient for you."

"That too. It's better for us both for now if we don't spend any more time together." His head moved in a jerky nod, and then he was out of the room.

"Just leave, then. And stay out of my life," I yelled at the door.

All the energy that I'd funneled into building the nest came rushing back to me now as I tore it all apart. In a half hour, I had it bundled up outside my room, had called the maid, and was texting Rain while ignoring the messages from my mom, my dad, and... oh shit. Tarquin. I'd missed seven messages from him.

Shit. Unfaithful. I suppose, technically, I had been. And I couldn't let that stand.

My friends and I had ruthlessly mocked the guys we'd known who had been too chicken to break up with their exes in person. Rain in particular felt like ghosting was a killable offense, and she had good reason to feel that way, since her own mysterious true mate, who she'd met on a trip years before, had done that exact thing to her.

But breaking up via text was almost as bad. I needed a bestie consult, stat. Quickly, I typed out the most vital information about the past day, then went back to organizing my horrific wardrobe. Rain didn't text back, which worried me. She would never ignore my messages.

So I was on my own. I needed a plan. I would stay put for the rest of the day, get myself cleaned up and under control. But I was not going to be stuck in my cabin for the rest of this cruise.

And when I went up on deck, I was going to make certain the alpha who'd rejected me got to appreciate just how *inconvenient* a pissed-off omega could be.

But first, I had a confession to make.

Mustering all the courage I had, I walked over to the window, watching the ocean pass by while I dialed Tarquin.

Chapter 12

Sunshine

"Soleil, I missed you all day yesterday!" Sylvia shouted from the pool as I stepped onto the main deck the next day. I'd considered staying in my cabin, but Rain had finally replied to my texts and insisted I leave my room. If I let some "random alpha" keep me from enjoying a week on a luxury yacht, she'd said, she would give me infinite shit when I got home.

"Thanks, Miss Ennui! I wasn't feeling my best, but I'm fine now," I replied. Sylvia waved and went back to playing water volleyball. I smiled at her black swimsuit. It exposed her sharpie tattoos, and if I wasn't mistaken, two of the other kids also had written something on their arms and shoulders.

"My little trendsetter," I murmured, then almost stumbled when I remembered I wasn't her betasitter anymore.

But that didn't mean I couldn't be her friend.

The deck chairs were mostly taken, and I waved at the people I knew best as I crossed to the pool's edge. With no clouds in sight, the sunlight was almost too bright, and the breeze was the tiniest bit cool, but I spied an empty lounger

125

next to a couple of betas I hadn't met before, and sat down. I pulled off my t-shirt, exposing the daisy-printed bikini top, and ignored the eyes I could feel on me as I lay back and untied my improvised cover-up skirt. I had on the gold bikini bottoms again, and this time, more than one person paid attention.

"Can I get you a drink, omeg—I mean, Soleil?" The redhead alpha's voice was soft as honey, and her scent of tart cherries and cloves wasn't nearly as overwhelming out here on deck. When I accepted, she waved the waiter over.

"Good morning, Miss Soleil," he said. "What will you have today?"

"Oh, just fizzy water, please. I wasn't feeling great yesterday. Have you heard anything more about your sister? Rebecca, right?" He'd been the crew member who took my suitcase to my room on the first day, and he'd told me a few things about his younger sister who had recently been diagnosed with leukemia.

"Mum texted. She made it through her second round of chemo yesterday, Miss Soleil. Thank you for remembering."

"Don't forget to text me your folks' address. I'll send her one of those fruit bouquets when we get back to Georgetown, too. I know when I'm sick, pineapple and strawberries are all that tastes good."

He took our drink orders, and I turned back to the alpha with a smile. The breeze had shifted direction slightly, and I subtly covered my nose as she asked where I had been the day before.

"Oh, I um... I wasn't feeling well," I said, shifting on the lounger. My ass was still sore, and I couldn't get comfortable. "Probably too much sun?"

"Or too much heat," she mused with a smile. After our drinks came, she stared at me for long enough that I felt distinctly uncomfortable, like a bug under a microscope. "What are you doing here, Soleil? You're no more a betasitter than I am."

"I promise I really am," I replied. "Or at least I was before today. I even owned an agency." I took a gulp of fizzy water and burped softly. "Of course, I may not even be able to keep the business once I get home."

She hummed. "Care to tell me how you ended up on Giovanni Grantham's yacht?"

"I can't. I signed an NDA." I held up a finger. "Which is probably unenforceable, now that I think about it. But still. It's the principle of the thing."

"Kindness and principles. More beautiful with every word."

What in the heck was going on? Had I rolled in some sort of alpha catnip? I felt a blush flare up on my chest.

"Ms. Jacks, please don't misunderstand. You're very attractive, but I'm not looking for any more alphas in my life right now. In fact, I just got rid of one yesterday morning, thank goodness."

"Thank goodness?"

"Yes. I never should have led him on like I did... but now that he's more or less out of my life, I'm so relieved. Is that awful to admit? That I'm glad he's not going to—" The sound of shattering glass behind me, and a scream from the pool, had me jumping up to see what had happened.

The door behind me that led to the bar had somehow shattered, the glass now in tiny particles. "What happened?" I slipped on my sandals and hurried over to check on Sylvia. "Are you okay?"

"Fine, Soleil. You?"

"Not a scratch on me. I'll go inside, though."

I felt someone wrapping my cover-up around me, and smelled cherries and cloves. "Not a scratch, no. But you do have some lovely handprints there. Keep this on while we walk and talk."

I wanted to die. This glamorous woman had seen my spank marks?

She burst out laughing. "Don't worry, sweetheart. They are very lovely 'spank marks,' and they'll be gone soon enough."

"Oh, crap. I said that out loud. Sorry."

"Never apologize for calling a woman glamorous. 'I can live for two months on a good compliment.'"

"Mark Twain," I said, recognizing the quote.

"Well-read on top of all the rest? I do like you, Miss Fairweather." She nodded as if she'd decided something, then gestured for me to follow her toward the walkway around the side of the boat. "You said you might not be able to keep your business. You have your own company?"

"Yes. For now, at least."

"Tell me about it."

So I did. I shared everything from my reason for starting it with Rain, our experiences with the first clients, the anonymous donation that helped us get our LLC set up, even my accidental engagement. She listened carefully, and was extremely thoughtful about staying downwind when she noticed I was overwhelmed by her scent.

"It sounds like you need a fairy godmother, and a little help with your parents to get them to see your potential. Not just as an omega, or some alpha's fiancée."

"Ex-fiancée, as of yesterday."

She burst into laughter. "You broke up with—what was his name? Goldtoe-Camembert?"

Goldtoe-Camembert. I snorted. "Socks and cheese? Yeah. I know it was chicken shit, but I did it on the phone. Thank goodness we had enough signal for a call. He took it pretty well, but we've been friends since our playdough-eating days. I'm pretty sure he saw it coming."

She was shaking her head, her arms wrapped around her middle like she might burst out laughing again at any moment. "You said earlier that you'd gotten rid of an alpha. I thought you meant... Oh, this is rich. He has no idea, does he?" I opened my mouth to ask who she meant, but she continued. "All right, Soleil Fairweather. When you get home, I want you to ask your parents to call me for a meeting. I'd like to invest in your little company, if you think you can stand to have me come by to meet your 'betasitters,' and stink up your office space every once in a while."

"Oh, Ms. Jacks, you don't stink. Your smell is... fine. It's just—"

"Not for you. I know how it works. My mother and father were true mates." She smiled and looked out over the ocean, the wind whipping her curls around her neck. "My mother said she always thought alphas smelled like stagnant water until she met my dad. And his aroma reminded her of almond cake. That was how she knew he was the one."

"Have you... I mean, do you have a special someone? An omega?"

"Not just an omega," she said, so softly the wind almost drowned out her words. "I found my true mate. But she doesn't seem to realize who I am to her."

I took her hand in mine and squeezed it. "Then she's an idiot, Ms. Jacks. You're not for me, but you're generous and kind, and any omega would be lucky as heck to have you."

"Thank you. I keep hoping she'll wake up, before it's too late. And call me Anne-Marie." Her eyes flitted to the top of the ship, where Lorelei stood alone at the railing. Watching us, with an expression that made me let go of Anne-Marie's hand and step away.

"Is Lorelei...?" I let out a whistle when Anne-Marie nodded slightly. "That's a lot. She's beautiful. But—"

"Yes. I know. When I boarded the yacht and shook her hand... Whew. That scent. Cinnamon and marshmallows. I thought I'd faint. My favorite scents in the world." A dimple flashed in her cheek, but her eyes were filled with pain as she stared back up at where Lorelei had been. "Now I need to get out of the wind, and you need some sunscreen." She held open a door to the ship's interior hall. "Out of curiosity, what's your favorite scent, young omega?"

I inhaled, wishing the salt air had a hint of his aroma in it, even if I was mad at him. "Mocha. Espresso with dark chocolate and cream."

Her quiet words followed me as I walked back to the bar. "He has no idea."

The afternoon was perfect, not a cloud in the sky, and the choppy seas had calmed as we sailed toward the private island where the wedding was to take place the day after tomorrow. I'd slathered on sunscreen, but also pulled a huge towel over my front to keep from burning, and was sipping a lemonade when I heard a chuckle behind me.

It was Alphonse. "Mind if I join you?" he asked as he pulled a deck chair over, scraping it across the teak. "Hot day. You keeping an eye on the kid?"

I murmured agreement, and tried to ignore him as he ordered a drink and settled into his chair. It was hard to pretend an alpha wasn't just staring at you from only a few feet away, though. Ogling.

I kept my attention on Sylvia, even if Clotilde had quietly informed me that she'd been asked to take over any official duties. Apparently, Giovanni had made sure everyone knew I wasn't her betasitter anymore. Most of the crew had whispered apologies, and the au pairs had all drifted over to check on me and let me know they had my back.

When my ex-boss finally appeared on the pool deck, wearing navy swim trunks and a white linen button-down open in the front, no one would speak to him.

But they all gave him looks that said plenty.

"Uncle G!" Sylvia called from the pool. "You're going to play?" They'd strung the volleyball net up again, and a game was just beginning. He walked past me without a word, but his glare at Alphonse didn't go unnoticed.

"Doesn't like me near you, huh?" Alphonse mused as soon as Giovanni was in the pool. "Good work. I gotta tell you, I'm surprised. I've never seen Grumpy Grantham off his game."

I did not like hearing that nickname from his mouth. "Excuse me," I said quietly. "I need to go inside. Too much sun." I stood, being careful to keep the towel over my front, and my back to the unoccupied side of the deck, as I gathered my things.

"I meant what I said before," he told me, his voice full of false solicitude. "I'll help you with your little heat issues—holy shit, omega. Where you been hiding all that?"

An unexpected gust of wind had caught the edge of the towel and wrapped the cloth over the top of my head. I couldn't see, but I could hear. Alphonse wolf-whistled, and I could sense him coming closer. I backed away and tripped over what felt like a chair, landing with a jolt on my already sore ass. "Ouch." I scrambled to get the towel away from my face, blinking into the harsh sunlight that was suddenly blotted out by a tall shadow.

"Sunshine, did he hurt you?"

I stood, keeping my balance on the deck chair, and turned

131

just in time to freak out at the scene before me. Giovanni had his hand around Alphonse's neck and must have grabbed him in some kind of Vulcan nerve pinch, because the larger alpha was on his knees on the deck, his hands tight around Giovanni's wrist.

But my alpha wasn't paying his sister's fiancé a single bit of attention. His hot gaze was on me, and I felt myself melt a little. "I'm fine."

I hadn't seen him for over a day, and he looked... rough. He had dark stubble on his jawline, and his eyes were blood-shot. But that same passionate fire still sparked as he took me in. I tried to remember what an asshole he'd been to me in my room, but my brain was skipping those parts and going straight back to the moment when he counted fingers, and.... *Soleil, stop thinking about Mr. Fingerfucker, and remember Mr. Stay in Your Room! He didn't want you. He was glad to leave.*

He rejected you.

The memory had me straightening up. "He didn't touch me. I fell."

"My mistake," Giovanni said, stepping back and letting go of Alphonse. "My apologies."

Alphonse rounded on him, and it looked like he was going to charge him, but Sylvia stepped up next to her uncle. "Why'd you leave the pool, Uncle G? We need you on our side."

His eyes shot to me, then Alphonse. "How about Miss Soleil plays on your team? I need to have a chat with Mr. Dubois."

Sylvia snorted. "You're really mad at her, huh?" She winked at me. "Please don't come on my team, Soleil. Especially right now. We're in the deep end."

Giovanni's frown grew more pronounced. "Why should that matter?"

"Don't you know she's a sinker?" Sylvia laughed, but her eyes stayed on Alphonse the whole time. Watching for danger.

"What the hell does..." Giovanni stepped back. "Dubois, I'll meet you in the conference room, level three." Alphonse muttered a curse and stalked away. Giovanni exhaled, shaking his head at me. "I told you to stay in your room, Sunshine. Get back there now."

"I'm not your betasitter. I'm just a guest," I said, taking a deep breath. I didn't mind the way his eyes snagged on my boobs.

"No, you're a stowaway," he muttered. "Do as I say." When I shook my head, he barked the order. "Go to your cabin, now!"

Fuck. My feet were moving before I even realized what was happening. One of the worst things about being an omega was how our biology responded to an alpha's bark. It was nearly irresistible to deny a command given in that tone.

I heard him call out, "Sylvia, get back here!" but she was right there with me, her hand in mine as I half-ran to obey his order.

By the time we got to my hallway, the alpha command had more or less worn off, and Sylvia pulled me to a stop. "He barked at you!" she screeched. "Uncle G barked at you! What a complete fuc—"

I had my hand over her mouth before the word could come out. "I may not be your betasitter, but that's not appropriate language," I cautioned her, though I felt the same way.

An alpha's bark was a psychological weapon, and for him to have used it in front of Sylvia and the other guests who'd witnessed the encounter with Alphonse was borderline unforgivable. It shocked me that an alpha like him, so in control at all times, so polished and urbane, could lose his grip so publicly.

"Mmmfhmm," Sylvia mumbled, her lips moving under my fingers. I removed my hand, and she glared at me. "The question is why aren't *you* cursing? Uncle G was completely out of line." She growled like an angry puppy. "This is literally why they invented four-letter words, Soleil."

"You're not wrong. But if you want to sound classy, and not get into trouble, you use old insults and swear words. Like Shakespearean or older," I cautioned. "No f-bombs allowed."

She crossed her arms over her chest. "I don't know any of those."

"Well, it's a good thing we have the internet and some time on our hands." I opened my cabin door, gladder than ever that I'd deconstructed the nest and had the maid clean the room thoroughly. For the first time in days, it didn't smell like sweat, sex, and pheromones. "Come on in."

In a few minutes, we were seated on my bed, immersed in Shakespearean slang.

"I really like this one," I muttered, jotting it in my notes. "Away, thou cream-faced loon." Sylvia giggled. She'd hardly stopped doing so since we entered the room.

"Off with you, you cullionly barbermonger!" she whispered to herself as she scribbled the line on her arm in permanent marker.

"Sylvia!" I covered my face with my hands. "It's an hour until dinner. Your mom is going to hate that."

"My mom probably won't notice," she said with a huff. "She's always around Alphonse, and when she's not, she's looking for him. She hasn't figured out where he goes. But I know."

"Where is he?"

"The wedding planner's cabin," she said, still scribbling. "Her name's Muffin—can you believe it? At least, that's what he calls her. I saw him come out of there yesterday, and he had lipstick on his neck and his clothes were disgusting."

Holy crap. "Did you tell anyone?"

She gave me a look that indicated she thought I'd lost my mind. "Who would listen to me? Mom already knows I can't stand Alphonse."

"Tell your uncle?" I suggested.

"Ugh, he's been so weird on this whole trip. Barking at you? I've never once heard him bark in my entire life. I didn't know he was that kind of alpha."

"I think he just hit his limit," I offered weakly.

"I think he's been grumpy for too long. He never would have done that sort of thing a few years ago. Even a few months ago." Her lips grew pinched. "Plus, he fired you for being an omega, no matter what he tells anyone else. We all know it. It's total discrimination. We're starting a petition."

"An omega? You think... Who thinks... What kind of a petition?" I sputtered.

"Come on, Soleil. You didn't need to tell me or anyone. I mean, you smell awesome, almost as good as my mom. And you act... I don't know. Nicer? It was weird. At first, I thought maybe you weren't one; people always say omegas don't like other peoples' kids. And you like me, right?" She swallowed and looked down. "You didn't want to stay in your room and not hang out with me, did you?"

Tears stung my eyes. "No. I think you're amazing, Sylvia. I was so mad at your uncle for telling me to stay away."

"And then he used his bark on you, like a feral alpha or something. I'm going to give him so much grief for that, don't you worry. I'll tell him he's acting like a..." She peeked down at her tablet. "An embossed carbuncle!"

"Now that I'm not your betasitter, I can tell you that I agree. He was being a bit of a carbuncle." We giggled and rolled onto our backs, staring at the ceiling. She felt like a younger sister to me. I wanted to protect her from the world.

"Now that you're not my betasitter, you could talk to Mom.

You're an adult, and an omega like her. Maybe she'd listen to you," she said after a moment, sitting up on her knees. She had changed into one of my t-shirts and a pair of my shorts, which embarrassingly fit her far better than they did me. "Tonight at dinner, I could distract Alphonse, and you could talk to her."

"Honestly, I'm not sure that would work. Your uncle has tried, and... sometimes love is blind." I sighed. "At this point, she'd probably have to catch him in the middle of a felony."

"Or something," Sylvia mused. "If she caught him... I don't know, hurting someone on the boat? Like, before the wedding."

I sat up, alarmed at where this was going. "Like tonight? Sylvia, it's too late. We'll be at the island tomorrow night. There's no time for elaborate schemes. Or sketchy ones. Promise me you won't do anything or put yourself in any danger."

Sylvia's chin firmed, exactly like her uncle's did when he'd made a decision. "I'll make her listen. I'll talk to her tonight."

I could smell a hint of my scent filling the room, calming her, soothing her mood. I stood, giving her a gentle hug. "Good for you. I hope she hears what you're saying. Now, you need to get dressed for dinner. Maybe wear one of the pastel princess dresses. You didn't cut them all up. It'll catch your mom off guard; she might listen to you."

"You'll come, too?" she asked as I opened the door. "I'm not... I'm not brave on my own. Not like you."

"Like me?" I wanted to laugh, but she looked so serious. "I'm a total chicken. I'm not the tiniest bit brave."

She blinked. "You are. You stood up to Uncle G, and my mom, and threw up on Alphonse, and you wore that tiny bikini out in front of everyone—which was like, whoa, Soleil! For a sinker, you sure rock the swimwear."

"Hey, I need the lifeguards at the pool to keep a close eye on me. Every time I try to get a little tan, I risk my life."

She burst out laughing. "Pretty sure Uncle G was going to have a heart attack when he saw you. He was watching you the whole day. When you were talking to Ms. Jacks, he was behind you, and then he slammed the door shut, and it broke everywhere..." She waggled her eyebrows up and down, then skipped away, while I tried to process everything she'd just said. "See you at dinner!"

Chapter 13

Grumpy

"Where is Alphonse, G? I haven't seen him all day." Lore stood at the glass window of the bar, looking out at the deck. Anne-Marie Jacks was outside, chatting with her sister, but her gaze kept returning to Lorelei.

I took a large swallow of my drink, trying to think of a way to tell Lore what I knew, without destroying her. I knew where her trash fire fiancé was, and who he was with. The boat's cameras had caught him sneaking in and out of the wedding planner's room enough times that even an ostrich like my sister wouldn't be able to deny he was fooling around.

But telling her was harder than I'd imagined. I helped her onto her bar stool and waved at the waiter to leave us alone. "Lore, where did you find that wedding planner? Muffuletta, or Mimsy, or whatever."

"Oh, Muffin? She's an old family friend of Alphonse's. She's not the best, but Fons asked me to give her a chance, so she could get some exposure. She's some sort of distant cousin."

I almost choked on my drink. "I hope very distant. Lore... I

138

need you to know, he's been slipping in and out of her cabin at all hours."

"Yes, they're planning some sort of surprise. Something romantic, I'm sure. Or wild. A dance up the aisle?" Her laughter was brittle.

She thought they'd been dancing? Perhaps the horizontal mambo.

I cradled my head in my hands. I'd had too much to drink this afternoon. Hell, since this morning, after I'd heard my omega tell Anne-Marie that she was glad she'd gotten rid of me. Her words were etched on my brain, seared into my soul.

I'm not looking for any more alphas in my life right now. I never should have led him on like I did. Now that he's out of my life, more or less, I'm so relieved. Is that awful to admit?

I'd been standing close enough that every word was perfectly clear. Agonizingly painful.

Then, seeing her in that tiny, mismatched bikini. Defending her from Alphonse. Barking at her like some brute... I'd never humiliated myself like that in public before. My niece had looked at me like I was some kind of monster.

I'd felt like one.

I'd felt too much on this trip, in every way. Every emotion. I wasn't used to it. This week couldn't end soon enough. But first, I had to break my sister's heart.

"Lorelei, I have footage of them. He's not planning a romantic surprise. Not for you, anyway. He's involved with her."

"Do you have a camera inside the cabin?" Her tone was resigned. Almost like she'd expected this.

"Right outside."

"That's not proof."

"God, do you need to see him fucking her to believe it?"

She stifled a sob. Fuck, I was a monster.

"Lore, I'm so sorry. I don't want to hurt you. I'm trying to protect you and Sylvia." Before I could say anything else, the door opened, and Anne-Marie stepped inside. A rush of wind followed her in, and her strong alpha scent of cloves and cherries filled the room.

"Oh, my apologies. I didn't mean to interrupt," she began. She ran a hand through her windswept curls, that seemed at odds with her severe white pantsuit. "I'll just go."

To my surprise, Lorelei blushed and stammered, "No, please. We, um, were done with this conversation. You can have my seat."

"Well, I came to speak with you, Lorelei. But... perhaps I could walk you to dinner?" Anne-Marie held her hand out, and Lorelei took it. At that very moment, the setting sun sent a ray of golden light through the upper windows of the bar, illuminating both their faces.

I hadn't ever seen my sister's eyes as bright and joy-filled as they were at that moment. She was mesmerized by the alpha. And Anne-Marie looked like she'd just discovered her greatest dream come true, in Lorelei's smile. "Shall we?"

"I'd like that." My sister gave me a wide-eyed look as Anne-Marie escorted her from the bar. "G? Go ahead and send me the video. And thank you."

And then they were gone.

I poured myself another drink, then went to dinner. I wasn't sure how Lorelei would handle Alphonse's indiscretions, but I had a feeling she would have help drying her tears.

"Uncle G!" Sylvia greeted me at the door to the dining room, and grabbed my hand tightly.

"Excuse me, young lady. I'm not sure we've been introduced. I'm Giovanni Grantham." I stroked my chin, peering down at Sylvia, who was wearing a fluffy lavender dress and a frown.

"I don't have time for teasing, and I'm still mad at you for being so mean to Soleil. But I need to tell you about something," she said, pulling me down to her ear. "It's an emergency, about Mom's fiancé."

"Soon to be ex-fiancé," I whispered, just as the man in question walked into the dining room, a few feet ahead of the wedding planner, who shot him a very intimate look before she went to her table. How could Lorelei not have seen it all along?

Love really was blind.

"Come tell me about your day, Sylvia," Alphonse said, ignoring me as he pulled out Sylvia's chair.

"I'm going to sit with my friends," she replied. "At the kids' table."

"The kids' table?" I muttered. "Since when are the children seated separately? But good idea. See if you can snag me a chair; I'll change into a diaper and a onesie if I have to." Her frightened smile tugged at my protective instincts, and I leaned down, hugging her close. "Stay as far from Alphonse as you can. I'll catch you up later. Stick with the au pair, okay?"

"Nah," she said, her eyes sparkling. "I'll stay with my betasitter."

"Your—" At that moment, the soft elevator music shifted inexplicably to steel drums, the air filled with the perfume of a thousand tropical flowers, and the sun rose inside the dining room.

Or at least, that's what it seemed like.

Soleil stood inside the dining room door, chatting with my CFO Yvette, seemingly unaware that every eye in the place was on her. I wasn't sure anyone could look away.

I knew I couldn't.

Tonight, she was dressed in a wild assortment of colors. She had on a fuchsia silk top with small golden padlocks down the center in place of buttons, and a bright purple miniskirt that stopped an inch below her crotch, if that. At the bottoms of her shapely legs, she wore what had to be five-inch red high heels. In one hand, she gripped a small purse that had tiny charms shaped like keys trailing down from one handle.

Shit. Were they the keys to the locks down her front? I'd never been so turned on, incensed, and amused before.

Slowly, the occupants of the dining room started talking again, many of them calling out to greet Soleil as she teetered on those ridiculous shoes over to what I assumed was the children's table.

One of my sister's friends approached me, initially asking about the wedding but quickly segueing into a subtle promotion of a new product his company was bringing to market. I nodded, pretending to listen, but my eyes were on my omega.

Everyone loved her, and for no reason other than that she was herself. She was probably one of the least affluent people in the room, but I watched as a half-dozen social climbers scrambled out of their chairs to go and chat with her. Complimenting her outfit, when almost every one of the other women wore some version of a little black or white dress by a designer who was a household name: Versace, Balenciaga, Dolce & Gabbana. I wondered how many of them would be on the phone to their designers within an hour of dinner, asking for something like hers.

But her clothing wasn't what made everyone want to be near her. She personified her name. She was sunlight, and warmth, and when you were in her presence, she was the only thing you could see.

But she wasn't looking at me. She didn't see me, didn't want me. She was glad I'd told her to stay away... and then she'd disobeyed me when I demanded she remain in her cabin.

Naughty Sunshine. I stared at her as she flitted like a butterfly, her face carefully angled away from me. Obviously aware of where I stood, and just as obviously intent on not making eye contact. Her cheeks were turning that perfect shade of pink, though, and I knew why.

The head waiter cleared his throat by my side. "The first course is ready, sir, and cannot be delayed. Is your sister dining with us tonight?"

I glanced at the head table. Alphonse was chatting with Yvette, who looked like she'd rather drink poison than sit next to him. But Lorelei's seat was empty, as was mine and Sylvia's. I sent Yvette an apologetic nod and replied to the waiter. "Go ahead and serve it. And have one of your crew add an extra chair next to where my niece is sitting. I'll be dining at that table tonight."

"At the children's table?" I heard him mutter as he raced to follow my instructions.

I circled the room, greeting a few of the people I knew from other social events and business dealings. When I neared the table, the waiter had already placed a chair directly between Sylvia and Soleil. Sylvia was wriggling on her seat like a puppy, and I raised one eyebrow. "Ants in your pants, Silly?"

"Uncle G," she hissed, her gaze darting to a dark-haired teenage boy sitting diagonally to her.

"Who the hell is that?" I sent the young man a look that promised a long, slow, painful death if he so much as—

"That's a child," Soleil muttered, her lips hardly moving, though she kept her smile pasted on. "He's very sweet, and Sylvia has a little crush. It's harmless."

"He'll be even more harmless at the bottom of the ocean," I said, placing my napkin on my lap.

143

She leaned forward to fiddle with her silverware. "Why are you sitting here?"

"My yacht," I replied stiffly. "I can sit where I like. Though I am almost certain I gave you very clear instructions to stay in your room, Sunshine." I leaned down to her ear. "You've earned a punishment."

She chewed at her lip, her cheeks even more pink, but then the food arrived, and she burst into laughter. "Oysters! Twice in one week. How lucky."

"Ew." Sylvia wrinkled her nose. "Do you like them? You can have mine." She shoved her plate closer to Soleil, and the other children at the table all offered theirs as well.

"Do you really like oysters?" I murmured.

"I detest them," she said. "But possibly not as much as a seven-year-old child. Wish me luck." She lifted one up to her mouth, mumbling something that sounded like "At least they're not hot jizz shots," and swallowed it down, only shuddering slightly.

I sighed heavily and waved the waiter over. "I'm afraid Miss Fairweather may end up eating a hundred oysters at this point. Can you ask Chef Juliette to prepare something slightly more... kid-friendly?" The waiter bustled away, and I realized the entire table was staring at me.

"Oh, dear," Soleil said. "Children? Hide your knives."

Instantly, every one of the young diners did exactly that. Sylvia tucked mine under the edge of the tablecloth, then grabbed my jacket sleeve. "Uncle G, I just want you to know, you've always been my favorite uncle."

"I'm your only uncle, Syl. Why is everyone acting like I just stepped in a pile of shi—shipwreck?" I corrected myself.

Under the table, Soleil's hand squeezed my leg. "Good boy," she whispered, still smiling.

My cock perked up like she'd patted him.

The answer to my question came in the next thirty seconds. Chef Juliette, ominously carrying a meat cleaver, emerged from the kitchen and arrowed across the dining room. "Did someone complain about the food?"

I opened my mouth to explain, but Soleil cleared her throat. "It was me. I'm afraid I had a rather traumatizing oyster experience recently. Even the scent... I'll need to dine alone in my room tonight, Juliette. I'm so sorry."

"Clear them away," the chef demanded, her face softening as she shook her head at Soleil. "Traumatizing oyster experience. I suppose some scents are just too much for delicate constitutions." She patted Soleil's blushing cheek, ordered fruit sorbets for the table from the head waiter, then glared at me and vanished.

The kids at the table burst into giggles and whispers after she was gone. I listened to their conversations, and realized they were all terrified about rumors they'd heard of my chef.

"Is it true?" Soleil murmured. "Did Juliette really stab her last employer?"

"He needed stabbing," I muttered back, eating the coconut sorbet and wondering how much coconut was safe to eat. I'd already started drinking coconut water and adding coconut milk to my coffee. Next thing I knew, I'd be jacking off with coconut oil... Actually, that thought had some merit.

I set down my spoon, feeling Soleil's attention on me, warming me from head to toe. Her eyes sparkled with curiosity as the main course arrived: filet mignon with portobello reduction, gratin Dauphinois, and seared broccolini in a lemon-sherry sauce.

Soleil whispered into my ear, her breath sending shivers up my spine, "Tell me what really happened with Juliette, if you're allowed. And if it wouldn't upset her for me to know."

I almost smiled. "I'm allowed. And she would tell you

herself. It wasn't reported widely in the press, since I had my people expunge most of the news articles after I hired her. Her previous employer was doing more than tasting the soup. He was sexually harassing Juliette, who had no interest in him. Or any man, as far as I know. He got drunk and took it too far one afternoon when I was at his chateau for his annual garden party."

"He did need stabbing," Soleil agreed, and I liked the bloodthirsty glint that accompanied her tight smile.

I turned to Sylvia to change the subject, and also because the proximity to Soleil was wreaking havoc on my composure. "So, Sylvia, you didn't want Soleil on your volleyball team today. Is she terrible at sports?"

"Well, she's pretty awful at swimming," Sylvia said with a laugh. "I tried to tell you, she's a sinker."

"A what now?"

Sylvia answered at length, quoting some sort of scientific journal she'd read that week, her voice filled with horrified fascination. Every word she said had my heart pounding faster.

When she finally finished explaining, Soleil had her head in her hands. "Miss Ennui, you can't just tell people about that. Now he knows how to murder me and dispose of the body with no evidence."

I took a long drink of water and realized my hand was trembling. "Do you mean to tell me, you came on board a yacht without knowing how to swim? What were you planning to do if you fell into the pool? Or god forbid, the ocean?"

She winked at me. "I suppose I'd either sink to the bottom of Davy Jones's locker, or hope to be rescued by a tall, dark and handsome yachtsman?" Her hand landed on top of mine for a brief moment. "Grumpy, you're shivering. Is it cold in here?" She leaned forward, her breasts practically spilling over her crossed arms.

"You're cold," I noted, trying not to stare at her hardened nipples. I didn't wait for an answer, but called over a waiter, who immediately brought my suit jacket. Taking it from him, I wrapped it around her shoulders.

She buried her face in the sleeve, inhaling deeply. "I wasn't cold," she muttered, ignoring my snort.

Before I could calm down enough to ask more about Soleil's genetic condition, my sister entered the room at last. She nodded to me, then crossed to Alphonse. They had a short, whispered conversation, before crossing to the door. I half-stood, but Lore shook her head at me.

I was not comfortable with that. I texted Captain Vance, telling him to assign a crew member to shadow them and make sure she got back to her room safely.

"You've turned her whole world upside down," I told Soleil, when the children were starting to excuse themselves. Sylvia had organized some movie showing on deck with ice cream sundaes. I loved the way she was at the center of the group as they crowded out of the room. "The way she's inter-acting with the other children. That confidence, that wit... She's amazing."

"I think so, too," Soleil murmured.

"I never realized how much she was like her father," I said, sipping my espresso. Another guest wandered close, and I shot him a glare. Soleil muffled a cough, then sipped her own.

"Simon Standish, yes? The actor."

"He was a gifted actor, the life of every party. Not like Lorelei. Especially not like me. We may pay for every party, but no one would care if we didn't show up for one. Or miss us if we stayed home."

"I'd miss you," Soleil said gently, then amended. "I mean, I'd miss your family. Sylvia."

"But not me."

"You said it yourself, Mr. Grantham," she replied. "It's better for us both if we aren't around each other. Though I never would have said such a thing." She rubbed at her face with the corner of her napkin. "I suppose it's good to know where I stand." She stood then. "For what it's worth, I don't agree with you. I think knowing you has made me stronger. And maybe knowing me will change you somehow."

Change me somehow? Bitterness churned in my gut. She hadn't changed me. She'd destroyed me, or at least the carefully constructed divide I'd placed between myself and the rest of the world.

She never would have said such a thing? I wished that were true.

But I wouldn't bring up what I had overheard, her relief to be rid of me. She had a right to her feelings. And she wasn't wrong. She was better off without me, and seeing her tonight had proved that. An entire ship full of the world's most annoying, pretentious elites had been not fawning over her, but just falling in... falling in love.

Something about her made it impossible not to dream of a life with her, wrapped up in her smiles, standing between her and anything that might hurt her. Holding her every night as I fell asleep, waking to her beauty every morning...

Fuck. I was falling in love with her.

But I didn't deserve her, even if I wished I were worthy of her love.

Chapter 14

Sunshine

"Are you cold now?" Giovanni's voice was almost covered by the sound of the wind rushing past as the yacht moved through the darkness.

"Not at all," I replied, clutching his jacket tighter around me. I was glad he couldn't see me, or smell the rush of perfume that had permeated his coat. I wasn't cold. But I also didn't want to give the coat back, so I added, "Thank you again for your jacket."

"It was nothing." His normal, stern tone was the same as always, but the heat in his gaze told a different story. And the questions he'd been asking about my life, as if he truly cared, had revealed a new facet to this enigmatic man.

We stood next to the railing on the topmost observation deck, Giovanni staring at the side of my face, and me marveling at the glittering moonlight that reflected off the sea. Was it possible that the man I was crushing on had a split personality disorder? Only earlier that day, he'd been barking at me, demanding I stay in my room, and generally making me feel like he hated me. Sure, I'd masturbated at least a dozen times to

149

the thought of that grumpy voice demanding that I come for him. But the way he spoke to me now was the opposite of that.

Now, he was talking to me like he was genuinely interested, and sharing his own stories about growing up with one much older sister and a succession of nannies in place of parents, when he wasn't away at boarding school. My heart broke a little more with every snippet of his past he showed me.

"No wonder you don't smile," I murmured, thinking my voice would be covered by the wind.

But he heard me. "I smile. Just not in public. And not around women."

"Why not?"

He sighed. "You know the nickname. You must have heard about the contest."

"The what?" I turned to face him, clutching his jacket around me as the wind pulled at it. "There was a contest?"

He groaned. "Yes. It's why I bought out that damned magazine. They'd decided to up their game—that instead of just speculating on who I'd end up with, they would challenge the 'women of the world' to try to crack Grumpy Grantham's face of steel. Or some sort of crap like that." He lifted an eyebrow while I tried to stifle a laugh and ended up snorting.

"Really? Like America's Grumpiest Bachelor: Make Him Smile Edition?"

"Hmm." He crossed his arms over his chest. "It sounds like fun until it's you being bombarded with women losing every scrap of dignity they possess for a cash prize."

I stifled the growl that tried to emerge from my throat at the thought of women chasing him. Possibly even *touching* him. *Grrrrr.*

"Is that your stomach?" Giovanni's eyebrows flew high.

It absolutely was not my stomach. But I wasn't about to admit I'd just experienced my first true omega growl. We only made that sound when we felt like an alpha was ours, and another woman was too close to the one we wanted to claim. Candy had made it when she met her true mate.

Could he be mine?

I banished that thought as fast as it had appeared. Giovanni Grantham, while he might be my fantasy man, was never going to belong to me. He could hardly stand me. He'd made no secret of it.

"You know omegas," I bullshitted breezily. "Sensitive digestion. So, women were chasing you? What did they do?"

He scowled. "They came at me in droves, night and day. One even drew a picture on her butt and mooned me on my way to work."

"Her butt wasn't nice?" I pressed my mouth shut against another impending growl.

He made a face. "It was my widowed neighbor, Georgiana Leopold. Eighty-seven years old, and at least that many wrinkles on her ass."

"Oh no."

"Oh yes. Three others tried to sneak in with singing telegrams. One rode a unicycle into my main office lobby, juggling dildos. Fourteen more women dressed like clowns."

I blinked, trying to picture it. "All at once?"

"No. One at a time, like water torture. Who the fuck thinks clowns make people laugh? That shit is terrifying."

I was wheezing with laughter as I sat on a narrow cushioned bench. "God, yes. What else?"

"Amateur comedians started taking jobs as hostesses at my favorite restaurants. My barber was out sick one week, and his replacement told some of the funniest jokes I've ever heard while she cut my hair. To be fair, if I hadn't noticed her phone on the counter, recording it all, I might have laughed."

"Laughing counted?"

"Apparently. People started speculating that I'd had Botox to freeze my face."

I giggled. "Did you?"

He turned toward me, his face completely blank. "Of course not. The Botox was for the wrinkles. I'm smiling on the inside right now, can't you tell?"

I completely lost it and fell back, holding my sides. "Oh, Grumpy, I can see it now. How long did it go on? How did I not hear about this?" One of my ridiculous heels had come off on the deck, and I took off the other one, wiggling my toes.

"I bought the company the week the contest started. And you know money can take care of a lot of things. Even bad publicity." He slid onto the seat next to me, and we both stared up at the stars.

"Money can't take care of everything, though," I said quietly. "It can't buy happiness."

"Are you sure about that?" Something in his tone made me peer into his face. He sounded almost mischievous, like he had something up his sleeve.

"Sylvia and Lorelei have money, but they're not happy. You have money and... well. Maybe you're just not very good at showing your inner joy to the world."

"Would your dad have a saying about that?"

"Absolutely. Something about... the sun is always shining, even when it's behind a cloud?"

His hand was on my cheek at that moment, and his eyes met mine. "I never thought much about the importance of sunshine until I met you, Soleil." His gaze was solemn. "I worked hard for my family, our employees, to keep our businesses afloat. To grow our fortune. But I never once thought about how much I needed more light in my life. I would give almost anything to be able to make you smile, and know I deserved it. That I'd earned it."

"I... I..." My mouth hung open, as I fought for words. How could I trust him, after all the things he'd said to me? My heart was racing, my breath coming faster. Was this a trick? "I don't know what to say."

"Say you forgive me. Give me another chance." My eyes stung at the perfect sincerity in his voice.

And then, directly below us, a child's scream split the air.

Chapter 15

Sylvia

I t was ridiculous how little attention parents paid to their own children. Well, not just parents. Adults in general.

I'd been hanging out on the portside walkway, just a few yards from the stupid wedding planner's room, for an hour. More than one adult had seen me here, but I'd pretended to be playing on Soleil's phone, and they ignored me.

I felt guilty that I'd snatched Soleil's purse at the end of dinner. She was so trusting, it was ridiculous. Maybe not all that trusting, I thought, feeling the lump in my pocket. The pepper spray I'd found along with her phone in her clutch had been a shocker. And a good surprise. I could protect myself if this plan went wrong.

Mom had disappeared somewhere, probably crying in her room like she had been for the past few days, though she hadn't answered when I'd knocked, and I hadn't heard her like the other times.

Alphonse had stomped off at the end of dinner, too. And I was worried he'd gone to yell at Mom. But I'd watched him go into the stupid wedding planner's room again. I'd seen him kissing her right here the day before, and wanted to tell Mom, but I knew she wouldn't believe me. I needed proof.

I held the phone up and started the video as soon as the door handle started to turn. Sure enough, Alphonse walked out, and the blonde woman followed, wearing nothing but a towel around her chest. "Al, come back tonight. I'll miss you." He grabbed her, giving her a kiss that looked like he was trying to scrape her face off.

"You know I gotta be careful, Muffin. She was asking all sorts of questions about you, and where I've been. I gotta play it safe until the wedding." He checked his phone. "The signal out here sucks ass. All right. Gotta go make nice with the bitch." His voice sounded weird. Not the usual weird, with that awful, muddled accent. But like he was a mob boss in some movie.

I wanted to jump up and tell him not to call my mom a bitch, but I held still, recording all the disgusting kissing.

"Bye, Alley Cat," the woman said, then slipped back into her room. Alphonse's room was in the other direction, but for some reason, he turned toward me. I scooted back into a maintenance doorway, trying to stay quiet, but the beads on Soleil's purse made a skittering sound on the deck.

"Who's there?" His face was twisted up and shadowy, like a horror movie villain in the jump scare scene. In a split second, he was striding toward me. "What the hell are you doing here, kid?" he demanded. "Didn't think you had a phone."

Crap. He'd noticed I was recording. "I was just watching a bunch of TikTok videos."

"Oh yeah?" he said, leaning down. "Lemme see what you're watching."

I shoved my hand in my pocket, grabbing the pepper spray. There was a hard catch on it, so it didn't go off accidentally, and I fumbled at it with my thumb. But before I could do anything, he'd grabbed me, his grip hard and tight on my arm, and yanked the phone out of my hand.

"I don't think you were watching anything, girlie. Not enough signal for it. You trying to break me and your mom up, huh? It's a shame what a little girl will do for attention."

He dragged me over to the railing, and suddenly, I wondered if he was going to throw me in. Heart racing, I tried to dig my heels into the deck, but my stupid ballet flats slid like it was buttered. I screamed, hoping someone would hear me over the wind. "What are you doing?"

"Drop the phone in the water," he ordered as he lifted me up and over the top rail, "and we'll forget this ever happened. I'll marry your mama, and you'll go off to Austria like a good daughter."

"No!" I shouted, trying to get away. He was holding me up by my wrist, and it felt like it might break. His other hand grabbed the phone, and I felt the railing under my butt.

The phone went flying into the water. "Now, apologize to your daddy," he said, with a smile on his ugly face.

My other hand came out of my pocket at that same instant, and I pressed my thumb hard on the top of the pepper spray. "You're not my daddy, asshole!" I yelled, spraying him straight in the eyes.

I got lucky. The wind was blowing just right that none of it flew back on me, and he let me go, cursing and pawing at his face.

"Serves you right!" I shouted.

But then I got unlucky. My shoes slipped on the railing, and I fell backward. I screamed as loud as I could, trying to grab anything to stop me from falling into the ocean.

Chapter 16

Sunshine

In one second, I was staring into the eyes of the man I had a feeling I was falling in love with. The next, I was running. Racing down stairs and along slick decking, for the sound of a scream I knew.

"Sylvia!" I yelled, turning a corner. Alphonse was on the walkway, barreling toward us, clawing at his face. For a moment, I thought he was going to attack me, and then I was shoved out of the way, against the brass railing.

Giovanni had Alphonse's shirt in his fists, shaking him. "Where is she? What have you done with her?" he shouted.

But I knew exactly where she was. I could see her tiny hand, holding the brass railing. Shaking.

"Sylvia!" I flung myself over the railing, my hand closing around her slender arm just as her fingers were losing their grip.

My grasp on her wasn't tight enough. "Help!" she sobbed, as her arm slipped. It felt like my shoulder was being pulled out of its socket, but I held on as hard as I could.

I wasn't strong enough.

"Help!" I screamed as Sylvia's face went white with terror, and she fell, a long, straight drop into the ocean.

Alphonse and Giovanni were fighting at the end of the deck, and no one else was nearby. No one would hear me over the wind, and even if they did, by the time they came to help, she would be too far away. Alone.

I had no choice.

I didn't hesitate. I threw up the lid on a nearby bench and grabbed the life jacket stored inside it. It had reflective tape, a flashing light, and—according to the brochure in my room about the boat's state-of-the-art features—a GPS tracker somewhere inside. All I needed to do was get to her before she was too far for me to paddle.

In seconds, I was diving over the edge of the railing, my arms through the heavy straps. I hit the water with a smacking sound, and my head went under immediately. But I didn't let go of the straps. For once, the feeling of terror that always hit me when I was submerged didn't make me freeze up, not with Sylvia out here in the ocean with me. There was no time to panic.

"Sylvia!" I shouted as the wake from the engines spun me out and away from the yacht. But I heard nothing, saw nothing.

The boat was moving away so fast, it seemed unbelievable. We would be alone out here in no time. I scanned the waves, kicking my feet to keep upright, and kept looking.

Then, at last, I saw a flash of moonlight on her lavender dress when the swell of a wave rose over the horizon. I kicked hard, using the life jacket like a kickboard. It took forever, paddling up and over the waves made by the boat's passage, but finally I reached her.

"Hang on," I called, grabbing her arm and pulling it over the edge of the jacket.

"Soleil," she sobbed. "You came for me. You came... to save me, and you can't... even swim."

"Sylvia, I can't even float." I laughed through my own tears and patted the life jacket. "Thank goodness for modern technology. Are you okay?"

"I was... stupid. I was getting video of Alphonse with the wedding planner, and he caught me. He threw your phone in the ocean." She clutched my arm with one hand, squeezing it. "I stole your purse. I'm so sorry."

She cried hysterically while I patted her hair, trying to hide my own growing panic. The yacht was so far away now, I could barely make it out. The flashing light on the life vest had gone on when we hit the water, but I worried it wasn't strong enough to see from a distance, especially with the lights on the boat being so bright. Surely Giovanni had seen us go overboard?

Sylvia's sobbed apologies forced me out of my own spiral of fear. "You don't need to apologize for a thing. Now, take a few deep breaths." I counted for her. "Three counts in, six counts out. And again. One, two, three, hold it... and exhale. Six, five, four..."

When she had it together, she asked, "Where did you learn that?"

"The Omega League," I answered, glad for the distraction. "They teach us all sorts of things. How to fold napkins, martial arts, what to say if a guy steps on your foot while you're dancing a polka."

She let out a shaky breath, the flashing light illuminating the tear tracks on her face every few seconds. "My mom was in a League. She said they taught her how to arrange flowers. That's how she met my dad. I wish they'd taught her how to recognize a bad alpha."

I asked, gently, "Did Alphonse try to throw you in?"

"I'm not sure. I pepper sprayed his face, and he let go of me.

I sort of slipped." It made me feel slightly better that perhaps the perpetrator wasn't a murderer. But he'd still endangered her life.

A wave carried us higher, and in the distance, I could see the yacht's lights. So far away. "Are they leaving us?" Sylvia sobbed.

"No, baby, I promise. Your Uncle G will take care of Alphonse, and then they'll come back here."

"How do you know for sure?"

"He's a billionaire, remember? The life jackets have GPS, and I'm pretty sure an alarm went off when I opened the bench to get this one." I wrapped one hand around her forearm. "I promise. We'll be okay."

"You're so brave," she said quietly. "I can't believe you jumped in for me when you can't even swim."

"I told you I can too swim!" I protested, hoping to distract her from the fact that now the yacht had vanished completely. "If your arms are getting tired, I'll even show you. Let's switch places. You put your arms through the straps so you don't have to hang on, and I'll demonstrate how a sinker won the Best Flutterkick three years running in Peewee Swim Class."

She sniffled. "You were held back in Peewee Swim Class twice, Soleil. That's nothing to be proud of. My arms are pretty tired, though."

I faked a smile to hide my nervousness at letting go of the straps, then chirped, "Okay, Sylvia. While you rest, I'll tell you about the time my best friend Candy took the cinnamon challenge in gym class and got kicked out of middle school for a month."

I was only halfway through the story when I heard a sound, a motor of some sort. Sylvia's head was higher than mine, and she saw the Zodiac lifeboat first. "Uncle G! Uncle G!" She waved her arms, and I got a face full of seawater.

"Sylvia, stop, calm down!" I shouted. "If you knock me off this floatie—" I managed to get a mouthful of salty water, and she quieted down immediately, grabbing my arms and holding tight.

"I've got you, Soleil. Don't fall."

I didn't. In a minute, the Zodiac was there, with Giovanni and two crew members. One of them had a hook on the end of a pole, and he used it to drag the life jacket closer. Then Giovanni pulled Sylvia and me into the small boat.

"Oh god, I thought we'd lost you," he rasped, hugging me and Sylvia both to his chest. "Oh, sweetheart. Oh, my love. I thought you'd both drowned. I thought I'd lost everything that mattered."

Sylvia's wide eyes met mine when he released us both slightly. "I think I'm the sweetheart," she whispered, "and you're the love." Giovanni crushed us both into his chest again, purring so loud it almost drowned out the motor as we sped back toward the yacht.

Sylvia recounted everything that had happened as we rode, now with silver blankets wrapped around us for possible shock. Once we reached the yacht and Sylvia had been carried aboard, Giovanni wrapped my legs around his waist. He didn't put me down until I was sitting next to Sylvia in the doctor's office.

Weeping copiously, Lorelei held her daughter while the doctor did a short examination, then pronounced her well. "No concussion, no water in her lungs from what I can hear. But she should not be alone. Stay with her, Lorelei, and stay awake. If her breathing changes, bring her back to me immediately."

"Keep her here," Giovanni ordered. "I'll have them bring in cots and some bedding. Dr. Rimbolt, please... my omega."

No one mentioned his slip, and the doctor had to convince Giovanni to let go of me so he could check me out. "You were very brave, Miss Soleil," he said eventually as he put his stethoscope away and jotted something on his tablet.

Sylvia gave a half-sob, half-laugh. "You don't even know how brave. She's a sinker. She can swim, but she can't float. She could have died."

All of a sudden, I was back in Giovanni's arms, and he was shuddering, as if he were the one going into shock. "It's okay, Grumpy. I'm okay. You found us. You saved us." I stopped. "Alphonse. Is he...?"

"He was a con artist," Lorelei said, her voice raw. "We went through his cabin. He and Muffin were working together."

From the open door, Anne-Marie snarled. "They've both been restrained, and he's under sedation until we get back to shore. We'll be home in two days, at the most. I'll make sure they both go to jail and stay there."

"You'll need a thorough checkup at a hospital, Soleil," Dr. Rimbolt said. "You're a very healthy woman, but after thirty minutes of exposure, and possible saltwater inhalation... Just to be safe, I want you both to get seen once you're ashore." I nodded.

"So," I joked weakly after the doctor slipped out of the room. "We're going home, huh? I guess that's good. I'd run out of clothes for the fancy dinners. Silver lining, right?"

Lorelei burst into tears at that. "This is all my fault. If I had seen what kind of man he was, if I had listened to you, Sylvia. To you, G." She took Sylvia's hands in hers, staring down into her pale face. "I can never make it up to you, but I can try. I will try." Then she and Sylvia were holding each other, and Anne-Marie was standing behind them, her heart in her eyes.

"Take me to my cabin?" I asked when Giovanni picked me up.

"No," he growled. "Mine." I wasn't certain he was talking about his cabin or me. Maybe both.

After he unlocked his door, he ushered me into the bathroom, kneeling at my feet as he removed my ruined top and skirt. He didn't touch me sexually at all, and wouldn't meet my eyes.

"Thank you for coming for us, Grumpy."

He went still for a moment, silent, his shoulders bowed. Then he unfolded a washcloth and lathered it up with a soap that smelled like coconuts, not answering. The warm water from the shower felt like paradise, but his hands on me, taking care of me, were even better.

"Your soap smells like me," I murmured as he ran the warm cloth over my legs, and my feet. He didn't answer, gently separating my legs and methodically wiping away every trace of salt. When he lifted one arm and saw a bruise forming there, he let out a small groan, like he was the one hurt. "I must have hit it when I jumped after her," I mused. "It's not painful."

He didn't speak, but his touch became even gentler. His hands were trembling as he washed my stomach, then my breasts, then my neck.

"Turn around," he instructed quietly. He washed my hair, then massaged conditioner through it. I held myself up on the wall as pleasure warred with exhaustion. When I was rinsed, he lifted me out of the shower and set me on a cushioned bench, where I drifted in and out of awareness as he dried me, then gently brushed out my hair.

I was almost asleep as he carried me to his bed, and must have been dreaming when he kissed my head, stroking my hair over the pillow, singing the same song my dad had sung to me when I was a little girl, though his voice had never held this much pain when he did.

You are my sunshine, my only sunshine...

163

I woke up alone, shadows flying across the blanket over me. Slowly, I realized they were shadows of clouds, moving fast because the boat was racing along.

"You slept well." Giovanni's voice was low and quiet.

I sat up, the covers falling to my waist. He was seated in a chair against the wall, beside a table that held a silver dome-covered plate and a carafe of water. He had on the same clothes as the night before, and hadn't shaved. Or slept, it looked like.

I felt cool air on my breasts and realized I was still naked, but his bloodshot eyes never dipped below my face.

"Did you sleep at all?" I asked, then coughed. My throat was terribly dry, as if I'd swallowed sandpaper.

In an instant, a glass of cool water was being pressed into my hands. I drank, as Giovanni perched on the edge of the bed, his gaze fixed on me.

"Have you been watching me sleep, Edward?" I teased. He didn't reply, and I added a Twilight movie marathon to the list of things I would subject this alpha to if I ever got him tied down and at my mercy. "What are you staring at?"

He exhaled, then answered, "The bravest woman I've ever met in my life."

I fell back on my pillow, laughing.

"Why would you laugh at that? You dove into the open ocean to save a child you just met this week. You can't even swim—" I started to interrupt, but he cut me off. "I watched you place yourself between Sylvia and Alphonse more than once, and stand up to her mother, and me, when we acted reprehensibly toward you." His voice broke.

"Lorelei texted me early this morning. Sylvia told her all the things you said to her last night, to keep her calm in the water. How you knew I would come for you." I watched a tear roll down his face, though he didn't seem aware he was crying. "That you believed in me, and I was already on my way. How you put her arms through the life jacket when she got tired, even though it put you in more danger." Another silent tear. "We can never repay you for what you did. And I can never deserve the faith you had in me."

Wow. I pinched my arm lightly, just to check if I was still dreaming. Then I laid one hand over his. His skin was warm, and I wanted to feel more of it.

"Are you hungry?" he asked, his voice quiet, respectful.

"I could eat," I said, and in seconds, there was a plate with toast, butter, marmalade, a small crystal cup of berries with yogurt, a boiled egg, and one link of sausage, still warm. Giovanni fed me a bite at a time, his focus entirely on my lips, and wiped the corners of my mouth when the food was gone. Not once did he glance at my boobs, or comment on the fact that by the end of the meal, my nipples could be used to facet diamonds, they were so hard.

"Still hungry?" he asked.

"Thirsty," I replied, inhaling deeply. For an instant, his gaze flickered to my chest, but he merely stood and brought more water to the bed.

Damnit.

A low, warm swirling began in my core, and I felt the familiar stirrings of lust. If the sudden rush of mocha scent was any indication, Giovanni was feeling it, too. Only he wasn't going to do anything about it.

I let the sheet fall a little farther down, so that it was barely covering my hips.

His voice was raspy as he cleared up the remains of my breakfast. "We turned the yacht around as soon as we found you. The closest port with a decent medical facility is George-town, so we're headed straight home. Your parents will be waiting when we get there."

"How long?"

"Thirty hours, give or take." His eyes scanned me. "If you're not feeling well, if you need to be home sooner, I can have a helicopter here—"

I interrupted. "You know how you said I was brave? I'm not. If I were brave, I'd be able to tell you what I wanted. To ask for what I need."

"Anything you want," he vowed, staring into my eyes. "Anything at all, I will give it to you."

"Anything? Are you sure you want to go there, Grumpy? Because I have a long, long list of things I want. Need." I moved my hands to my nipples, twisting and pulling at them gently until they ached.

He groaned. "Anything, Sunshine. I'm yours."

"Mine." Oh, I liked the sound of that. This perfect, perfectly maddening alpha, all mine. I pinched my nipples harder, then slowly moved one hand down my stomach until it vanished beneath the sheet. The sounds of our breathing, and my fingers moving through wetness, created a strange sort of music in the otherwise silent room.

"The doctor said you needed rest," he rasped, though his hands were on my breasts before he was done with the sentence.

"Then I'd better lie still here for a while, and let you make me feel better. That's what I need." I met his hungry gaze. "I need you to make me come. And then I need you to fuck me so hard I won't remember yesterday at all." He shook his head, and a cramp shot through my gut. Was he going to deny me again? "Just once, Grumpy. Just for once, give me what I need. You said I needed to ask for what I wanted in bed, right? Well, I'm asking. Give me your body."

"Just once," he agreed, and was suddenly bracing himself over me, his hands on the blanket, pinning me down, his clothes still. Fucking. On.

I growled. "No. No more of this 'me nude, you clothed' crap. If you're not naked in one minute, I'm going to show you what a grumpy omega looks like. Strip."

"Yes, ma'am," he said, the corner of his lips twitching as he moved down the bed, pulling the blanket off, his stubble scratching at every inch of the soft flesh he exposed on his way. Then I was naked, lying on the bed, and he was stripping away his clothing. I watched, my core beginning to heat, my thighs damp, as he tossed away his tie, then his belt, then his shirt.

"Mine," I muttered, and he threw it to me. While he toed off his socks and shoes, I wrapped his shirt around a pillow and began moving the blanket to the edges of the bed. "Need more." I licked my lips as he pulled off his trousers.

"More blankets?" he crooned gently. "Are you going to build a little nest for me here, sweet omega?"

"Maybe, asshole alpha," I huffed, holding my hand out for the trousers. They went over another pillow. He pulled off the tight black briefs that had hidden the rest of him, while leaning over to open a drawer for more blankets. I took in the lines of his back, his ass, his thighs. He was as perfect as a classical sculpture, with sparse, dark hairs giving depth and texture to the honed, bronzed shapes of him.

When he turned around though, the classical lines were interrupted by his outsized... "Campari. At least a Campari," I whispered as he tossed the blankets to me, his cock bobbing as he grabbed a few more pillows off the floor. I reached down and patted my mound gently. "Hope you're thirsty, girl. Really, really thirsty."

Giovanni made a strange choking sound. "Are you talking to your vagina?" I grinned up at him, trying to hide my nervousness, though he looked a little off his game now, too.

Good.

"Um, don't you talk to your dick? You know, positive affirmations, little check-ins on the state of the peen-ion?" Something weird was happening on the side of his face. Like a little seizure, or a muscle spasm. I went on, ignoring it. "If I had an enormous sausage like that, I'd talk to it all the dang time."

"You would?" He stepped forward, his knees bumping the edge of the mattress. His face twitched more. Was he trying to smile?

"Come on, it's bigger than some of my friends' chihuahuas, Grumpy. And look how it's nodding at me. It agrees with me." His cheek spasmed again, and I stopped, blinking up at him, then at his cock that was slowly rising to attention a degree at a time. "I salute you, Captain Campari," I whispered, as I crawled across the bed. "You are the finest of all the wine-bottle-sized penises in the world."

"The doctor didn't say you had a head injury. Better call him," Giovanni muttered, shifting his weight. Quick as a wink, I grabbed his penis with one hand and his thigh with the other.

"I don't think so, Captain. You said you'd give me anything I want. Well, I want to see if I can get this monster dick in my mouth, *capisce?* I want to taste you." He groaned as I let go of his thigh and cupped his balls. "I want to play with you, and get comfortable with you, and then maybe see if there is any way I can fit you inside me."

"It'll fit," he promised as I closed my lips around the tip of his cock, lapping up the pre-cum that had beaded up there. "We'll make it fit."

I didn't answer, but hummed around the smooth head, which was a mouthful all on its own, though it wasn't nearly as thick as the base. I'd never liked giving head the few times I'd tried. My nose was too sensitive, and... well, warm oysters came to mind when I thought of the taste of the guy I'd experimented with.

But Giovanni tasted rich and salty, and mixed with the

mocha scent that was thick in the room, I realized it was all about the man attached to the peen. "I'd suck a whole bag of your dicks," I mumbled around the mouthful I had, ignoring Grumpy's "What?"

It wasn't talking time now. It was time to get to work, recreating the porn videos I'd watched, or at least a few of the books I'd read. I swallowed and took him into my mouth a bit deeper, moving my hand to the base of his sac and scraping his perineum gently with my nails. The werewolf shifter king in my favorite book had particularly liked that.

He muttered something about me torturing him.

Smiling on the inside, I swallowed again, while I took his knot in my other hand and squeezed hard. A small rush of pre-cum filled my mouth. It was absolutely delicious.

He whimpered, and I almost laughed around his girth as I began to feed more of him in, until I choked. Damnit, I didn't even have a third of him in my mouth. I made a frustrated sound and tried again, choking once more.

"Good girl," he whispered. "Don't force it. You're doing so well. Breathe, and move, and relax your throat." He purred slightly, and something about that noise made my muscles listen to him. He moaned while I swallowed, letting my mouth and throat massage him as I managed a little more with each dip of my head. "Let me help?" I tasted more of his salty-sweet release in the back of my throat, and felt his hands on my hair, moving me back and forth in a gentle, even rhythm. "Is this all right, Sunshine? Can I move you like this?"

I looked up, blinking the tears away that had gathered at some point. "Mmhm," I agreed.

"Oh, good Sunshine. Such a sweet, hot mouth. You want me to fuck it? Fuck into you, come down your throat, and fill up your belly?"

I tried to nod again, but his grip was firm on the sides of my head now, and he was thrusting, the head of his cock pushing deeper. I closed my eyes and focused on relaxing. I was drenched with slick, my thighs dripping. I felt like I was floating, like I was powerless and eminently powerful at the same time.

"God, I've never felt anything like this perfect mouth on me, Sunshine. You hungry for my cum? You want me to cover you in it, feed it to you?" I hummed again, and he laughed, a dark, tempting sound. "My little cum slut. I'd like to wake you up every day like this. Stuff my cock in between those pink lips and fill your belly. Watch you choke around me, watch your pretty pussy get sloppy wet while I fuck your face. Touch yourself, Sunshine. Put some fingers in that wet pussy."

I did just that, dipping into my drenched entrance, then pulling the fingers out. I showed them to him while I swallowed again around his girth, then rubbed my slick over the knot that was swelling at the base of his cock.

"Shit," he cursed, pulling out of my mouth. "Naughty girl, you almost made me come in your mouth."

"That was the plan," I teased, licking my fingers clean. He swooped down and kissed me, tasting himself, and me, and growling in satisfaction.

"You know your slick is an aphrodisiac. It makes me more sensitive. Makes me come harder, more often... My cum is like that for you, too."

"It is?" I pouted as he kissed me, his hands moving over my breasts, my waist, as if he was memorizing my shape. "Then why not let me have it?"

"Because we don't have long enough right now for all the things I want to do to you. With you. And when I come in you now, it's going to be in your tight pussy, while I stare into your gorgeous face." He buried his own face in my hair, and I heard him mumble something.

My love? Beloved? Believe it?

"Need to get you ready, princess," he said, moving down and gently parting my thighs with his hands. He dove into my pussy, using his lips, tongue, teeth, and even his nose to drive me to one peak, and then another. He stared up at me, his face glossy with my slick after my third orgasm. "Almost ready, baby," he murmured. "I need to know, before we're lost in the moment... I promise I won't bite you. I know we can't be together. But... will you let me knot you, Omega? Will you give me that memory?"

I almost burst into tears. I *wanted* him to bite me, claim me, show the whole world that he was proud of me. That he loved me.

But I knew that was a fantasy that would never come true.

I bit the inside of my cheek hard to keep from crying, and forced a small smile. At least I could have this. This memory.

"Please, Grumpy. I need you."

Chapter 17

Grumpy

I 'd said something wrong. I knew it. And I knew better than to brush off my misgivings at the slightly charred coconut smell that tainted the lush sweetness of my beloved's scent. But she'd said she needed me.

And I knew I'd never be able to give her what she needed again.

She would go home to her fiancé, to the man she'd promised herself to. And even though I'd set everything in place for her to have a choice that wasn't him—that wasn't marriage, and the small, safe existence her parents seemed to want for her—I couldn't be certain that she'd take the path I'd laid out for her.

Her choices lay in the future, though. Mine lay beneath me, panting with want, flushed and almost feverish with need. I slid up the bed and lowered my face to hers, kissing her gently, slowly. "Are you certain, princess?"

Her scent changed, softening slightly as she stared into my eyes with a look that I didn't dare hope was something deeper than lust. "Yes. I'm sure."

"Then I'm going to fuck you now, love. I'm going to take my time, so it won't hurt." I set the head of my cock at her entrance and rubbed it back and forth in the slippery mess we'd made of her. Slowly, I pushed forward, feeling her walls stretch around the thick head, welcoming me. Her eyes flared wide. "Are you okay?"

"God, yes. It feels... so *good*. More, please." Her lashes fluttered as I pressed forward another inch, stopping when she whimpered. "It burns. Let me just... Give me a moment."

I held still, my pulse hammering wildly in my throat, echoed by the one in my knot. I was seconds away from falling into a rut, where I would fuck her with no thought to her comfort, only to making her mine, breeding her. Filling her so full of my seed that her pussy would leak for days.

Fucking my baby into her.

The thought alone had me pressing deeper. I blinked away the red-tinged haze that threatened to overwhelm me, and pulled out.

"What—no!" she cried, grabbing my arm. "I can fit you in. I just needed to take a breath." Her voice was desperate, and I comforted her immediately, purring slightly.

"No, my Sunshine. I'm not leaving. I'm just switching positions." In one smooth movement, I flipped us, so I was lying on my back and she was sitting on top of me. "This way you can control how much and when, okay? I'm going to hold on here," I explained, grasping two of the stainless-steel bars of the headboard. "Now, I want you to play with your clit and sit up over me. Ride me, my love. Take as much or as little as you want."

"I want all of you," she said, and the promise hung in the air like a sunbeam. She lifted herself up and started circling her clit with two fingers, her wet heat enveloping the top of me. "I want every inch of you. Every part of you. I want you." With each word, she moved, taking in no more than an inch at a time.

I allowed myself to fantasize that she meant more than just my cock. That she meant me. With all my imperfections. My temper and my sour disposition. Even after the things I'd said and done to push her away.

"I want you, too," I told her, wishing she could read my thoughts. "I want all of you, princess."

It was agony. It was ecstasy. Her thighs were splayed out wide to make space, and she shuddered and breathed shakily as she forced more and more of me into her. Finally, her pussy had taken all of me, up to my knot. "I did it," she said proudly.

"You did it, sweetheart. Look at your perfect cunt letting me inside."

"Not all of you," she whined. "Your knot."

"Not yet. But you can do it. And even if you don't, this is the best I've ever felt. If I could stay like this forever, it would be more than enough."

She smiled and started riding me slowly, then picked up her tempo. I let go with one hand and reached down to take over at her clit, loving the sounds she made as she chased her pleasure. Her eyes were closed, her face pink, and her hair darkened with sweat. She was a goddess.

How was I ever going to let her go?

Suddenly, her walls grew tighter around me as she started to come. I circled faster, feeling the waves of her climax begin to move from deep inside her. "Now," I grunted. "Push down hard on me, Sunshine. Push my knot into you." I thrust up at the exact moment she let out a breath on a wail, and her tight walls expanded just enough to let me in.

Her walls strangled my cock, pressing so hard on my knot it bordered on painful. It was a pain I never wanted to end. A pleasure that, even if it meant I died, I would go happily.

I loved this woman. Loved her no matter what happened next, whatever pains or pleasures lay in store.

"Sunshine!" I felt the ropes of cum pouring out of me, filling her. My knot expanded as I came, locking us together. She screamed again as another wave of bliss poured over her, then collapsed on my chest.

Fuck. I needed to rut her. Had to...

"Fuck me, please," she begged. "I need *more.*" Her pussy was milking my knot even as she lay still, but I stroked her hair from her face, making sure. Tears shone in her eyes, but her lips were curled in a sweet, perfect smile.

Gently, I flipped us again, moving as carefully as possible. Each mini-thrust drove more of my release out of me and into her, each burst causing her to shudder with renewed pleasure.

"So good," she whimpered, her turquoise eyes fixing on the place where our bodies were joined, as I pressed my knot into her deeper, as if I could somehow be so far inside her, we would never be separated. "Don't stop."

"I won't."

I kept moving, staring at her face, my heart breaking even as I rode wave after wave of pleasure. I had billions of dollars. Investments and assets all over the world. I had everything money could buy.

But I would give it all up if I could have this funny, brilliant, charismatic woman instead.

Chapter 18

Sunshine

I stood on the deck of the yacht, watching the tender that would carry us to the port in Georgetown come closer, and wondering where it had all gone so wrong. Lorelei and Anne-Marie waited with me, both of them politely ignoring the tears that were falling like rain down my cheeks.

Sylvia was the noisy one, complaining about how far her home was from mine, and insisting I allow her mother to talk to my parents so I could stay on as her betasitter. "They never taught us the laws about omegas were so disgusting and repressive. It's repulsive! It's... barbaric! The people who made up those laws are..."

She ran out of words, and I hugged her tightly. "Cullionly barbermongers? Foam-faced toads? Carbuncles?"

"My Uncle G is the carbuncle. He has all this money, but he can't use some of it to help omegas get basic human rights? I'm going to have a very serious conversation with him," she declared. "And then I'm going to start a protest. The kids of like twelve Prime Ministers and Presidents are in my school."

"Invite me to the planning sessions," I suggested. "I'd be

176

delighted to help you make t-shirts." Her hug got tighter. "If my parents allow it, I'd love to come see you. I may not be allowed to be your betasitter, but they can't stop me from being your friend." I held up my arm, where she'd written all her contact info in Sharpie marker, since I no longer had a phone to save it in.

Sylvia muttered about why a grown woman would need permission to visit a friend, but Lorelei took my hand. "Soleil, you didn't need to do that. I'm having a courier send over a replacement phone, and I'll make sure you get everyone's contact info."

"Thanks, Lorelei," I said, and swallowed hard. "Have you... seen your brother today?" He'd vanished from his cabin an hour after he'd knotted me, and I hadn't seen him since. I'd been able to have dinner the night before in the small family lounge with a very small subset of guests, including Veronika, Clotilde, and Juliette, and I'd slept in his room, hoping he would return. But he was avoiding me.

Lorelei sighed. "He's on the yacht somewhere. He escorted Alphonse and Muffin to the dock and delivered them into police custody first thing this morning, then returned with a detective to gather evidence."

"Oh." Maybe he'd just been too busy to say goodbye. "Do you think he'll come to...?" My question trailed off as she shook her head.

"He feels so guilty for you and Sylvia being put in danger. When really, it's all my fault. Please forgive me, Soleil. And forgive my brother for being an idiot?"

I didn't know what to say. The tender was pulling up alongside the yacht, and a crew member was operating the electric ramp for me to descend.

Weirdly, the ocean water between us and the tender didn't seem frightening anymore. Like I'd already survived the worst danger the ocean presented. Who would have thought the greatest danger to me was the man who'd fished me out of it?

I was almost certain there was no one who could keep me from drowning in my pain.

"He gave me this for you." Lorelei handed me an envelope, then wrapped me in a hug. "Don't give up on him."

"Um, I hate to say this, but he's the one—" I managed to squeak, before Sylvia was hugging me again.

"I'll text you every day, and we can video chat. We can cook together," she half-shouted. "And work on our crafting projects and... and..." Lorelei bundled her into her arms, gently escorting her away.

Anne-Marie helped me step onto the tender, and one of the crew carried my luggage on and helped me into a seat. "Have you thought about my offer?" she murmured, as the engine of the smaller boat revved. "Can I be your fairy godmother investor?"

"If I have a pumpkin and any mice left when my parents get done with me, I'd love that." She pressed a kiss to my cool cheek, then stepped away.

The tender moved away from the yacht quickly. I swiveled in my seat until my neck hurt, looking for him. I saw a few of my friends waving from the second level, kids jumping up and down, but no one else. I knew the yacht was huge, but it seemed to grow smaller so quickly, diminishing the way a dream does when you start to wake up.

Slipping from my grasp.

Had it ever really happened? Had I fallen in love with a tall, dark, handsome stranger? The only things that made it seem real were the sickeningly empty hole in my chest where my heart had been... and the solitary figure on the topmost observation deck, who stood and watched me leave him.

I cried all the way to shore. The crewmembers very politely

ignored me, except to press a small packet of tissues into one hand. I almost smiled at the gold lettering on the edge of each tissue, with a tiny, embossed yacht.

"Soleil!" My mom and dad had me in their arms the instant my mismatched sandals hit the pier.

Dad kissed my forehead and turned away, but not before I saw tears streaking down his cheeks. "Okay, okay," he said. "I'll go get the car. We're taking you straight to the hospital."

"The hospital?" I asked, before I remembered Dr. Rimbolt's instructions to get a thorough exam.

Mom made a strange hissing noise. "That *man* was going to have an ambulance waiting for you. Insisted on it, until we reminded him that what he did was essentially kidnapping, and we would call in the FBI if we needed to. He terrified us, said you almost died. If his darling sister Lorelei hadn't called, we would have both had heart attacks."

"Lorelei called you?" I asked, then really took in my mom's state. She was always put together, her clothing and hair neat, her makeup polished. But now she looked like she'd been on a battlefield somewhere. Her hair was tossed up in a messy bun, her face bare, and her clothing a wreck. The buttons on her blouse were off by one, there was a strange-looking stain that smelled a bit like coffee, and... I clapped a hand over my mouth. She had on two different shoes, one navy and one black pump.

"Yes. She did call, to tell us all about her daughter and all you did for them. And promised to watch you until you were back in our arms. If she hadn't... I think your dad was going to phone in some sort of mercenary person to go and bring you back."

"Dad knows a merc?"

She waved a hand in the air, like she was shooing a fly. "He was asking around at the country club. But that's not impor- tant." She drew a shaky breath, then took both of my hands in a tight but trembling grip. "Why did you go? Why didn't you tell us?"

"Mom, oh god, I'm so sorry," I said into her hair as she pulled me in for another bone-crushing hug. "I just... I couldn't stay and marry Tarquin. And I knew I would. You were so excited, and Dad was already inviting him to tennis, and he smells like gym socks and runny cheese, and I just couldn't."

She laughed as we rocked back and forth. "Why didn't you say something before? We thought you liked Tarquin."

"I did. I do. He's a dear friend. But I only said yes because..." I glanced back at the boat. The tender had reached it, and more passengers were loading up. There was no figure on the observation deck now. "Because I didn't think there would be anyone better."

"What do you mean by that—" she began, but then Dad was there, escorting us to the waiting car. He and Mom began to bicker about the best way to get to the hospital during the lunch rush.

At the hospital, there was a nurse waiting at the door with a wheelchair, which we all thought was strange. Then she wheeled me right past the Admissions desk and up to a private floor where there were no other patients at all, and it got even stranger.

"What is this?" Mom asked, touching a gorgeous etched glass sculpture inside the examination room. There was a matching chandelier overhead, and the regular exam table was flanked by three gorgeous forest-green leather chairs that complemented the lighter green and cream walls. Dad was in a separate waiting room, drinking some sort of herbal tea that an honest-to-goodness concierge had made for him.

We'd been to this hospital before, but it sure hadn't been like this.

The nurse had taken my vitals, drawn blood, then had me

give a urine sample in the bathroom next door for some reason. She apologized for the doctor running late, and left us here.

"I've never seen a hospital room like this," Mom said, opening a mini-fridge that had chilled bottles of water, organic orange juice, and tiny Dom Perignon champagne bottles. "Did your billionaire set this up for you? Are we expected to make mimosas while we wait?"

"He's not my billionaire, Mom. But I guess you can if you want? I saved his niece; maybe this is his way of saying thank you." My throat started to close up just thinking of Giovanni, so I hopped off the examination table and grabbed a pamphlet, thumbing through it to hide the impending tears.

Mom sucked in a sharp breath. "Why are you reading about gonorrhea, Soleil? Is there something you want to tell me about last week?" She grabbed a cut crystal glass and poured straight champagne into it, taking a swig like she was preparing for the worst.

"No, Mom, jeez!" I flung the pamphlet across the room as if it were infested with clap cooties... right as the door opened and the doctor entered. The pamphlet hit her directly in the chest, and she let out a short laugh. "Oh god, I'm so sorry!" I apologized. "I didn't mean to throw that. And also, I do not need that, I swear. Totally clap free. No STDs here, nope. Not any."

I slapped a hand over my face. For all I knew, I did have an STD. I'd had unprotected sex with Giovanni.

Oh god. What if I was pregnant? He'd made it clear there was no future for us.

It was entirely possible I could have the clap *and* a baby on board. For all I knew, he'd renovated my entire vaj with his Campari-bottle dick.

I'd never even thought about internal injuries. What if I could never feel pleasure again? He'd practically made pancakes out of me while he was filling me with his baby batter... *Oh god, babies.*

I put a hand to my flat stomach. Omegas had twins far more often than betas. I could be pregnant with twins.

Across the room, my mom slumped down into one of the chairs. "Baby... batter? Pancakes? Twins?"

I blinked at the doctor, who was fighting not to laugh. "I'm doing that thing where I say it all out loud, aren't I?"

"Afraid so, sweet girl."

I let out a huge sigh. "Mom? I think you may want to step outside for this." Mom nodded weakly, taking the champagne as she left.

The doctor's dark eyes, familiar somehow, glittered with humor as she escorted my mother from the room. When she returned, sat in a chair next to me. "I think you may have a story to tell. I received some records from Dr. Rimbolt, so I know a bit. But why do you think you might be pregnant, Soleil?"

It all came out in a rush of unstoppable tears and frantic explanations. There was a pile of about ten used tissues on the side table next to me when I finally moaned, "And I'm not sure he'd even care if I was pregnant. He might not ever want to see me again."

The doctor hummed slightly as she helped me up to the table and began her own exam. She did a very thorough check over my entire body, inside and out. "Why would you think your alpha wouldn't want to be with you?"

"He's not my alpha."

Her eyebrow arched. "You must know that mini-heats like this, at your age, are almost always precipitated by one event."

"Great stress?" I said with a weak smile.

"Meeting your true mate should not be stressful, Soleil. What did that idiot do?" She sounded pissed.

"Well, he avoided me after... you know."

"The Campari sex?"

"Yeah." I blushed. "Sorry I went into such graphic detail. But after that, he vanished. He didn't even say goodbye. And he made sure during it to tell me it was... a one-time thing." I grabbed another tissue and held it over my face. "I can't think about what it means if he really is my true mate and... and didn't want me."

The pain at even voicing the words was excruciating. My heart ached. My skin stung. When I told the doctor what I was feeling, she said solemnly, "Mate rejection can be debilitating. I'll write you a prescription for some pain meds."

Oh god, I needed to call Rain. She'd lived through this, though I wasn't sure how. She'd be able to help me.

The doctor stabbed the end of her pen at her tablet, muttering something that sounded like "Stupid ass alphas" while I regained my composure. Once I'd stopped sniffling, she put down her tablet and sighed. "Well, it's a good thing we took all the samples we did. I'll have some initial answers for you in a few minutes. Now, if I were speaking as Giovanni's doctor, I would not be allowed to tell you that you have nothing to worry about regarding STDs. He has full physical checkups every six months in this hospital."

"Every six months? Is he ill?"

"No. He just likes to visit his aunt."

"His... aunt? Oh." I felt the mother of all blushes start to spread from my chest, up my neck, over my ears, and across my entire scalp. "Oh god, I said all that to..."

She held out a hand. "To his Aunt Marguerite."

"You... you weren't on the wedding cruise."

"Lucky break. I was on call this week." She muttered, "And praying Lorelei would come to her senses before the big day." She smiled gently when she looked up and noticed my red face.

"His mother, Raquel, is my older sister. Gio donated the money for this entire wing of the hospital a few years ago, so I could settle close to my grandchildren. Normally, I work in the neonatal intensive care unit, but I have extensive training in obstetrics as well." She peered at the tablet in her hand. "And everything looks fine. But I'm afraid we won't know just yet if you are expecting. That test is inconclusive, though the levels are a little unusual. Still, it's only been a week since your first... introduction to his sperm."

I covered my face with both hands. Had I actually told his aunt about the cum scooping?

Yes. Yes, I had.

"I need to find a large body of water and throw myself in it," I moaned.

"Oh, sweet girl," the doctor said, and suddenly, I was enveloped in an unexpected hug. "You saved my great-niece's life. You're the true mate to my idiot nephew. If you are expecting and decide to go through with the pregnancy, you will be *family*. Even if Gio never pulls his head out of his ass. Whatever happens next, I promise, you won't be doing it alone."

An hour later, I was carrying a bag full of prescriptions, including antibiotics "just in case there was anything nasty in the water with you," a home pregnancy test kit, and all the tiny bottles of orange juice and champagne we could fit.

"Don't worry, I'll make sure Gio gets billed for every last one," Dr. Marguerite had promised. She'd also reminded me that our conversations were totally confidential, even if she was his aunt, and made an appointment for me to come back in two weeks for another pregnancy test.

After we got home and had dinner, it was nine p.m., and I was half-asleep. Dad wanted to have "the talk" immediately, but Mom reminded him that the doctor had said I needed rest after my traumatic events. I was almost certain she hadn't mentioned the pregnancy question to him.

The next morning, it was obvious she had. Dad's face was pinched and slightly tinged with gray.

"So, you found out about my business," I finally said at the breakfast table, when neither of them spoke. They stayed quiet. "I'm sorry I went behind your backs."

"That's the least of what you needed to apologize for, young lady—" Dad started, getting ready to bluster.

But Mom cut him off. "I'm sorry you had to, Soleil. I'm sorry we failed you as parents."

"What?" I asked.

"What?" Dad parroted.

Mom sighed. "Peter, look at what she had to do to get our attention." I opened my mouth to protest, but she held up a finger. "If we had listened to you, if we had given you a home where you knew the truth was more important than smiling and pretending—" Dad tried to say something, but she held up a very different finger in his direction. "You will shut up, Peter Fairweather, or regret it for the rest of your days. Our daughter could have died because you thought you knew what she needed. Thought she needed a man, an alpha, instead of her dream."

She took a deep breath. "It ends now. Soleil, you need to call Tarquin to take his ring back. Peter, you need to sit down with me and figure out how we're going to support our daughter if she *is* pregnant."

"I want to keep the business," I said quietly.

Dad shook his head. "Soleil, if you are..." He swallowed hard, looking like he'd smelled hot oysters. "You know, expecting. Then you can't work as a betasitter. No one wants a pregnant woman watching their kids."

"What an asshole thing to say," I spat out, standing up.

185

"And you're wrong. One of our long-term jobs was filled by an omega who is pregnant. And another by an omega who has a child of her own, and they both got rave reviews from their clients. Not everyone is so pig-headed and regressive." Dad's jaw opened and shut, like some sort of marionette. I supposed I'd never talked back to him like that.

No, not talked back. Stood my ground. Stood up for myself and what I needed.

Mom was politely clapping from her seat. "Brava, Soleil."

"Where did that come from?" Dad stood, crossing his arms over his chest and glaring at both of us. "That's not my sunshine."

I didn't even try to smile. "No. I'm not your sunshine anymore. I've changed. I'm *my* sunshine now. And I'm going to live my life how I want to."

Which apparently, meant eating six macarons in the kitchen, crying on Mom's shoulder, and then going to my room to sleep.

Mom knocked on the door a few hours later, saying a package had come for me. I opened it with her watching, and I wasn't sure which one of us screamed louder. "Who would send you that?" she wondered aloud as I held up the iPhone to my window.

"I think it was Lorelei, Sylvia's mom," I said, watching the light catch the inlaid crystals—I was not going to allow myself to think they were diamonds—that covered the entire back of the case. They were yellow and white stones, the pattern a sun with rays shooting out to the sides. The home button was a much larger crystal. I swallowed hard. It had to be just a crystal, because it if wasn't...

"What kind of phone is that? It says iPhone, but a 'King's Button'? What king?" Mom muttered to herself, looking inside the box, while I powered on the phone. It was already charged, and my own home screen—a picture of Rain, Candy, and me eating funnel cakes at the State Fair—was almost entirely covered with texts and notifications.

"There's a note in the box," Mom told me.

"Read it?"

She unfolded it. "Dearest Soleil, there is no way I can begin to repay you for your heroic actions in saving my daughter. The least I can do is replace your phone. Please call on me if there is anything, large or small, that I can help you with. With deep gratitude, Lorelei Grantham."

The phone in my hand buzzed, and I peeked at the screen. Sylvia was texting me. My pin number was the same as it had been, which seemed more than a little suspicious, until I realized Sylvia had to have sneaked it when she took my original phone.

"Don't lose that phone," Mom wheezed, sitting down on the edge of my bed and blinking at a piece of paper. "Although it came with its own insurance policy in case you do." I peered up at her. "It's eighteen-karat yellow, white and rose gold, with 140 diamonds on the edge strip. The back, the sunburst, has another 800 diamonds." She showed me the paper.

"Holy shit. *Four million dollars?*" I stared at the home button, which was apparently a six and a half carat diamond, and burst out laughing. "I've got to call Rain."

"She's out of town, darling. She's been blowing up my phone checking on you, and I told her what was going on. She wanted to come back as soon as you got home, but the job she's on turned out to be more involved than she'd thought. She said she'd tell you all about it when she can 'escape the alphahole.'"

Escape? "Where is she?"

"She couldn't say, since she signed what she called an unreasonable addendum to her NDA." Mom's eyes narrowed at that, and I made a mental note to check in on Blue Skies' files as soon as possible and see if she'd left a note there.

"Should I be worried?"

"I don't think so. She said the addendum also meant a triple bonus." Mom stood, shaking her head. "My little girl, a secret businesswoman. No matter what your dad says, I'm so damned proud of you."

I wiped my face. When had I started crying? "Thanks, Mom."

She smiled softly. "Now, I'll go help Belva get lunch together. You use that ridiculous phone to call Tarquin over. You owe him an apology. And a ring."

Chapter 19

Sunshine

My suitcase was already in my room, and as I unpacked it, memories of the week piled up along with the terrible clothes. The stories the crew had told me about their families and loves. Clotilde and Veronika's friendship. Sylvia's emergence from her cocoon of anger and sorrow, into a sharp-witted but sweet-natured, black-draped butterfly. Anne-Marie and her offer to help Blue Skies.

I didn't let myself think of him.

I shot off a quick text to Sylvia, then another to Tarquin, and finally one more to Rain about Anne-Marie. Rain's long stream of "Call me, bitch!" texts that had ended suddenly two days before worried me, but there were no additional notes in the files online. I had to trust she'd be okay. Rain's mom always said Rain was a "real nutcutter," and it was true. Anyone who'd ever been on her bad side knew that was the last place in the world you wanted to be.

I unpacked everything and hung the clothing back up, knowing that I could never give away the things I'd worn the week I met my true mate, even if it was all tacky and too small.

At the bottom of the case was a gray silk tie, one of Giovanni's. I pressed it to my nose, inhaling the already fading scent of him. It was wet with my tears by the time I could muster the strength to tuck it under my pillow.

"Why wasn't I enough for him?"

There was no answer. There probably never would be.

I searched the internet for ways to cope with the loss of a true mate until my phone buzzed. Tarquin was out front.

"Hey," I said quietly, when I met him outside. He was seated on the porch swing, staring down at his clasped hands, but jumped up when I spoke.

"Oh, Soleil, I was so worried about you." He crossed to me and grabbed my shoulders, staring into my face with sweet concern. "Your parents told me all about what happened on the boat. Throwing yourself into the open ocean after a little girl? You're ridiculously brave, you know."

I sniffled, pulling the ring out of my pocket and holding it out to him. "So brave I dumped you on the phone, Tarq. You deserve better."

"I mean, yeah," he said with an awkward laugh as he turned the ring over in his hand. "And like you told me, I'm going to find it. Find the woman who's just right for me. In fact, um..." He blushed. "I have a date today, in an hour or so."

I laughed. "Who's the lucky girl?" I didn't feel the slightest bit jealous of her. I was envious of him, and his hopefulness.

"I joined this online dating app, Knotmate.com. I got a 99.5% match with an omega named Supriya in Northeast Georgetown, can you believe it?" He told me all about the woman he'd been chatting with nonstop for the past few days.

"Wow, Tarq. That's incredible. She was right here under your nose all along?"

"Yeah." He sighed happily. "We sent each other scent samples, and Supriya said mine reminded her of the happiest day of her life, when her dad took her to Paris, and they ate camembert on the Seine." We both grinned at each other like fools before Tarquin threw his arms around me again. "But it took you being brave enough to let me go, for me to get the chance to meet her. Thank you for being amazing... and thanks for breaking up with me." He twisted his lips. "Can I admit now that the chemistry just wasn't right?"

I fought back a laugh. "What, our engagement kiss wasn't everything you dreamed of?" He stammered for a moment before I put him out of his misery. "I'll admit it, Tarq. It wasn't a great kiss, and that wasn't your fault. I would not have made a very good wife for you. But I hope we can stay good friends."

"I hope so, too, Soleil. I had no business proposing. You're amazing, and sweet, but it was my parents—"

"Who made it seem inevitable?" I nodded. "Mine too."

He shrugged. "They wanted it so much. More than we did, which was the problem, right? We need to follow our hearts, not theirs." He pulled the ring back out from his pocket. "Soleil, I've known you since we were little. And even though you never complained, I know it hurt a lot when you lost all those big dreams you had growing up. Keep the ring."

When I protested, he shook his head. "I want you to sell it. Use the money to pay for whatever scheme you and Rain have cooked up—yeah, of course I knew you had something going on," he said with a laugh. "Come on. You can't lie to save yourself. But this ring might help your dream come true as well. That illegal underground fighting ring you and Rain are running, or whatever it is."

I punched him in the arm lightly, then held the ring up to the light. It sparkled like a thousand possibilities. We could rent office space with this. Advertise. Get the apartment for Rain and me...

But not with his money. We needed to do this on our own.

So we could show the world someday that it *could* be done. That omegas could run a company, be their own bosses.

"Oh, Tarq, you are the sweetest alpha," I muttered into his shoulder, holding my breath and hugging him as hard as I could. He threw an arm around my shoulder as I slipped the ring back on my finger, just for the moment. I held it out, admiring it, then slipped it back off, pressing it into his hand. "You keep it. You may need it on your date."

He grinned. "An engagement on our first date? That's moving a little fast, Soleil."

I shrugged. "When you know, you know."

"And you... you knew, didn't you? You've met someone, too." He lifted my chin and peered into my face. "Aw, Sol. I can't stand seeing you cry. Who do I need to beat up?"

I laughed at the mental picture of Tarquin trying to fight Grumpy. "No one. Just... why couldn't I love *your* scent?" I stuck out my lip in a pout.

"Must be a you thing, Sol. I've heard I smell amazing. Wine and cheese and yeast bread? I'm every omega's dream. Now, let me go smooth things over with your dad."

Laughing, we went back inside.

Chapter 20

Grumpy

The paparazzi that hung around Georgetown Mercy Hospital were sleeping on the job when my chauffeur pulled up that day. "Or maybe they've decided they hate me, too," I muttered as only one pap snapped a quick photo, then went back to scrolling on his phone.

I took the elevator up to my family's private level, trying to ignore the way my joints and bones ached. I was only forty-two, but in the two weeks since I'd returned to my home city, I had aged twenty years. I had what felt like arthritis, the flu, and hives. My heart ached. My skin burned. Everything hurt, and itched, and it was only getting worse by the day.

Of course, I knew what was wrong with me. But it would never be right. And I'd have to learn to live with it, so she could have the life she wanted.

Aunt Marguerite greeted me at the door, her face screwed up like I'd stepped in dog shit on my way in. "What are you doing here?" I asked her. "I made an appointment with Rimbolt."

"I'm here to see another patient," she spat back, visibly

angry. "You need to leave."

"What the hell?" I stepped back. "What is it with the women in this family?"

"The women are fine. It's the idiot men who need to have some sense knocked into them." She squared her shoulders and pasted a broad smile on her face. "Let's try again. Hello, little Gio. How are you today? Have you destroyed any young omegas' lives this week, or are you turning over a new leaf?"

I rolled my eyes. "Have you been gossiping with Sylvia and Lorelei?" Sylvia had taken to texting me the most bizarre insults—most of which I had to look up to understand—since we'd gotten back. She'd addressed me as "Carbuncle G" the last few times I'd seen her, ranted for a while about the perfidy of men, then gone silent, glaring daggers at me.

Lorelei, when she wasn't fluttering her eyelashes over Anne-Marie and rebuilding her relationship with Sylvia, just gave me *I'm not mad, I'm disappointed* looks and sighed. She and Anne-Marie had tried to talk to me about Soleil two days after our return, ambushing me in my home office, but I'd shut them down.

"Gio, you can't give up on that girl," Lorelei implored, pacing on *the Aubusson rug as I drank another glass of Balvenie DCS, my third that afternoon. "She loves you; anyone could see it. And you felt something for her, too. Why won't you give it a chance?"*

Anne-Marie watched from the chaise longue by the window. When I didn't answer, she mused aloud, "You know, I was there on the yacht, when you heard her saying she'd gotten rid of an alpha. I already told you, she wasn't referring to you, Giovanni. She had just broken up with her fiancé. He was the one she didn't want."

I poured another three fingers of whiskey, then hesitated

before adding a fourth. Not five, though. Five would be far too...

My blood went hot for a second as I flashed back to the first time I'd touched her, felt her inside. Watched her dissolve into a whimpering ball of ecstasy and need, felt her squirting around my fingers.

Fuck, even drinking was reminding me of her.

Lorelei whirled around, her eyes shining with tears. "Why can't you get over your pride, and go after her? Go to her house, knock on the door, find out if there's any hope. She's your true mate, Giovanni." Her gaze flew to Anne-Marie, and the sparks between them were almost visible. "I can't imagine a life without mine, now that she's here. Please don't throw this gift away."

I set down my glass gingerly. It felt like if I moved suddenly, I might fly apart. "I did go to her house," I admitted softly. I ignored their gasps. "I had my driver, Lewis, take me not long after we were home. She was outside, on her front porch. With her fiancé." I took another drink. "I asked Lewis to slow down, so I could be sure of what I was witnessing. Maybe she was breaking up with him, I thought. Maybe she was giving back his things, I don't know. But I watched..."

My breathing hitched, remembering. The way she'd smiled like he'd lit up her entire world when he pulled the ring out of his pocket. How she'd slid it on, her affection palpable even from a distance.

How they'd embraced.

I'd rolled down the window, wanting to call out, and heard the young alpha promise to smooth things over with her dad.

"Maybe she did mean that on the yacht, Anne-Marie," I said, my voice creaking. Creaking, like the old man I was. Or was becoming. "But she's with him now. And he's... he'll be better for her than me."

. . .

I'd collapsed on my desk then. Lorelei had panicked, calling an ambulance that I had to send away. Dr. Rimbolt had already warned me about what might happen as the days passed. The exhaustion returned full force now, facing down my angry aunt.

"Marguerite, I don't want to be rude. But I'm not feeling well. Can we schedule the verbal evisceration for later in the week?" I staggered as I tried to move past her.

"Oh god, Gio, what's wrong with you?"

Dr. Rimbolt stepped around the corner and helped her guide me into the larger consulting room. My aunt demanded again to know what had happened to me. "Well, Marguerite," he said with a sigh as he took my vitals. "This is what happens when a stubborn alpha won't do as nature intends."

"So she *is* your true mate, like Lorelei suspected." Marguerite's lips got so tight, they almost vanished. "How you could abandon that young woman is beyond comprehension. If it was just you suffering, that would be one thing! But to leave her now when she may need you most..."

"What do you mean?" I demanded, my blood going cold. "What do you mean she needs me?" I glared at Rimbolt. "You said omegas don't feel the loss of the bond like alphas. You said there would be no side effects for her—"

"Not severe ones, no," he said, cutting me off with a curious look at my aunt. "At least, not that I know of. Marguerite? Has there been some recent research? Is the girl ill?"

My aunt's lips pursed. "I can't say."

"But she came to see you two weeks ago, right?" I interrupted her stare-off with Rimbolt. "She wasn't sick from being in the ocean?"

Something flashed in her eyes. "You should contact her and find out what's wrong, Gio."

"Is she ill?" Rimbolt looked concerned. "Were there side effects from her misadventure?"

Exasperated, she huffed, "I can't violate patient confidentiality, Herb. You know that."

"Please, Marguerite. Should I have called the helicopter to evacuate her that day? I'll never forgive myself if—"

Her eyes slid to mine, then away. "No, that's not the issue." She leaned close to Rimbolt, speaking quickly and quietly. "Some slight concern with elevated hCG, but only at twenty-four."

Dr. Rimbolt tapped the side of his nose. "Ah, I see. I saw the tech setting up the ultrasound."

"Exactly."

"What the fuck are you two *talking* about? Is my omega sick?"

"That," Aunt Marguerite snapped, poking a finger into my chest. "That right there is the problem. She's your omega. But if you don't make it right... well, let's just say, she won't be alone."

"I know she won't. She's got a fucking fiancé," I spat out. "Why do you think I'm suffering like this? It's for her. So she can have... what she wants. *Who* she wants."

Aunt Marguerite stared at me while I panted. "My god. Lorelei really did get all the brains, didn't she?" With that, she turned on her heel and walked out.

Dr Rimbolt did his exam in silence, only humming a bit. Then he directed me to a chair, and sighed. "It's not good, Giovanni. I'm afraid the symptoms will only get worse."

Worse? I wasn't sure I would be able to work if the pain got much more severe. I'd barely been able to keep up with the aftermath of the "Alphonse Dubois debacle" in the past two weeks. Meetings with Storm Security officials, federal agents, and even Interpol. I felt like an hourglass, running out of sand.

But I had to keep my companies afloat. My family

protected. There had to be something I could do. "I've heard they have some treatments. I read about some clinical study—"

"I know the one you mean. Paxson Pharma pulled it in December. A friend of mine is on the board. There were potentially lethal side effects. Some of the alphas in the trial had coronary infarctions."

"What else can I do? It's been two weeks, and I can hardly work. I can't think."

"This is just the beginning, son." I didn't like the look in his eyes, like he was trying to find the gentlest way to break terrible news.

"Wait, I know a guy. Victor Castleton. He's doing fine." I stopped, wondering if that was true. I'd texted him nine months before, when he was down in South America, but not since.

Rimbolt let out a low whistle. "I don't see how. The pain must have become unbearable as time passed." He rubbed his chin, lost in thought. "Unless he never actually had sexual relations with his omega. Since you did have unprotected sexual relations with Miss Soleil, even if you didn't fully claim her with your bite—"

My heart skipped a beat. "How did you know that?"

"That you had sexual relations?

"No. That they were unprotected."

His eyes shifted around the room, looking everywhere but at me. "Ah. Can we pretend I didn't let that slip, Giovanni? I could lose my license."

"What's the ultrasound for, Rimbolt?" I demanded, sudden strength flowing into me as I stood, towering over the smaller man.

He didn't answer, and I took a deep breath, ready to remind him I was his employer... and my lungs filled with a hint of coconut and hibiscus.

She was here.

Chapter 21

Sunshine

"Come right in, Soleil," the doctor said, meeting me outside the office on the private floor of the hospital, for some reason. She seemed slightly nervous today, which worried me. "You look fabulous. How have you been feeling?"

I'd dressed in my favorite sunshine yellow Jimmy Choo heels, with a puffy yellow skirt, a chunky, hand-tooled leather belt, and a bright orange silk shell with Swarovski crystals stitched along the neckline. It was "a lot," according to Mom, but I'd sent my friend Candy a picture, and she'd told me she was calling the police since I'd start a riot downtown in this.

It was good having girlfriends who knew when to blow sunshine up your skirt.

I smiled at Marguerite. "You want the truth, or you want me to say I'm fine?"

She took both my hands in hers. "Always the truth, young one. How are you feeling? What's been happening?"

"Physically, I'm fine. Well, I have to take the painkillers you prescribed most days. Mentally? I'm a wreck."

The nurse opened the door behind her and nodded. Marguerite bustled us both in, and when we reached the examination room, she sat next to me in one of the green chairs. "Now, tell me what's going on."

"I don't want to trash talk your nephew to you, Marguerite," I said with a weak smile.

"Oh, there's nothing you could say I haven't already thought. He hasn't been in touch?"

"Well, in a roundabout way, I suppose he has. He sent attorneys to speak with my parents. He formed some kind of trust for me, with a hundred million dollars in an account I was only allowed to use if I was given their permission to have my own accounts, run a business, and even move out." I giggled at the shock on her face. "Yeah, my dad's expression was the same as yours when he heard it. I mean, who can turn down that kind of money?" I winked. "My dad always said I was one in a billion."

Her jaw snapped shut. "You turned it down?"

"Well, yeah. It was a grand gesture, but not the kind that matters, right? I told that jerk I didn't want his money. I wanted his... I wanted..." I breathed through the wave of sadness. I was getting used to doing that now. In a few seconds, I had control again. "It's always been important that we make it on our own."

"We?"

"Yes. Rain and me. I mean, we have another friend, Candy Paxson, who already said she'd buy us an entire block of offices."

Her eyes flew wide. "Candy Paxson? Nicholas Paxson's new bride?"

"Yeah. So money isn't really the issue anymore. Honestly, I wouldn't mind taking a slight hand-up from a friend. Rain, on the other hand, is super stubborn about accepting what she sees as charity. She's never had much money, not since she was young. It matters to both of us that we omegas make this happen independently."

"You're trying to prove it can be done."

I smiled. "Anyway, we scheduled enough bookings over the past few months to cover what we need to rent a small office. And Mom went around Dad and gave permission for me to have my own bank accounts, and be on the paperwork for the business—legally, that is. He didn't want her to—he still thinks all I need is an alpha—but she's turning out to be pretty badass, to be honest."

Marguerite slapped a hand over her mouth, and I wasn't sure if she was stifling laughter or a sob. After a few seconds, she said, "Can I adopt you?"

"I'll let you know after the tests. Because what happens if I am pregnant? Then your great-nephew or niece would also be your grandchild, and I'd be sexually attracted to my own cousin... Knocked up by my cousin?" I fanned my face while she snorted. "Isn't that a cable reality show with banjos in it? No can do. Let's just stay friends."

When we could finally stop laughing, she tapped on her tablet with the end of her pen. "All right, beautiful girl. You said you waited to test again. So we're going to do another urine sample and then, if we need to, a quick ultrasound." She handed me a specimen cup, then stuck her head out the door, looking around.

So weird.

"An ultrasound?" I asked, but she was already bustling me out into the hallway and to the ladies' room.

When I was done, I washed my hands, picked up the sample with a paper towel wrapped around it, and stepped back out into the hallway, wondering where I was supposed to leave it. There was a faint hint of coffee and chocolate in the air, and I inhaled deeply, feeling better than I had in days. The tight pinch in my chest almost vanished as I breathed. The nurse came scooting down the hallway at that very moment, remarking at how fast I'd been, and looking flustered.

"Yep, that's me. Fastest urethra in the tri-state area." She blinked at me, like I'd lost my mind, so I held the sample out to her and changed the subject. "I didn't know the tea bar had coffee. Is there any chance I can get a mocha?"

She shook her head, taking the cup. "There isn't. Do you drink tea? We only have decaf, herbal varieties."

That was weird. I could've sworn I smelled mocha... Maybe it was hers, and she wasn't sharing.

"Not usually. I guess I'll have to get used to it," I said, smiling grimly, and nodded at the cup in her hand. A door opened to my side as I added, "If it turns out I'm pregnant."

The voice that had haunted my dreams for two weeks boomed in my ear. "Pregnant?"

I spun around so fast, the heel of one of my Jimmy Choos actually snapped. Before I could even start the mourning process for my favorite heels, I felt myself going down, my arms windmilling.

But once again, I didn't fall.

Giovanni had caught me. Again.

"Sunshine?"

I closed my eyes and moaned softly, from embarrassment and a sudden wave of lust.

He lifted me in his stupidly muscular arms. "Rimbolt! Marguerite! She needs medical attention!"

"I don't," I insisted as he carried me into the room he'd just come out of. "I mean, I do. I'm at the doctor's office. Wait. What are you doing here?" I opened my eyes, worried.

He set me down on the examination table, his hands still on my upper arms, staring into my face like he was in shock. "I'm... I'm..."

He looked terrible, like he'd lost twenty pounds in the past two weeks. His hair was a mess, he had five-day stubble, and his eyes were bloodshot. Even his clothing was in disarray. I looked down and bit my lip to keep from laughing. He had on two different dress shoes: one matte black, the other a glossy charcoal.

"I'm... I'm..."

How hard had I hit the guy? "I don't know, Grumpy, but I think you may have a concussion. Let's ask one of these nice doctors to examine y—" Before I could finish my sentence, he'd picked me back up and crushed me to him in a hug that made my ribs creak slightly. "Can't... breathe..." I squeaked.

Immediately, he set me down on a chair and kneeled in front of me, my left hand held before his face like it was one of the wonders of the world. "You're not wearing the ring," he whispered. "You're not engaged."

"I haven't been for a while," I said, confused. "Wait. You thought I'd have had sex with you if I was engaged?"

"No one would blame you. It was medically necessary sex," he answered, still staring at my hand. "A lifesaving encounter."

I rolled my eyes, ignoring the muffled laughter of the doctors and nurse just outside the room. "I'm known to do that on occasion, I suppose." Giovanni just bowed his head. His shoulders were shaking, and when he looked up, his face was a mask of despair and pain.

"Save me," he whispered. "I'm begging you."

"Save you?" I wasn't sure what he meant, but right then, I would have jumped into an ocean without a life preserver to know.

"I'm in love with you, Soleil Annette Fairweather. I can't live without you. When you walked out of my life, the sun vanished. It's so dark, princess. Won't you give me another chance to show you how I feel? To deserve your love?"

His hand was so large next to mine, and I found myself smiling as I noted the muscles on them. "First, you have to tell the truth," I said, and his gaze shot to mine. "Do you have a personal trainer for your fingers?"

He nodded slowly. "All billionaires do, Sunshine. You'll get one, too, if you'll be mine. My beloved betasitter."

Beloved?

All of a sudden, I felt like I'd swallowed my tongue. Had he just said what I thought? "Your betasitter? Aren't you a little old for one?"

"I am. And that's why I let you go. I know I'm too old for you, princess. Too old. Too grumpy. I don't deserve you. But I need you. And maybe... you need me, too?"

I chewed at my lip. Was this all because he thought I might be pregnant? My heart pounding, I called out, "Marguerite, am I pregnant?"

Even through the door, her voice was clear. "We haven't run the test yet."

"Does it matter, Grumpy? Will you still want me if I'm not pregnant?"

"Fuck yes. And if you're not, then you will be soon," he replied with a snarl. Then he picked me up, threw me over one shoulder, and carried me caveman-style out of the office. The nurse squeaked, but gave me a thumbs up. Dr. Rimbolt just laughed. I waved at them all as I bounced along down the hall. Grumpy was almost running now.

"What are you doing?" Aunt Marguerite shouted. "Where are you going?"

"Home," Giovanni called back, mashing the elevator button so hard I thought it would break.

"My home?" I squeaked.

"No, Sunshine. Our home."

The air in the elevator as we descended was so thick with

pheromones, our scents mingling, that when it finally opened back up at the ground floor, most of the people waiting at the bottom all backed away, fanning their faces. Two of them started making out almost instantly, the tidal wave of our combined pheromones working their magic. One old man made a snarky comment about "Kids these days."

"Hear that, Grumpy?" I whispered in his ear. "You're a kid."

He didn't answer, and from the sound of the constant rumbling growl that he was making, I had a feeling he was past words.

I pressed my lower half closer to him as he strode toward the main hospital doors. The growl was vibrating up from his chest to my torso, and it reminded me of the first time I'd taken a tandem ride on a friend's motorbike in high school.

The air around us blossomed, and Giovani finally managed words. "Whatever you're thinking about, stop. I'll take you right against the doors of the hospital, Sunshine. I'm hanging by a fucking thread." He let me slip down so my arms were around his neck, and I wrapped my legs around his waist.

"I was remembering my first orgasm," I whispered in his ear. "I was riding behind Steve Dorfermeyer on his motorbike our junior year of high school. The vibrations were all I need-ed." I pressed my pelvis against him, glad I'd worn a skirt long enough to cover everything that was going on below. "If you don't stop growling, Grumpy, I'm not going to be able to control myself." I ground my pelvis into him, holding my breath slightly. Almost... there...

"No, no, no, little brat," Giovanni muttered, moving even faster toward the doors now. "The next orgasm you have is going to be on my cock, in our bedroom, and you're going to beg me for it."

Our bedroom.

"Grumpy? When you said you wanted me to be yours... what did you mean?" He didn't answer, just kept moving, and I couldn't stop the tiny sob that crept out. It had sounded like he wanted me to be with him from now on.

But he'd pulled away from me so many times now. He'd let me go. How could I be sure this was for real?

For forever?

"Sunshine, no, don't cry. Why are you crying?" The sunlight outside was almost too harsh, and I ducked my head, not wanting him to see my fear, my uncertainty.

"It's just... you let me go. I don't know if I can do whatever this is, if you're going to leave me again." I forced out the next words. "And you might. You keep saying I'm too young. I know I'm not *enough* for someone like you."

I didn't know what was happening next, but suddenly, I was standing, and Giovanni was on one knee in front of me, my hands gripped in his. His face was ravaged, his dark eyes haunted. "Sunshine, no. I made such terrible mistakes. Trust me when I say, I know letting you go, even for just days, was wrong." A tiny glimmer in his eye flared, then vanished. "My own family isn't speaking with me. Chef Juliette refuses to cook for me. My CFO sends me links to therapists and self-help books every damned day."

I almost smiled at that. "It was weeks, not days. Two weeks."

"I swear on my life, from now on, I will spend every day I have showing you how perfect for me you are. No, just how perfect you are." He closed his eyes. "You are beloved by everyone who meets you. When you walk into a room, you change the atmosphere. You make everyone who meets you... better." He squeezed my hands gently. "You made *me* better. You taught me how to love."

I tried to speak, but he went down on both knees now.

"Soleil Fairweather, I am a miserable asshole. I do not deserve you, but I can't seem to let you go, to let you have the life you should with a better man." He opened his dark eyes, equal parts longing and hope reflected in them. "Please tell me you'll forgive me. Make my days bright, my life worth something. Please love me, and never leave me again."

I swallowed hard. It seemed like fireworks were going off all around us, just like at the end of the princess movies I'd watched as a little girl. "Grumpy, I don't know why you think you don't deserve me. But I'm not dumb enough to turn down a man who makes my heart sing, and makes my lady bits pray for mercy. I forgive you. I love you."

There was something happening around us. Shouting, more fireworks, some sort of argument, but I couldn't look away from the miracle in front of me.

My grumpy alpha was smiling.

Chapter 22

Grumpy

The paparazzi were having a field day, snapping thousands of pictures, calling out questions. I didn't care, until one of them jostled Soleil.

Then I leaped up, growling. "Touch her and die, asshole," I barked.

The photographer, a weedy-looking guy with a ball cap and a goatee, literally fainted.

"Um, not that hearing you say those exact words isn't the fulfillment of one of my most cherished fantasies, Grumpy," Soleil said behind me, "but I think we should go back to the... the house now." A sudden wash of coconut and flowers rushed around me.

"Fuck, Sunshine," I breathed. Her skin had gone a bright pink, and sweat dotted her brow.

"Yeah, that's the plan, right?" she muttered.

In seconds, I had her in the car, gave the driver instructions, and we were off. I rolled up the partition between the front and back seats, then pulled her seat belt around her, buckling her in. I pulled out my phone and tapped a few instructions to my staff at home, making sure the house would be ready.

"Grumpy?" Soleil was panting with need, but her expression was hesitant and uncertain.

"Yes, my love?"

She wouldn't meet my eyes, fiddling with the seat belt buckle instead. "You were at the hospital. You were sick?"

"Yes. Rejection sickness. It's nature's punishment for being the world's stupidest alpha," I joked. But she didn't laugh.

"You suffered for two weeks with it. You weren't there for me, were you? You were there to see Dr. Rimbolt."

"I was. I've been very ill. And extremely busy as well." She stayed quiet for a moment too long, her scent turning bitter, and I found myself rushing to explain. "When I came ashore, federal investigators met me at the pier. Alphonse Dubois' second cousin Muffin, as it turns out, was a scam artist, and the one with the brains, although that's being generous.

"Alphonse was an attendant in the rehab facility Lorelei checked into six months ago. At his cousin's urging, Alphonse befriended my sister, then convinced her he was in love. He had no real criminal record, only parking tickets and a DUI from a decade before. His cousin, on the other hand, was the person of interest to the FBI and Interpol. She's wanted in three countries for embezzlement, fraud, you name it." I rubbed my brow. "I've been tied up getting to the bottom of the mess for almost the entire two weeks."

"How is your sister?"

"Lorelei feels wretched that she fell for him, but he did treat her well when they were together. Still, she thinks she should have seen it earlier."

"Love is blind, right?" Soleil muttered, still looking down. I tipped her chin up.

"I don't think so. I think love was staring me in the face the whole time, and I was the blind one." I blew a cool breath over her sweat-dampened brow. "I came by your house, you know."

"You did?" she gasped, her eyes widening.

"You were on your front porch, and you weren't alone. I saw that alpha give you the ring, and you put it on. You two looked good together."

"But... that's not what was happening. We weren't together; he was trying to get me to sell the damn ring and invest in my company."

I fought back a curse. "You didn't take it?"

"Of course not. If you'd bothered to ask, if you'd come inside..."

"I'm sorry. I thought I was doing what you wanted, driving away. I thought the pain I felt was what I deserved, for hurting you."

"I never want you to hurt, Grumpy." The corners of her lips turned up slightly. "Unless you're into that sort of thing." She twisted toward me and reached for the buttons of my shirt, undoing two before I grabbed her hands.

"Wait until we're home, princess. I'll take care of you, I promise."

She whined. "Why not start now? I've never had hot car sex. It might be fun. Let's find out." She licked up the side of my throat, and I was tempted to give in. But I knew better. My control was hanging by a frayed thread.

"If I fuck you now, Sunshine, I will knot you right here, and we'll be in this car for hours." She nodded like she understood, but let out a small sob.

No, I couldn't let her suffer. Not for one more second.

I leaned up against her, reaching over, and shoved her puffy yellow skirt around the tops of her thighs. "I can help take the edge off, princess. Just do what I say, all right? Hold still."

She nodded furiously, hissing when I wrapped the thin

strap at one side of her panties around my fingers and snapped it, pulling them off. Her scent was overwhelming, and my mouth watered as I sucked in a deep breath.

"Pinch your nipples, Sunshine. You keep busy up there, and I'll take care of the rest."

She muttered something, her head thrashing back and forth as I worked her clit, smearing it with the juices that were flowing from her onto the leather seat. She begged for more, already getting lost in a pre-heat haze. I found myself smiling wickedly as I thought of how many times I was going to make her come. How she'd beg me for more.

I smiled through her first orgasm, and her second, fighting for control as I wrested hers away. By the time we reached our destination, she was out of her mind with want, her skin almost painfully hot.

And I was almost feral with lust.

Lewis opened the door to the Rolls, keeping his gaze averted, though I could see his half-hidden smile. My butler stood on the step with the front door already open wide, and I nodded my thanks as I raced past.

I ran with her in my arms all the way into my bedroom, where I slammed the door behind us. The curtains in this room had been closed, so it was dark even in the middle of the day, and the bed was piled high with blankets. My staff had done well, and they deserved the raises I would give them.

Now it was time to take care of my omega.

Omega. *Wait.* I remembered all the things I'd known long ago about what omegas needed in heats.

"Sunshine, what else do you need?" I murmured, kissing her sweat-soaked brow. "Can I get you anything?"

"You. Knot," she replied, blinking up at me like an angry kitten.

I blew a cool stream of air across her face, smiling again at her impatient, grumpy expression. "Do you need anything more, love?"

"Yes," she said, a snarl transforming her normally sweet face into a fierce, slightly terrifying one. "I want your cock, your knot, your tongue, and if you don't get in that bed now and give me those, I'll settle for taking your balls instead and making them into earrings!" Her voice had risen to a hysterical shout at the end.

"And they call *me* the grumpy one," I muttered, and threw her into the middle of my California king-sized bed. She almost vanished into the fluffy down comforters on top. One small hand emerged, her middle finger pointing straight to the ceiling.

"And they call me the omega," she sassed back, fighting her way out of the comforters. Or under them? Yes, the little temptress had gone under them. It almost looked like she was swimming. "You're supposed to be an alpha, right? Jeez, I don't have this many blankets on my bed."

"Little brat, I'll show you an alpha," I replied, stripping off my clothes as fast as possible. One of my platinum cufflinks pinged across the room; two of my shirt buttons did, too. I didn't care. The comforters looked like snowdrifts, hiding my omega from me, but I could see the covers moving and hear her muffled giggles. "You'd better be naked by the time I get in there."

"You'll never find me," she called back. "I'm buried in a thousand-thread-count avalanche!"

Naked, I grabbed the corner of the thick duvet and pulled it off in a giant movement. She was naked, as I'd told her to be. "Good girl," I growled. "How should I reward such lovely obedience?"

"I'm sure you'll think of something." Her face was wreathed in a smile, and as I crawled across the mattress to her,

I found myself returning it. "I love your smile, Grumpy. I want to see it every day," she whispered as I lowered my face to hers, our kiss beginning as a question and ending as a carnal promise of more to come. She writhed beneath me, pressing her soft curves up into the hard planes of my stomach.

"Anything for you, Sunshine." I rained kisses across her forehead and down her neck, moving to her breasts as she arched her back and moaned lightly. "I will give you anything you want," I vowed, then sucked her right nipple, drawing on it hard.

"I will give you everything you need." I moved to the other breast, then down to her stomach, licking the slight hollows by her hips.

"Give you a baby." I traced a gentle line down her mound, burying my nose in her dampness and inhaling her luscious scent.

"Give you all of me," I breathed into her as I set my lips around her clit and sucked gently, my hands holding her hips in place, keeping her where I wanted her.

I would keep her forever, even if I didn't deserve her.

I nibbled, licked, sucked, drawing on every past experience I had to make this moment with my omega the best she had ever felt. I wanted her to be addicted to me. I wanted to be all she could see, feel, dream of.

I wanted to own her thoughts, her soul, the way she owned mine.

I brought her to her peak once, twice, then used my fingers and tongue in tandem to see if I could coax another orgasm from her before I made love to her.

Because that's what I was doing. Making love. Treasuring her. Being gentle, tender...

"Grumpy," she whimpered, her voice more than slightly distraught. "Maybe... you are... too old for me."

I stopped moving. "What did you say?"

"I said, stop fucking around and get your cock in me." She punctuated her demand with a slightly hysterical giggle. I sat up, wiping my face off, and moved up so I was staring into her flushed face. Those blue green eyes twinkled with mischief and affection. And impatience. "Where's the asshole who pulls my hair, hm? What does a girl have to do around here to get chok —*oof!*"

"You think you're ready for this, princess?" I growled, notching the head of my cock to her entrance. My hand spanned her throat, and I put the tiniest bit of pressure on the sides of her neck while I worked the thick head in an inch or so.

Her answer was muffled—"Aye aye, Captain Campari"— and then her eyelids fluttered shut as I began thrusting.

"I love how tight you are, Sunshine," I purred. The orgasms had made her walls thicken and swell, and I almost had to force my way in, though she was so wet, her slick gushed out all around my cock. "Spread wider, princess. Need to get my whole cock into you in the next thrust."

Her eyes flared open, filled with desire and a hint of fear. "Open, now, naughty girl," I said, and she obeyed, spreading her slender thighs. "Yes, just like that, brat. You'll regret that sass in the morning." I laughed as I moved my hand behind her head, grabbing hold of her hair and tugging her head back slightly. Her nipples jutted up toward the ceiling like an offering. I leaned down and took a nipple in between my lips, sucking hard as I pressed my hips forward.

She arched her back, and I thrust inside, plunging my full length into her. It was so good, so hot, for a second, I was afraid I would come right then. She was shuddering, making a soft mewling noise when I finally got control of myself and started fucking her.

"Whose naughty girl are you, Sunshine?" Her pussy was so

tight, it felt like she was trying to force me out as I plowed her. "Whose wet little cunt is this?" I pulled her hair tighter, and set my tongue and teeth to work on her nipples as I fucked her into another climax. "Answer me, or I'll fuck your tight little ass next."

"Yours," she screamed as she came again. When she stopped shuddering, I pulled out, and flipped her over. "Knot, Alpha," she whined.

"Present, Omega."

"I can't, I'm too... Can't move." She mumbled against the sheet.

"Present," I repeated, smacking the round globe of her ass with my hand once, then again, loving the way it jiggled and the way the skin flushed pink. "Present for me, or I stop fucking and start spanking."

Honest to god, I could almost hear the gears turning in her brain as she weighed the two options. Oh, I'd spank her again. But not until she was mine.

I laughed, then infused my next command with just a hint of an alpha bark. "Present, Omega." Her ass shot up in the air as her body obeyed my command, her knees on the sheet, and her arms stretched out in front of her. "Good girl," I praised, as I spread her ass cheeks wide. "God, I can't wait to get inside this little hole, too, princess."

"You... you can't possibly," she mumbled against the sheet.

"Oh, I like a challenge." Her ass was already drenched with her sticky wetness, but I swiped my thumb just inside her pussy, then pressed it gently against the outside of her ass. "Have you ever let anyone inside here, baby?" I murmured low.

She shivered, then mumbled, "No."

I crouched over her, keeping my thumb flush with her tight

hole and bumping the head of my cock against her pussy again. "Have you ever used a toy in here, princess?"

Softer. "No."

My inner alpha roared. "Oh, baby, then we'd better start soon. I'll get you a plug. Maybe a pretty one with a yellow diamond on it. Train this ass, bigger plugs every week, until you can take my cock in here." She moaned as I fucked into her and let my thumb breach her hole at the same time, feeling the tight ring of muscles there as they clenched, then relaxed. "Good girl. Let me in. Oh, so tight, princess. Gonna have to stretch you every day. Fuck your mouth in the morning, fill your hot pussy with my cum every night, then plug this little ass so you can get ready for your alpha's cock."

I leaned down and whispered into her ear, "Someday, you'll take my knot there, princess. You'll beg me for it. You'll want me to stretch you wide, and make it hurt so... damn... good."

She cursed into the mattress as I slammed into her pussy with each word, her walls clenching around me, my engorged knot pressing against the opening to her cunt. I grabbed her thighs and pounded into her, watching her for signs of her next orgasm.

I felt the fluttering of her cunt around my cock as I slowed, and knew the time had come. "Now, Omega. Come for your alpha."

She cried out and spasmed, losing the ability to support her weight. I took over for her, lifting her hips and pressing forward as she came, taking advantage of that moment where she was lost in her pleasure to push past the entrance and inside her.

My knot began to swell, locking us together, and she cried out again as she came. She milked me, my cum pouring out into her, filling her up.

I set my teeth to the juncture between her neck and shoulder, and bit down, her hot blood filling my mouth. "Mine." I reared back, taking in the marks on her flushed skin that would stay for the rest of our lives. Binding us together, connecting not only our bodies, but our emotions. I could feel her ecstasy in my own veins, her acceptance and desire. "My omega. My mate."

"Mine," she hissed back. Quick as a snake, she darted to one side, sinking her dull teeth into my forearm.

It was the sweetest pain I'd ever felt, and the angry, restless part of me—the part that had never smiled in years, that had been angry at the entire world—calmed.

"Mine," she whispered again as I licked her neck, soothing the wound I'd made there. My alpha instincts were satisfied. It would heal into silver scars, visible every time her neck was exposed, and show the world she was mine.

"I am, Sunshine. You claimed me so well. I'm yours. Forever." A pulse of joy, tinged with wonder and a deep satisfaction, filled my thoughts. I knew she could feel my emotions as well, and hoped the depth of my love soothed any lingering doubts.

After a moment, I rolled her onto her side. She slept with me, sometimes snoring softly, sometimes waking to ride me. My cock never softened, though my knot went down enough for me to carry her to the bathroom for water and a quick shower, then back to bed where we began the process again. And again. I was lost in a wild rut, and I fucked her through the night.

Until finally, we slept.

Chapter 23

Sunshine

I woke happy and rested, and so sore it felt like I'd ridden rodeo bulls all night long. Or at least an alpha the size of a bull. I winced as I gently pressed one hand to my mound, moving the other one over to where I thought I'd find Giovanni.

But he was gone.

A small clock was on the side table, showing the time and date. Friday already? "We fucked for two days?" I asked the empty room.

My stomach answered with a mighty growl. I pressed a hand on it. The mini-heat had kept me from feeling hunger, though I had hazy memories of Giovanni making me drink water and—most embarrassingly—carrying me to the bathroom so I could pee. But now I needed food. The pillows were starting to remind me of marshmallows.

My purse was sitting on the table as well, and I grabbed it, pulling out my diamond-encrusted phone. I'd never seen so many notifications in my life. But the only one that I clicked on was the one from Dr. Marguerite Grantham.

Holy shit.

Before I could process what she'd written, I heard a deep baritone, singing the melody to a song I'd heard a thousand times. "The other night dear, as I lay sleeping..." The door opened, and Giovanni stepped through, carrying a platter of what had to be breakfast, judging by the delectable smells. He was already dressed, in his signature suit and tie. Silver cufflinks winked at his wrists, and I felt myself frowning.

Was this it? Was he going back to work, like this was a normal day? I didn't know if Giovanni was a workaholic, or... or much about him at all. Besides my Internet stalking, and the conversations we'd had on the boat, he was practically a stranger.

Except I could feel the waves of affection, gratitude, and the bedrock solid promise of protection and care that emanated from the bite mark on my shoulder. He was a good man, and now, a happy one.

And a clothed one.

"Sunshine, what's this? I'm supposed to be the grumpy one, not you," he teased, sitting on the edge of the bed.

"You're dressed. I thought..." I squiggled back down the bed, tucking my face under the sheet.

He tugged it down. "What did you think?" He caught my chin gently in one hand. "Tell me, princess. What did you think?"

I closed my eyes so I didn't have to see his reaction. "I thought we'd be able to spend some time together. Get to know each other. I mean..." I placed a hand over the mate mark, liking the slightly painful, pleasurable throb. It was a good distraction from the ache in my heart. "It's okay. Have a good day at work."

His laughter shook the bed. "Sunshine, I'm not going to work. I just got dressed so I wouldn't shock the staff."

"You put on cufflinks to get coffee?" I blurted out. "Is this a billionaire thing?"

His cheeks darkened, and he shifted slightly. "No. I have a few odd habits. Lorelei always made fun of me for them. I just like wearing suits."

"Well, they're sexy on you, for sure," I said, with a sniff. "But on to more important questions. Is that you or is that—"

"A mocha latte? It is indeed." He grinned, and my brain stopped working again. Was that a dimple in his right cheek? Oh, my. It was. A tiny, hypnotic dimple. "Sunshine? Sunshine, what are you staring at? You really do need coffee."

I really, really did. But I knew better. "Orange juice, I think." I sat up, taking the cut-crystal glass. The sheet fell back, and Giovanni gazed at my breasts like he hadn't practically sucked my nips off the night before. Not that I was complaining.

I sipped the juice while he unloaded the rest of the tray onto the bedside table. There were warm croissants, crystal pots of butter and wild strawberry jam, a boiled egg in a tiny Wedgwood egg cup, and one sausage. "One sausage?" I muttered as he began slicing it up. I was way hungrier than that. "That can't possibly be enough."

"It's a big sausage, sweetheart. I'm pretty sure you'll be satisfied." He wiggled his eyebrows like a pervert.

"I'm not sharing," I warned as he offered me a bite. "I really, really like sausage."

"I know." He chuckled, rubbing the front of his pants with his free hand. "Maybe too much. I think you sprained my knot."

Once I finished laughing and could talk again, I told him, "You have a wonderful laugh, Grumpy. And a gorgeous smile. How could you hide it for so long?"

"I never had a reason to smile until now."

I swallowed a huge gulp of my juice to keep from bursting into tears.

Then, when he'd finished feeding me cut-up pieces of sausage—interspersed with long, delicious, breakfast-flavored kisses—he reached into a pocket. "You know the paparazzi already posted pictures from two days ago," he said, showing me his phone. There were dozens of articles with #grumpysmile and #grumpynomore, and a headline of "The Smile that Broke a Thousand Hearts." That picture showed Grumpy on his knees, smiling up at me.

My expression was the same as I imagined it would be if I'd just taken a blow to the head. "I look like an eejit."

"You look radiant," Giovanni said softly, almost to himself. "I'll show this picture to our grandchildren someday."

I choked on a swallow of my juice. Giovanni reacted like I'd gone into cardiac arrest, patting my back and muttering alarming things about delayed drowning and lung infections. When I finally could speak again, I rasped, "Chill out. I'm fine."

"You were *choking*."

I rolled my eyes. "You can't just drop a word like grandchildren into a conversation and expect me to stay relaxed. I mean... children."

"You don't want children? I mean, you don't have to. You're young. You have plenty of time. Or you may not even want them. Your business will take time, and attention. I know that." It was almost cute how he was trying to mask his disappointment, and blabbering. "Not all women want to start families at your—"

"I'd better want them. Or at least one," I interrupted, holding up my phone. "And you'd better, too."

He peered down at my screen, reading the words his aunt

had sent me that morning. "You're... pregnant? But... you were in heat last night."

I snorted. "Apparently, back in your day, they didn't teach sex ed. Or at least not how omegas work. Normal heat cycles are fertile times, and mini-heats, or mating heats are, too." I felt my face burning. How was it that I had to explain this to a man eighteen years older than me?

Then I remembered the "man" part. I knew some politicians in our country thought babies were gestated in the stomach. And that women could choose to be fertile or not. *Ugh.*

Giovanni finished the explanation for me. "But mating heats between true mates can recur until there's a claiming bite. I'd forgotten."

I barely stopped myself from commenting that memories faded with age. We would have years for me to tease him. "Anyway, you've got strong swimmers, I guess. I got pregnant on the boat, from that one night. Although it might have been from the time you did that cum dump truck maneuver that was weirdly gross and sexy at the same—*oof!*"

He'd wrapped his arm around me, hugging me so close I couldn't talk, or breathe. For some reason, he was shaking. Trembling.

I sniffled as he rocked me back and forth, and waited for him to wrap his mind around the news. Not that I had. In less than nine months, I'd be a mother. And this overbearing, intelligent, handsome growly alpha would be a father. A daddy.

"I'm not calling you Daddy," I whispered in his ear. "I know we have that age gap thing going, but no. That's not on my list of potential kinks."

Giovanni kneeled beside the bed and opened the bedside table. "I don't care what you call me. Grumpy, Gio, Asshole... Sir." He raised one eyebrow. I knew how much he liked me calling him that.

"Understood, sir."

"Good. I was hoping, though..." Suddenly, he had a small, hand-carved box in his hand, with what looked like threads of gold and platinum and a dozen brightly colored gemstones decorating the lid. He placed the box in my hand. "I was hoping I could call you my wife."

The box opened with a quiet snick, and I gasped. Nestled in sapphire velvet was an art deco-style ring crafted in gold and platinum, with three emerald-cut yellow diamonds on the top. The central stone was the largest yellow diamond I'd ever seen.

"I had it the day I went to your house. I just never dreamed I'd be able to see you wear it... will you?"

"Grumpy," I wheezed, pulling the ring out of the box.

"Not grumpy anymore. Not if you say I do, my love," he rasped. "When I met you, you had on a yellow dress, and it was as if the sun came out from behind a cloud that had covered my entire life. Be my wife. Be my sunshine." He slipped the ring on my finger, and it warmed instantly.

"I do!" I shouted, tackling him and pressing kisses to his face, giving a few extras to the cute dimple that kept popping up. "I'll be your Sunshine for the rest of our lives."

Chapter 24

Sunshine

"Okay, with you as maid of honor, Candy as matron of honor, Flora doing the flower arrangements, Valentina making the cakes, and Laurel as wedding coordinator, I think my wedding will either be the best one this century, or a cautionary tale for all future brides."

Rain rubbed her temples with her forefingers. "Forget brides. You'll either set omega rights forward a decade, or back a hundred years."

I ignored her, focusing my attention on the macarons on my plate. I couldn't have caffeine now, but I could have pastries, and Chez Palette's were the best. Thank goodness I didn't have morning sickness.

Honestly, of the two of us, Rain was the one who looked sick. She'd been dropped off by a uniformed driver in a Bentley again today, wearing a couture dress that I had seen in a recent magazine. She'd gotten back in town two days after Giovanni had proposed. But when I demanded she tell me her story, she'd burst into tears and begged me not to make her talk about it yet.

So I didn't. Instead, I made her my maid of honor and gave her a shit ton of work to take her mind off the guy who'd made her cry.

For the past three weeks, we'd met daily in the back office of Chez Palette, since Giovanni wanted us to be married as soon as possible. Today, she'd seemed particularly distraught, but between the stack of baked goods, the waves of my calming omega pheromones I'd been accidentally pumping out, and the graphic descriptions of everything Grumpy and I had gotten up to in bed so far, she was smiling through her tears.

She sucked down half her black coffee in one swallow, and went on. "The announcements at least were a hit on Instagram."

"They were so cute, right? The little suns on the fronts with the yellow Swarovski crystals, and the envelope origami boats..."

She glared at me. "Don't remind me, Soleil. I still have the paper cuts from stuffing all five hundred envelopes. As I was saying, from the announcements to the pornographic bachelorette party favors, which one of our League friends leaked to the press—"

I glared back. "They were not *pornographic*. They were sex positive."

She frowned. "Tiny bottles of lube instead of bubbles, plus his and hers cock rings and lipstick vibes? By the way, Flora said she had anal beads in hers as well."

"I made a few special ones," I said, sipping my horrifically decaffeinated mocha.

"I thought we were trying to avoid the omega stereotype. Just be more circumspect with the wedding favors themselves, okay?"

"We are. We're doing certificates for planted trees in old growth forests, carbon offsets for the entire wedding, and wooden carved boats in bottles made by the omega artists' co-op downtown. Every company we've contracted with is at least partly omega-run."

"As long as the reception has great food—not shaped like penises this time—then we should avoid a catastrophe." She glared even harder, and I tried to look innocent. I had ordered individual dick-shaped petit fours for the bachelorette party, and somehow a picture of Rain putting her mouth around one, with a very convincing O face, had found its way into my *Blackmail for Eternity* photo album.

"Got it," I said with a thumbs up, then dove back into the enormous stack of macarons on my plate. "Good food and drinks. Not that I can even drink the cocktails."

"Don't act like you're not drinking Captain Campari every night." Her lips twitched into a smile when I pretended to be embarrassed. "I'm so glad you practiced that party trick," she mumbled. "Have you shown him the double cherry stem knotting maneuver I taught you?"

"I'm saving that for the honeymoon," I replied with a wink. "A girl's gotta have some secrets, right?"

"Secrets. Sure. Everybody loves secrets," she muttered, then squared her shoulders and tore into an éclair like she was biting off someone's head.

The *little* head. *Ouch.*

Before I could find a way to ask if she'd been visualizing any peen in particular with that bite, she mumbled, "I saw a huge deposit in the Blue Skies account with Tarquin's name on it. I thought you said you gave back the ring?"

I handed her a napkin. "I did. But he was introducing me to his new girlfriend, and she asked about our business. So I told them what we did, and he bought advance vouchers for two months of betasitting for a friend who's just moved to town.

Paid premium, too." I rolled my eyes as she began to bluster about staffing shortages. "Don't worry. I'll either hire qualified staff, or do it myself."

Her face froze, and a dollop of éclair cream dropped from her open mouth. "You're going to keep running Blue Skies with me?"

My own jaw dropped. "Is this why you've been so down? Of course I am! It's half mine. Legally now! I'm not letting you buy me out, either."

"But... you'll be married in six more weeks. And almost out of your first trimester. You're telling me Giovanni Grantham is going to let his pregnant wife run a temp agency? Betasit?"

"Let?" I rolled my eyes. "Do you really think he could stop me from doing whatever I want?"

"He's an alpha, Soleil. And a billionaire. Don't act like he's not stronger than you."

"Physically? Sure." I fluttered my eyelashes, letting a burst of my omega pheromones out on purpose. "But you remember that story my dad always told about the guy with the coat on, and the sunshine?"

"The one about how the cold wind couldn't make him take his clothes off, but the sunshine did?" Rain grinned. "Your dad is such a pervert."

"It wasn't the man's clothes—it was just his coat, Rain," I said, smacking her arm. "Get it right. Anyway, I'm working my irresistible magic on Grumpy. While the paparazzi are so wild, he wants me to take a break. So I'll do the web stuff, the writing. Online interviews and even the bookkeeping, if I have to. But once we're married, I'm back in the betasitting biz."

She pretended she wasn't crying, and I pretended not to notice. After a few minutes, she said, "Right. We have to make a final decision on the reception theme today."

"I was thinking we'd do a nautical theme. You know, teeny-tiny bikinis on the waitstaff. Knots. Yachts. Warm oyster shots." She sputtered with laughter, while I took one last swig of my mocha. "Oh, and by the way, Rainbow? I've made one decision." I licked my lips, giving her my million-dollar smile.

"I'm definitely a swallow girl."

Epilogue

Grumpy

It was raining outside on our wedding day, but inside the Northeast Georgetown Country Club, the sunshine was blinding.

At least, my Sunshine was. She stood just inside the doors at the far end of the great ballroom, slowly making her way toward me in a daffodil yellow Danasha gown, her father's arm in hers. For some reason, nearly every person she passed reached out to her, to kiss her hand, or speak a few words, so her trip down the aisle was taking far longer than it should.

But I got it. They all loved her. Everyone who met her had to.

Smiling, her father shrugged, as if in apology. I smiled back, ignoring the wedding photographer who buzzed in front of me, taking yet another picture of what a tabloid had dubbed "Grumpy's Gorgeous Grin."

To one side of the assembled guests, a twelve-piece string orchestra played Vivaldi. Lorelei, who had gotten ordained especially for this event, stood behind a podium. My father and his girlfriend, and my mother and her two boyfriends, sat on the front row on either side of my sister's true mate, who fully deserved the seventy-thousand-dollar bottle of whiskey I'd promised her in exchange for keeping our parents apart.

I found myself grinning wider when I remembered Soleil's excitement at being asked to be the matron of honor at Anne-Marie and Lorelei's wedding the following year. She was already making plans for an "epic double bachelorette extravaganza" with unforgettable party favors. Then she'd mentioned something about ordering an extra "double bride-zil-do strap-on" to use at home.

I'd gently, yet thoroughly, spanked that idea right out of her. She'd liked it so much that she'd teased me about it a few more times. Life with Soleil would never be dull.

Sylvia stood at my side, dressed in a deep navy gown with yellow accents. In her hand was a basket with rolled-up copies of a pamphlet she and Soleil had written. All our wedding gifts were donations to a political action group that was introducing legislation at the state and federal levels to help level the playing field for omegas.

Sylvia had stopped wearing all black, and had turned into a social shark. She'd been present at every dinner and social event Lorelei allowed her to attend in the past few months, intent on winning my wealthy friends to her cause. "If I don't change the world, Uncle G, who will?" she'd asked at the rehearsal dinner. "What happens if I turn out to be an omega? I don't want to have to sneak around to follow my dreams, like Soleil. To live the life I deserve."

She'd convinced Nicholas Paxson, the head of Paxson pharma, to donate five million to her political action committee. Of course, all my groomsmen had given plenty; she'd saucily informed Storm Halder the week before that since he was my best man, he had to donate ten million.

"Anything for my bestie," he'd replied, making all our

friends laugh. We hadn't been friends until Soleil had walked into my life, merely business acquaintances. But now, he felt almost like the brother I'd never had.

And he wasn't the only new friend Soleil had brought into my life. At some point in the past two months, she and her friends had gotten together and decided all the men in their lives needed to bond. I wouldn't admit it to Soleil, but I was having more fun with her—and her noisy, young, whipcrack smart friends—than I had in decades. It didn't hurt that most of the fiancés and husbands that came with her Omega Leaguers were around my age.

What was even better was that I didn't hurt anymore. The symptoms that had plagued me when I'd left her had vanished completely with our claiming bites. Hell, the twinge in my elbow from playing tennis in college had disappeared as well. I felt twenty years younger.

Sylvia whispered, "Uncle G? I'm so glad you're marrying my betasitter. She's good for you."

I tapped her on the nose. "I think she's good for all of us, Silly." She wrapped her arms around my waist, and I leaned down for a hug. "I hear you decided to stay at the reception instead of going to the kids' movie night?" Lorelei had rented out the historic Majestic Theatre next door and was showing back-to-back family-friendly movies there.

Sylvia smirked. "I would go, but Senator Olan is going to be at your party, and he's on the House Ways and Means committee. I'm going to convince him to let one of our bills come up for a vote this session." She peered up at me with a sweet, wide-eyed expression. "How do I look?"

I pulled out my pocket handkerchief and rubbed at her neck. "Sorry, Silly, but you had a tiny bit of Sartre showing there. It's harder to look innocent and earnest when your neck reads 'Hell is other people.'"

She just rolled her eyes, muttered, "But it's true," and smiled beatifically at the one groomsman she hadn't fleeced yet.

Finally, my bride approached, and her father placed her hand in mine.

Sylvia whispered, "You sure about this, Soleil? Uncle G's pretty old. Grumpy. Smells weird. Frowns an awful lot." She winked and took the bridal bouquet of daisies and yellow roses when I huffed at her.

Soleil wrinkled her nose at my niece. "Why did I ask you to be my bridesmaid again, Ennui?"

"Because you love me?"

Soleil tucked a strand of dark hair behind Sylvia's ear. "I absolutely do."

"I love you, too, Soleil. I love you so much." The two hugged for a long moment while Lorelei wiped at her tears, and I fought to keep my composure.

Once she could speak, Lorelei addressed the crowd. "Ladies and gentlemen, we are gathered here today to join the lives of two people who met on a boat, though one of them couldn't swim. Or even float. And the other had been lost—not at sea, but buried in his work—for decades. Caring for his family, but waiting for the right woman to brighten up his life."

At that moment, a sunbeam broke through the clouds outside and light streamed through the tall windows. Soleil's hair was illuminated like a halo, the diamonds woven into the strands shining like constellations of fire.

I was almost certain the wedding photographer swooned.

Soleil's hand was warm in mine, her eyes spilling silent, joyful tears as we said our vows and gave our lives to each other.

"You may kiss the bride," my sister finally announced.

I didn't just kiss her. I ravished her, showing her and the whole world how much I loved my true mate.

Soleil giggled into my neck when she finally broke away, blushing furiously. "Grumpy, be careful. You'll wake up Captain Campari."

"The captain's been awake since the minute you walked in this room. And he's decided he's done being a respectable seaman. It's time for a little piracy."

She wrinkled her nose. "Privacy?"

"That, too," I replied with a grin. Then I lifted her in my arms and carried her down the aisle and out into the sunlight.

Epilogue

Sunshine

"Come on, husband. It's time for you to swab my decks so I can walk Captain Campari's massive plank," I demanded, kicking my shoes off. Whoever had invented heels needed to be brought back from the grave and forced to face the millions of poor souls who'd paid the price for his crimes against womankind. "If I can walk, that is." I dug my bare toes into the soft rug by our bed.

We'd just gotten back home after the wedding reception. Honestly, a large part of me wanted to *stay* home, but our families were desperate to celebrate with us—and my parents wanted to see the yacht that had brought their new son-in-law into our family. We'd decided to take a very short, intimate honeymoon wedding cruise on the Little Duchess XI. There would only be twenty-five of us sailing this time, and while Giovanni had experienced what he called a heart attack—but Dr. Rimbolt had more accurately labeled a temper tantrum—when I suggested the cruise, he'd calmed down about it.

Of course, he'd commissioned an entire line of cruise wear for me that had small air pockets as part of the designs, so if I fell into the ocean or pool, I would already be wearing a life preserver. My new underwear looked like thin, colorful bubble wrap, and I cringed every time I tried on the poofy shorts and tops.

I figured I'd humor him until we were out at sea, then distract him in our stateroom until he forgot to worry. I giggled, thinking of the distractions I had in mind. I'd been holding off on showing him Rain's party trick for a while...

"Are you sure you didn't have anything to drink at the reception?" Gio teased as he slipped out of his flat, comfortable wingtips.

"You know I didn't," I said, pulling the pins out of my hair. "Unless you count that little trip to the ladies' room where I swallowed your —"

He pulled me into him, kissing me silent for a long minute. Every one of his kisses today had made my head spin. Not that I'd tell Giovanni that; he'd have me back at the hospital faster than I could say "drunk on love." I ran my hands down his back, grabbing hold of what I liked to call Sunshine's Personal Wedding Cake.

"Tell the truth. Billionaires have personal trainers for every single muscle, don't you? Finger trainers, butt trainers, ab trainers..."

He nodded, pushing me away and undoing his shirt buttons. "Eight ab trainers at least," he replied, his face severe. "One for each ab." He pulled the shirt free and leaned down to slip off his socks. "Let's not get started on the specialists I had to hire for my toes. You think phalangeal muscles like these just happen?" He stared at his wiggling toes, then up at me, his expression perfectly blank.

I bit the inside of my cheek to keep from laughing. "Of course not. Your toes are..."

"I think the word you're looking for is 'swole,' Sunshine." He flexed his toes, making a grunting noise.

I fell back on the bed, laughing. "How do you keep a straight face all the time, Grumpy?"

"Decades of practice, princess."

"I want muscle trainers," I teased. finally pulling the last of the crystal strands free of my hair and letting it fall down my back. "Hot ones, with abs for days."

He pulled me back up, thrusting his pelvis against my gown. "You're only getting one trainer. But I promise I'll make you so sore, you'll never miss the others." I ran my fingers over the place where I'd marked him, loving the way he shivered every time. "Now get naked, naughty girl. It's time for a little plank walking."

"Aye aye, captain," I said with a jaunty salute. I tried not to drool as he bent over to take off his trousers. When I got undressed, I sort of flung everything on the ground to deal with later. I'd learned that Giovanni hung each piece of his clothing up meticulously, every time.

"Attention to detail," he called it when I teased him about it. "It's how I kept my company afloat."

I appreciated the trait now. Giovanni paid attention to every detail of my body, and had gone to great lengths in his efforts to wring as many orgasms as humanly possible from me every day so far.

The tux he'd worn to the wedding was the sexiest thing I'd ever seen him wear, and the dark gray bow tie hung loose around his neck. It reminded me of the first time we'd met. I pulled it off his neck, then turned around and pulled my long hair to the front, exposing the five million buttons on my back for him to undo.

While he muttered curses about fasteners, I dropped the silk tie to the floor and kicked it under the bed to retrieve later.

Omegas were scent hoarders, and I had an impressive collection of my favorite things he'd worn in a secret box in my closet. This was definitely going in there.

I let my dress fall to the ground and turned around. "You like your wedding present? My besties picked it out."

My friends had gotten me a set of the world's most comfortable fetish wear to go under my wedding dress. It was made of golden, shimmering narrow leather straps that went around each breast, crisscrossed my abdomen—even making room for the tiny baby belly that gently curved out below my ribs—and continued down to where it culminated in a set of buckled garters on my upper thighs. I also had on a pair of the laciest, prettiest underwear, that looked like a gold foil bikini bottom pressed onto my skin.

Giovanni's voice was a harsh growl as he looped two fingers through the straps under my breasts and pulled me toward him. "Tell your friends I'll buy them their own yachts if they keep giving you this sort of thing." He pulled harder, and my back arched, exposing my nipples to him. "Damnit, princess, if I'd known you were wearing this all day, I would have thrown you down in the ballroom and fucked you right there."

"Better late than never, Grumpy," I said breathlessly. "Let's go to bed?"

He surprised me by shaking his head. "I have a present for you, too."

"Another one?" He picked me up and carried me to the door. "Let me put on a robe!"

"No wife of mine will ever wear clothing," he growled, squeezing my ass so hard, the underwear tore. He grumbled an apology and ripped them the rest of the way off, dropping them to the floor. "That's better. Start out as you mean to go on, right? Naked."

I groaned. "Now who sounds like the fortune cookie? Please, don't embarrass me."

"I would never. You think my staff would risk their lives by coming into this wing when I've told them to stay out? They all know anyway. Some of them even helped with your wedding present." He carried me down the hall and opened the door into a short hallway with another door at the end, painted a subtle golden-yellow.

"What is it?" I breathed, but he'd already opened the door and was setting me on my feet. "A nest?"

He stroked my cheek with the backs of his fingers. "On my boat, that evening when you'd made that little nest with your twin mattress in your cabin... I knew if I ever had the chance to be with you, I'd make sure you had a nest you could be proud of. A perfect place, just for you."

It *was* perfect. The room was the ideal size for a nest, about fifteen feet square. A small open door on one side led to a closet-sized bathroom, but other than that, there were no windows. The ceiling was low, and fairy lights had somehow been embedded into the surface, making it look like a night sky. The walls were painted a soft blue-green.

"The exact color of your eyes," Grumpy said, dropping a kiss on my forehead. "I made them remix the paint twelve times."

Except for a small walkway around each edge, the floor was covered with an enormous square mattress, mounded high with blankets and pillows in every shade of yellow, green, and blue. A small table in one corner had a bottle of water and two glasses on top, and what looked like a carved wooden treasure chest underneath.

The best thing about the entire room was the aroma.

"It even smells right!" I threw myself onto the bed and

pulled a pillow over my nose, inhaling our mingled scents. "How can it already smell like us?"

His cheeks darkened. "You know how you steal my belts and ties? Well, I've been sneaking things out of our laundry, and the maids have been pulling sheets and blankets. Not the really dirty ones, just a few. If anything's not right, just let me know, and I'll make sure—"

"Don't change *anything*. Just... how?" I laughed, rolling over. "How did you get this done without me knowing?"

He shook his head at me, smiling again. "Billionaire, remember? I paid them to work quietly." He shucked off his dress shirt and slithered out of his boxers, staring down at me. "May I enter your nest, my sweet omega?"

"Yes, Alpha. You may."

He slid in next to me, patiently waiting as I moved the pillows and blankets into the exact places where I instinctively knew they needed to be. When everything was just right, I leaped on top of him, kissing him thoroughly. He let me stay there for a while, then gently flipped me over on my back, using the harness I still wore.

"This could come in handy. We should order a few more."

"One in your size? I don't know if they make them that big," I teased, as he grasped the leather straps at the tops of my thighs and pulled my legs apart, then instructed me to hold my legs up.

He purred as he began nibbling his way down to my clit. "Oh, Sunshine. Haven't I taught you by now? We can stretch almost anything to fit." He reached down and tapped the exposed gemstone on the plug he'd slipped into my ass halfway through the reception. "I'm glad to see you're still wearing this. I wouldn't want to have to spank you on our wedding night."

I felt a blush work its way up from my chest to my ears. "I mean, I can take it out now..." He was still laughing as his mouth closed around my clit, and he began doing what he did best.

Which, as it turned out, wasn't building up companies, or intimidating his competitors. It was making his wife come again and again, until I almost blacked out. Sometimes, I did.

"Present, Omega," he demanded, though he was already using the leather straps to move me into position. "Up on your knees, arms in front, spread those legs a little wider. That's right." He grabbed some pillows and placed them under me for support. "You tell me if it gets to be too much. If it hurts."

I moaned and stretched my arms out. "You know I kind of like the hurting parts."

"Naughty girl," he purred, and started to feed his cock into my swollen pussy. "I'm going to fuck you hard, and fast, and fill this aching pussy up with my cock." He leaned over me, his warm chest pressing down on my back as he slid into me, the stretch of him still almost too much at first. It was even more intense with the plug in my ass. He whispered, "But I'm not going to fill your dripping cunt with my cum. I'm going to pull that pretty little plug out, stuff my thick cock into you, and come inside your ass tonight, sweet Sunshine."

All I could do was moan in answer at his filthy words as he made terrible, wicked promises about how much he would make me love it. I was nervous, and he knew it. But he also knew just how to relax me.

I came again, and while I was still spasming, felt him working the plug in my ass, moving in and out through the ring of muscles there, before pulling it free. He slid across the nest to the wooden treasure chest and opened it. I almost laughed at what I could see on top: a plethora of sex toys, dildos, and containers filled with god only knew what sorts of lubricants and oils.

He opened a small bottle of lube, then stroked the liquid

over his engorged cock and knot, staring at my ass the whole time. I swallowed hard, still a little uncertain as to whether I could take his knot there.

I guess I'd find out.

He worked my clit with one hand for a moment, and as I began to relax again, he used two lube-slicked fingers to stretch my ass a little more.

I was pretty sure my willingness to try anything in bed at least once had shocked him, especially since I'd been relatively inexperienced. It wouldn't have been a surprise to anyone who'd seen what I had on my e-reader, though. I'd witnessed almost every perverted sex act that existed, only on the page, not in real life.

Well, I'd watched my fair share of alpha porn, too.

The past few weeks had been so busy that we hadn't had time to experiment too much. But I thought I was ready to cross this last line. He'd fucked the head of his cock into my ass once, and the sensation had made me come almost instantly, which had shocked us both.

"Relax, princess." He purred louder, sending me into an almost trancelike state as he pressed into me. The head of him breaching me felt amazing—there was pressure, but no real pain, none of the burning and stretching I'd worried about. An intense fullness, though, and I knew it would get more so. "Feel good?"

"So far," I whimpered, "so good."

"Ah yes, my sweet, dirty girl," he murmured as he leaned forward and grasped my hips. "Push back a little, take more of me. You're so tight, so fucking hot. You like this, don't you? Want more?"

"Yes," I managed to hiss, as he picked up his tempo, thrusting even farther into me. He wasn't too long for me to take him there, but the girth made it a struggle, and he had to go no more than a few centimeters further with each movement.

By the time I felt his thick knot pressing on my back entrance, I was panting. He moved one hand around to my clit and circled it with just the right pressure and speed that another orgasm—somehow connected to what he was doing inside me—barreled down on me.

"Come, princess. Come while I'm fucking this tight, perfect ass. Come so hard it drenches the sheets."

I did, my slick flowing freely, the sensations so powerful I almost didn't feel when he worked his knot into me, except the pressure of the climax kept going.

And then his knot expanded, and I screamed, the ecstasy and pressure blending together in a glorious whirlpool that threatened to drag me into unconsciousness. Giovanni roared out his release, his shout eclipsing mine. Hot liquid began to fill me, and I lost control of my body, the pillows and Giovanni's firm grip on my straps around my hips all that held me up.

"Oh, my naughty, perfect girl. I'm filling your ass with my cum—can you feel it?" He growled. "You're squeezing my knot so hard, so good. How does it feel, Omega? Tell me."

"It's so... *good.*" I squealed as he thrust the smallest bit deeper. After a moment, his hot release still filling me as his knot pumped inside me, he rolled us over, so we were spooning in the center of the nest.

The air swam with our combined scents, and I fell asleep with his knot still inside me.

When I woke, he was cleaning me gently with a warm cloth. At some point, he'd removed the leather lingerie, and the soft sheets felt like a caress on my skin. "Feeling all right, princess?" he asked, his hot gaze moving along my body. I returned the favor, making a mental catalog of all the places I was going to lick, bite, and suck as soon as possible.

"Thirsty," I finally said. "I'm a very thirsty girl."

In seconds, he was there with a glass of my favorite pomegranate-cranberry juice and a naked, muscular arm pulling me up to a seated position. I drank, then cuddled into his warm chest as he played with my hair, which was still crinkly from the hairspray.

"What would you like to do next?" he asked drowsily.

"Well, I'd love to tie you up and have my way with you—" His laughter cut me off. "Hey, we already had wedding night anal knotting. I think I should get at least one thing."

"Not tying me up," he grumbled, pulling out his phone to play some music from the built-in speakers. "God knows what you'd do."

Oh, God had no part in any of the plans I had for a tied-up Giovanni Grantham. I faked a sniffle, covering my face with my hands.

Grumpy's attention was on me in an instant. "What's wrong, princess?"

"Nothing. I just... I really wanted to try something." I hunched my shoulders up. "We have years ahead of us. I'm sure you'll let me tie you up someday." I let out another shaky breath.

Gently, he pulled my hands away from my face. "You little faker. You're not crying."

I stuck my lip out. "Come on, Grumpy. I won't do anything you wouldn't do." I scooted up so I could nibble his ear. "I'll even promise not to count any higher than three."

I'd never seen a man's eyes get that big that fast. When I burst out laughing, so did he. "What a naughty girl," he growled, tossing me back into the center of the bed. "Time for a spanking?"

I rolled over and wiggled my butt at him. "If you think

you've got enough energy for that and another round, Grumpy."

He did indeed have the energy for another round.

And many, many more.

Thank you for reading! Want another round of Soleil and Giovanni? Wonder what happened to Sylvia? Join Merri's newsletter for a free, flash-forward short story.
www.merribright.com

Please leave a review! This makes such an incredible difference for indie authors like me. A few words from you can make the sun shine.

Rain's story, Rainbow's Storm, is next! Pre-order today.

Acknowledgments

Some people deserve the first thank you. My unbelievably generous, kind, focused, and intelligent PA, Darcy Bennett, has been the sunshine in my life more days than I can count over the past few months! Thank you for shining your talent my way, Darcy.

Raewyn Ash got the dedication, so I'm not going to get sappy here. But you should all know that once again, she's the only reason you didn't have to wade through sopping channels and dripping caverns. Thank you as well to Kate at Y'all That Graphic for the wonderful cover and graphics!

My amazing Alpha, Beta, and Omega readers, I made you work for it this time, didn't I? Thank you to Alex, Bekka, Courtney, Elle, Liza, Lucila, Megan, Maria, and Tara. I'll mix you all your cocktail of choice when we meet in person someday. Just please don't ask for a Dirty Sanchez.

A special thanks to author friends Sarah Reynolds and Indie Sparks for handing me tissues and last-minute read-throughs.

My ARC reader team and my Merri's Mischief Makers brighten all my days. Thank you for your support, love, and for hanging in there with me as I experiment with Lonely Sausage books.

Also by Merri Bright

The Forgotten Angel Series

Lost Feather

Fallen Feather

Rising Feather

The Lost Lines Series

Vali's Stories:

The Omega's Mischief: A Short Story Prequel

The King's Omega: The Lost Lines Series Book 1

The Queen's Nest: A Lost Lines Series Novella

Haven's Story:

The Guards' Haven

Cilla's Story:

The Duchess's Designs

Roya's Story:

The Assassin's Promise

Wren's Story:

part one ∼ The Leviathan's Debt

part two ∼ The Wyvern's Redemption

About the Author

Merri Bright spends her days dreaming up naughty angels, misunderstood demons, sexy shifters, growly Alpha males, and frequently refuses to limit her heroines to just one love interest.

Please join Merri's Mischief Makers on Facebook where you'll discover random giveaways, sneak peeks of new novels, book recommendations, and silly/sexy/funny stuff. Or email her at merri@merribright.com.

www.ingramcontent.com/pod-product-compliance
Lightning Source LLC
Chambersburg PA
CBHW031213260626
47169CB00007B/2045